KEITH LAUMER

A TOM DOHERTY ASSOCIATES BOOK

Acknowledgements

Night of Delusions, © 1972 by Keith Laumer
"Thunderhead" © 1963 by Keith Laumer
"The Last Command" © 1971 by Keith Laumer

(The novel version, *Night of Delusions*, was originally published in 1972.)

KNIGHT OF DELUSIONS

A TOR Book
Published by Tom Doherty Associates, Inc.
49 West 24 Street
New York, NY 10010

Cover art by Tom Kidd

ISBN: 0-812-54362-9   Can. ISBN: 0-812-54363-7

First TOR edition: November 1982
Second printing: July 1988

Printed in the United States of America

0 9 8 7 6 5 4 3 2 1

She was sitting across the table from me, wrapped in a threadbare old cloth coat with a ratty squirrel skin collar. Her eyes looked into mine with a searching expression.

"Don't tell me," I said, sounding groggy even to me. "I was sitting here with my eyes crossed, singing old sea chanteys to myself in Amharic; so you sat down to see if I was all right. Good girl. I'm not all right. I'm about as far from all right as you can get and still count your own marbles."

She started to say something but I cut her off: "Let's not run through the rest of the lines; let's skip ahead to where you tell me I'm in danger, and I go charging out into the night to get my head bent some more."

"I don't know what you mean."

"I mean it seems we sat and talked like this before. We looked at each other in the same way then—"

"That's an old popular song."

"It seems to be. Everything seems to be something. Usually what it isn't. What are you?" I reached across and took her hand.

"Florin," she whispered. "Don't you remember me? I'm your wife."

Look for these TOR books by Keith Laumer

BEYOND THE IMPERIUM
THE BREAKING EARTH
THE GLORY GAME
THE INFINITY CAGE
KNIGHT OF DELUSIONS
THE MONITORS
ONCE THERE WAS A GIANT
THE OTHER SKY/THE HOUSE IN NOVEMBER
PLANET RUN
A TRACE OF MEMORY
WORLDS OF THE IMPERIUM

Knight of Delusions

I didn't hear anything: no hushed breathing, no stealthy slide of a shoe against the carpet. But I knew before I opened my eyes that there was someone in the room. I moved my hand under the edge of the blanket onto the worn butt of the Belgian-made Browning I keep by me for sentimental reasons, and said, "Let's have some light."

The dim-strip by the door went on. A medium-sized, medium-aged man in a plain gray suit stood by the door. He looked at me with a neutral expression on a face that was just a face. The bathroom door beside him was open a couple of inches.

"You interrupted a swell dream," I said. "I almost had my finger on the secret of it all. By the way, tell your partner to come on out and join the party."

The bathroom door opened wider and a thin, lantern-jawed man with a lot of bony wrist showing under his cuffs slid into view. He had scruffy reddish hair, a scruffy reddish complexion with plenty of tension lines, a neat row of dental implants that showed through a nervous grimace that he might have thought was a smile. I lifted a pack of smokes from the bedside table, snapped a weed out, used a lighter on it. They watched all this carefully, as if it were a trick they'd heard about and didn't want to miss. I blew out smoke and said, "Why not tell me about it? Unless it's a secret, of course."

"We have a job for you, Mr. Florin," the gray man said in a terse, confidential voice. "A delicate mission requiring a man of unusual abilities."

I let that ride.

"Our mode of entry was in the nature of a test," the bony man said. He had a prissy, high-pitched voice that didn't go with the rest of him. "Needless to say, you passed." He giggled.

The cigarette tasted terrible. I mashed it out in a glass ashtray with *Harry's Bar* on the bottom.

"Sorry you had the trouble for nothing," I said. "I'm not looking for work."

"We represent a very important man," Slim said, and showed me an expression like that of a man who worked for a very important man. It looked a lot like the expression of a man in need of a laxative.

"Would he have a name?" I said. "This very important man, I mean."

"No names; not for the present," the gray man said quickly. "May we sit down, Mr. Florin?"

I waved my free hand. The gray man took two steps and perched on the edge of the straight chair beside the dresser. Slim drifted off into the background and sank down into one of those big shapeless chairs you need a crane to get out of.

"Needless to say," the gray man said, "the pay will be commensurate with the gravity of the situation."

"Sure," I said. "What situation?"

"A situation involving the planetary security." He said it impressively, as if that settled everything.

"What's the planetary security got to do with me?"

"You're known to be the best man in the business. You're discreet, reliable, not easily frightened."

"And don't forget my winning smile," I said. "What business?"

"The confidential investigation business, of course."

"The personal escort aspect," Slim amplified.

"Bodyguarding," I said. "It's all right; you can say it right out loud. You don't have to make it sound elegant. But you overlooked a point. I'm on vacation—an extended vacation."

"This is important enough to warrant interrupting your holiday," Slim said.

"To you or to me?"

"Mr. Florin, you're aware of the tense—not to say desperate state—of public affairs today," the gray man said in a gray voice. "You know that public unrest has reached grave proportions—"

"You mean a lot of people are unhappy with the way things are going. Yeah, I know that; I recognize the sound of breaking glass when I hear it. But not me. I'm a contented man. I keep my head down and let the waves roll over me."

"Nonsense," the gray man said without visible emotion. He slipped a hand inside his jacket and brought out a flat leather folder, flipped it open. The little gold badge winked at me.

"Your government needs you, Mr. Florin," he said indifferently.

"Is this a pinch or a sales pitch?" I asked.

"Your cooperation will have to be voluntary, of course."

"That word 'voluntary' sure takes a beating," I said, and yawned, not entirely honestly.

The gray man almost smiled. "Your cynical pose is unconvincing. I'm familiar with your record in the war, Mr. Florin. Or may I say Colonel Florin?"

"Don't," I said. "Reminiscences bore me. The war was a long time ago. I was young and foolish. I had lots of big ideas. Somehow they didn't survive the peace."

"There is one man who can save the situation, placate the malcontents. I think you know the man I mean."

"Campaign oratory in the middle of the night is no substitute for sleep," I said. "If you've got a point, get to it."

"The Senator needs your help, Mr. Florin."

"What ties a small-time private cop to the Senator? He could buy the block where I live and have it torn down—with me in it."

"He knows you, Florin; knows of your past services. He reposes great confidence in you."

"What does he want me to do—ring door-bells?"

"He wants to see you; now, tonight."

"Don't tell me the rest," I said. "You've got a fast car waiting at the curb to whisk me off to headquarters."

"A copter," the gray man said. "On the roof."

"I should have thought of that," I said. "OK if I put my pants on before we go?"

* * *

It was a big room with deep rugs and damask walls and a fancy cornice and a big spiral chandelier that must have taken a family of Venetian glassblowers a year to put together. A big fellow with a long, solemn face and a big nose full of broken blood vessels met me just inside the door, shook my hand carefully, and led me over to a long table with a deep wax finish where four other men sat waiting.

"Gentlemen, Mr. Florin," he said. The boys behind the table had faces that were curiously alike, and had enough in common with a stuffed flounder to take the edge off my delight in meeting them. If they liked my looks they didn't say so.

"Mr. Florin has consented to assist us," Big Nose started . . . .

"Not quite," I cut in. "I agreed to listen." I looked at the five faces and they looked back. Nobody offered me a chair.

"These gentlemen," my host said, "are the

Senator's personal staff. You may have complete trust in their absolute discretion."

"Fine," I said in that breezy manner that's earned me so many friends over the years. "What are we being discreet about?"

One of the men leaned forward and clasped hands with himself. He was a wizened little fellow with pinched, clay-pale nostrils and eyes like a bird of prey.

"Mr. Florin, you're aware that anarchists and malcontents threaten our society," he said in a voice like the whisper of conscience. "The candidacy of the Senator for the office of World Leader is our sole hope for continued peaceful progress."

"Maybe. What's it got to do with me?"

A man with a face as round and soft as a saucer of lard spoke up: "The upcoming elections are the most important this planet has ever faced." He had a brisk, thin voice that gave me the feeling it should be coming from a much smaller, much leaner man, possibly hiding under the table. "The success of the Senator, and of the policies he represents, spell the difference between chaos and another chance for our world."

"Does the other party get equal time?"

"It goes without saying, Mr. Florin, that your loyalties lie with legal government; with law and order."

"But you said it anyway. I get the feeling," I went on before he could step on me, "that we're dancing around the edge of something; something that wants to get said, but nobody's saying it."

"Perhaps you've noticed," the plump man

said, "that in recent days the Senator's campaign has suffered a loss of momentum."

"I haven't been watching much telly lately."

"There have been complaints," the birdman said, "that he's repeating himself, failing to answer his opponents' attacks, that the dynamism is gone from his presentations. The complaints are justified. For three months now we've been feeding doctored tapes to the news services."

They were all looking at me. Silence hummed in the room. I glanced along the table, fixed on a man with bushy white hair and a mouth that was made to clamp onto a bulldog pipe.

"Are you telling me he's dead?" I said.

The white head shook slowly, almost regretfully.

"The Senator," he said solemnly, "is insane."

The silence after the punch line hung as heavy as a washer-load of wet laundry. Or maybe heavier. I shifted around in my chair and listened to some throat-clearing. Faraway horns too: d on a distant avenue. Wind boomed against the picture window with its view of lights laid out on the blackness all the way to the horizon.

"The burdens under which he's labored for the past three years would have broken an ordinary man in half the time," Lard Face said. "But the Senator is a fighter; as the pressure grew, he held on. But the strain told on him. He began to see enemies everywhere. In the end his obsessions hardened into a fixed delusional system. Now he thinks every hand is against him."

"He believes," Big Nose said, "that a kidnap plot is afoot. He imagines that his enemies intend to brainwash him, make him their puppet. Accordingly, it becomes his duty to escape."

"This is, of course, a transparent rationalization," said a lath-thin man with half a dozen hairs slicked across a bald dome; his eyes burned at me hot enough to broil steaks. "He avoids the pressures of the election—but for the noblest of reasons. By deluding himself that in sacrificing his hopes of high office he prevents his being used, he relieves himself of the burden of guilt for his failure to measure up to the challenge."

"Tragic," I said, "but not quite in my line. You need a head doctor, not a beat-up gumshoe."

"The finest neuropsychologists and psychiatrists in the country have attempted to bring the Senator back to reality, Mr. Florin," Big Nose said. "They failed. It is therefore our intention to bring reality to the Senator."

* * *

"Our plan is this," the bird-man said, leaning forward with what was almost an expression on his face. "The Senator is determined to venture out incognito to take his chances alone in the city. Very well—we'll see to it that he carries off his escape successfully."

"He imagines that by slipping free from his role as a man of great affairs—by casting off the restraints of power and position—he can lose himself in the masses," said Hot Eyes. "But he'll find matters are not so simple as that. The analysts who've studied his case assure us that his sense of duty will not be so easily laid to rest. Difficulties will arise, conjured from the depths of his own mind. And as these imaginary obstacles confront him—he will find that they're not after all imaginary."

"A man who believes himself to be persecuted by unseen enemies, threatened with death, is, by definition, psychotic," Lard Face said. "But if he is, indeed, hunted? *What if his fears are true?*"

"You see," said the hot-eyed man, "at some level, the man in the grip of hallucination knows the illusion for what it is. The victim of hysterical blindness will casually skirt a footstool placed in his path. But—when the imaginary dog *bites*—the shock will, we believe, drive him back from his safe retreat—not, after all, so safe—to the lesser harshness of reality."

"We'll make him sane by definition, Mr. Florin," Big Nose said. "And having established a one-to-one relationship with reality, we will lead him back to sanity."

"Neat," I said. "But who provides the pink elephants? Or is it silver men in the closet?"

"We're not without resources," Big Nose said grimly. "We've arranged for a portion of the city to be evacuated, with the exception of certain well-briefed personnel. We've set up highly sophisticated equipment, keyed to his cephalic pattern, responsive to his brain. His movements will be tracked, his fantasies monitored—and appropriate phenomena will be produced accordingly, matching his fears."

"If he conceives of himself as beset by wild beasts," Hot Eyes said, "wild beasts will appear. If he imagines the city is under bombardment—bombs will fall, with attendant detonations and fires and flying debris. If he dreams of assassins armed with knives, knife-wielding killers will attack. He will overcome these obstacles, of course; it's inherent in his nature that he'll not fantasize his own demise. And in facing and overcoming these dangers he will, we're convinced, face and defeat the real threat to his sanity."

I looked along the table at them. They seemed to be serious.

"You gentlemen are expecting a lot from some stock Trideo footage," I said. "The Senator may be as batty as Dracula's castle, but he's no fool."

Big Nose smiled bleakly. "We're prepared to offer a demonstration, Mr. Florin." He moved a finger and I heard the growl of heavy engines, and a crunching and grinding that got closer and louder. The ashtrays rattled on the table. The floor trembled; the chandelier danced. A picture fell off the wall, and then the wall bulged and fell in and the snout of a 10-mm. infinite repeater set in the bow of a Bolo Mark III pushed into the room and halted. I could smell the stink of dust and hot oil, hear the scream of idling turbines, the thud and rattle of bricks falling—

Big Nose lifted his finger again and the tank winked out and the wall was back in place, picture and all, and the only sound was me, swallowing, or trying to.

I got out my hanky and wiped my forehead and the back of my neck while they smiled at me in a nasty, superior way.

"Yeah," I said. "I take back that last crack."

"Believe me, Mr. Florin, everything the Senator experiences on his foray into the city will be utterly real—to him."

"It still sounds like a nutty scheme to me," I said. "If you brought me here to get the benefit of my advice, I say forget it."

"There's no question of forgetting it," Lard Face said. "Only of your cooperation."

"Where do I crawl into the picture?"

"When the Senator sets out on his adventure," Big Nose said, "you'll go with him."

"I've heard of people going crackers," I said. "I never heard of them taking a passenger along."

"You'll guard him, Florin. You'll see him through the very real dangers he'll face, in safety. And, incidentally, you'll provide the channel through which we monitor his progress."

"I see. And what, as the man said, is in it for me?"

The bird-man speared me with a look. "You fancy yourself as a soldier of fortune, a man of honor, a lone warrior against the forces of evil. Now, your peculiar talents are needed in a larger cause. You can't turn your back on the call of duty and at the same time maintain your self-image. Accordingly, you'll do as we wish!" He sat back with a look that was as pleased as a look of his could ever get.

"Well, maybe you've got a point there, counselor," I said. "But there are a couple of other things I pride myself on besides being Jack Armstrong-to-the-rescue. One of them is that I choose my own jobs. Your gun-boys wear clean shirts and don't pick their noses in public, but they're still gun-boys. It seemed like a good idea to come along and hear your pitch. But that doesn't mean I'm buying it."

"In spite of your affectation of the seamy life, Mr. Florin, you're a wealthy man—or could be, if you chose. What we're offering you is a professional challenge of a scope you would never otherwise have encountered."

"It's a new twist," I said. "You're daring me to take your dare."

"The choice is simple," Big Nose said. "You know the situation. The time is now. Will you help or will you not?"

"You warned me you had the advice of some high-powered psychologists," I said. "I should have known better than to argue."

"Don't denigrate yourself, Florin," Big Nose said. "It's the only decision you could have made in conscience."

"Let's have one point clear," I said. "If I sign on to guard the Senator, I do the job my way."

"That's understood," Big Nose said, sounding mildly surprised. "What else?"

"When does the experiment come off?"

"It's already under way. He's waiting for you now."

"He knows about me?"

"He imagines your arrival is a finesse devised by himself."

"You've got all the answers, I see," I said. "Maybe that's good—provided you know all the questions."

"We've covered every eventuality we could foresee. The rest is up to you."

* * *

Two of the committee—they called themselves the Inner Council—escorted me to a brightly lit room in the basement. Three silent men with deft hands fitted me into a new street-suit of a soft gray material that Big Nose said was more or less bulletproof, as well as being climate-controlled. They gave me two guns, one built into a finger-ring and the other a reasonable facsimile of a clip-pen. One of the technicians produced a small box of the type cultured pearls come in. Inside, nested in cotton, was a flake of pink plastic the size of a fish scale.

"This is a communication device," he said. "It will be attached to your scalp behind the ear where the hair will conceal it. You will heed it implicitly."

A pink-cheeked man I hadn't seen before came into the room and conferred with Big Nose in a whisper before he turned to me.

"If you're ready, Mr. Florin . . . ?" he said in a voice as soft as a last wish, and didn't wait for my answer. I looked back from the door. Four grim faces looked at me. Nobody waved bye-bye.

* * *

I had heard of the Senator's Summer Retreat. It was a modest cottage of eighty-five rooms crowded into fifty acres of lawn and garden in the foothills sixty miles northeast of the city. My pilot dropped me in a clump of big conifers among a lot of cool night air and piney odors half a mile upslope from the lights of the house. Following instructions, I sneaked down through the trees, making not much more noise than a bulk elk in mating season, and found the hole in the security fence right where they'd said it would be. A booted man with a slung power gun and a leashed dog paced past me fifty feet away without turning his head. Maybe he was following instructions too. When he had passed, I moved up to the house by short dashes from shadow to shadow, not falling down more than a couple of times. It all seemed pretty silly to me; but Big Nose had insisted the approach was important.

The service door was almost hidden behind a nice stand of ground juniper. My key let me into a small room full of the smell of disinfectant and buckets for me to put a foot in. Another door let onto a narrow hall. Lights showed in a foyer to the right; I went left, prowled up three flights of narrow stairs, came out in a corridor walled in gray silk that almost reminded me of something; but I brushed that thought away. Up ahead a soft light was shining from an open doorway. I went toward it, through it into dimness and richness and an odor of waxed woodwork and Havana leaf and old money.

He was standing by an open wall safe with his back toward me; he turned as I came through the door. I recognized the shaggy blond-going-gray hair, the square-cut jaw with the cleft that brought in the female vote, the big shoulders in the hand-tailoring. His eyes were blue and level and looked at me as calmly as if I were the butler he'd rung for.

"Florin," he said in a light, mellow voice that wasn't quite what I had expected. "You came." He put out his hand; he had a firm grip, well-manicured nails, no calluses.

"What can I do for you, Senator?" I said.

He paused for a moment before he answered, as if he were remembering an old joke.

"I suppose they've given you the story about how I've gone insane? How I imagine there's a plot afoot to kidnap me?" Before I thought of an answer he went on: "That's all lies, of course. The truth is quite otherwise."

"All right," I said. "I'm ready for it."

"They're going to kill me," he said matter-of-factly, "unless you can save my life."

* * *

He was giving me the old straight-from-the-shoulder look. He was the captain and I was the team and it was time for my hidden-ball play. I opened my mouth to ask the questions, but instead I went past him to the ivory telephone on the desk. He watched without saying a word while I checked it, checked the light fixtures, the big spray of slightly faded roses on the side table, the plumbing fixtures in the adjoining bathroom. I found three bugs and flushed them down the toilet.

"A properly spotted inductance mike can still hear us," I said. "So much for privacy in our modern world."

"How do things look—outside?" he asked.

"About as you'd expect," I hedged. He nodded as if that told him plenty. "By the way," I said, "have we met before, Senator?"

He shook his head, started a smile.

"Under the circumstances," I said, "I'd think you'd want to see some identification."

Maybe he looked a little confused, or maybe not. I'm not a great reader of expressions. "You're well known to me by reputation, Mr. Florin," he said, and looked at me as if that were my cue to whip out a chart of the secret passages in the castle walls, complete with an X marking the spot where the fast horses waited outside the postern gate.

"Maybe you'd better fill me in just a little, Senator," I said. "I wouldn't want to make any unnecessary mistakes."

"You know the political situation in the city," he said. "Anarchy, riots, lawless mobs roaming the streets. . . ." He waited for me to confirm that.

"The disorder is not so spontaneous as it may appear. The crowd is being manipulated for a purpose—the purpose being treason."

I got out one of my weeds and rolled it between my fingers.

"That's a pretty heavy word, Senator," I said. "You don't hear it much nowadays."

"No doubt Van Wouk spoke of the approaching elections, the dangers of political chaos, economic collapse, planetary disaster."

"He mentioned them."

"There's another thing which perhaps he

failed to mention. Our planet has been invaded."

I lit up my cigarette, snorted the stink of it out of my nostrils.

"It must have slipped his mind. Who's doing the invading?"

"The world has been under a single government for twenty years; obviously, there is no domestic enemy to launch an attack. . . ."

"So what does that leave? The little green men from Andromeda?"

"Not men," he said gravely. "As for Andromeda—I don't know."

"Funny," I said. "I haven't noticed them around."

"You don't believe me."

"Why should I?" I put it to him flatly.

He laughed a little. "Why, indeed?" The faint smile faded. "But suppose I give you proof."

"Go ahead."

"As you might have expected, I don't have it here; nothing that would convince you."

I nodded, watching him. He didn't look wild-eyed; but lots of them don't.

"I realize that what I'm telling you seems to lend credence to Van Wouk's story," he said calmly. "I took that risk. It's important that I be utterly candid with you."

"Sure."

"Let me make myself perfectly clear. You came here as Van Wouk's agent. I'm asking you to forget him and the council; to give me your personal loyalty."

"I was hired to bodyguard you, Senator," I said. "I intend to do my job. But you're not making it any easier. You tell me things that seem to call for the boys with the butterfly nets; you know I don't believe you; and then you ask me to back your play and I don't even know what your play is."

"I also told you things that Van Wouk didn't know I knew. The fact is, I maneuvered him, Florin." He looked strong, confident, sane, determined—except for a little hint of nerves around the eyes.

"I wanted you here, beside me," he said. "Van Wouk can think what he likes. I got you here, that's what counts. Score that one for me."

"All right, I'm here. Now what?"

"They've been in communication with the enemy—Van Wouk and his crowd. They intend to collaborate. They hope for special rewards under an alien regime; God knows what they've been promised. I intend to stop them."

"How?"

"I have a certain personal following, a small cadre of loyal men of ability. Van Wouk knows that; that's why he's determined on my death."

"What's he waiting for?"

"Raw murder would make a martyr of me. He prefers to discredit me first. The insanity story is the first step. With your help he hoped to drive me into actions that would both cause and justify my death."

"He sent me here to help you escape," I reminded him.

"Via a route leaked to me by his hireling. But I have resources of which he's unaware.

That's how I learned of the invasion—and of the other escape route."

"Why didn't you leave sooner?"

"I waited for you."

"What makes me that important?"

"I know my chances alone, Florin. I need a man like you with me—a man who won't quail in the face of danger."

"Don't let them kid you, Senator," I said. "I go down two collar sizes just at the idea of a manicure."

He twitched a little smile into position and let it drop. "You shame me, Florin. But of course you're famous for your sardonic humor. Forgive me if I seem less than appreciative. But quite frankly—I'm afraid. I'm not like you—the man of steel. My flesh is vulnerable. I shrink from the thought of death— particularly death by violence."

"Don't build me up into something I'm not, Senator. I'm human, don't ever doubt it. I like living, in spite of its drawbacks. If I've stuck my neck out a few times it was because that was less uncomfortable than the other choices."

"Then why are you here?"

"Curiosity, maybe."

He gave me the shadow smile. "Don't you want to find out if I'm really as crazy as Van Wouk says? Aren't you interested in seeing what I'll offer you as proof that we've been invaded by nonhumans?"

"It's a point."

He looked me in the eye. "I want you with me as my ally, faithful unto death. That—or nothing."

"You'd get that—or nothing."

"I know."

"You're aware that you'll be in deadly danger from the moment we deviate from Van Wouk's prepared script," he said.

"The thought had occurred to me."

"Good," he said, curt again. "Let's get on with it." He went to a closet and got out a trench coat that showed signs of heavy wear and pulled it on. It took a little of the shine off the distinguished look, but not enough. While he was busy with that, I took a look in the open wall safe. There was a bundle of official-looking documents wrapped with purple ribbon, letters, a thick sheaf of what looked like money except that it was printed in purple ink and had a picture of a lion on it and the words *Legal Tender of the Lastrian Concord For All Debts Public and Private*. There was also a flat handgun of a type I'd never seen.

"What's the Lastrian Concord, Senator?" I said.

"A trade organization in which I hold shares," he said after a hesitation. "Their currency is almost valueless now. I keep it as a souvenir of my bad financial judgment."

He wasn't watching me; I slid the play gun into my side pocket; the Senator was at the window, running his fingers along the gray metal frame.

"It's a long way down," I said. "But I suppose you've got a rope ladder in your sock."

"Better than that, Florin." There was a soft *snick!* and the sash swung into the room like a gate. No blustery night air blew in; there was a featureless gray wall eighteen inches away.

"A repeater panel in the wall," he said. "The house has a number of features Van Wouk would be surprised to know about."

"What was the other route, Senator?" I said. "The one Van Wouk expected you to use?"

"It's an official emergency exit; a panel at the back of the closet leads down to the garages. A guard is supposed to be bribed to supply a car. This way is somewhat less luxurious but considerably more private."

He stepped in ahead of me, slid away out of sight to the left. As I was about to follow, a cricket chirped behind my ear.

"Good work," a tiny voice whispered. *"Everything is proceeding nicely. Stay with him."*

I took a last look around the room and followed the Senator into his secret passage.

* * *

We came out onto the grounds in the shelter of a giant kapok tree that had cost somebody a lot of money to transplant alive. The Senator led the way without any dramatic dashes through an ornamental garden to a row of imported poplars, along that to the fence. From somewhere inside his coat he produced a set of snippers and some jumper wires. He cut a hole for us and we went through and were in a cornfield under the stars. The Senator had turned to me and started to say something when the alarm went off.

There were no jangling bells, no sirens; just the floodlights blossoming all across the grounds. I grabbed the Senator's arms as he started to look back.

"Don't look at the lights," I said. "Or is this part of your plan?"

"Come on—this way!" He set off at a run toward the wooded rise beyond the field. There was plenty of light leaking through the poplars to cast long shadows that scrambled ahead of us. I felt as conspicuous as a cockroach in a cocktail glass, but if there was an alternative course of action I couldn't think of it right then. There was another fence to get through; on the other side we were in light woods that got denser as the ground got steeper. We pulled up for a breather a quarter of a mile above the house, which floated peacefully in its pooled light down below. There were no armed men swarming across the lawn, no engines gunning down the drive, no copters whiffling into the air, no PA systems blaring.

"It's too easy," I said.

"What do you mean?" The Senator was breathing hard, but no harder than I was. He was in shape, a point for our side.

"They didn't switch those floods on just to light our way—or did they?"

"There's a rather elaborate system of electronic surveillance devices," he said, and I saw he was grinning. "Some time ago I took the precaution of tampering with the master panel in a small way."

"You think of everything, Senator. What comes next?"

"Radial 180 passes a mile to the west. However. . . ." He waved a hand toward the ridge above us. "Secondary 96 skirts the foothills, about seven miles from here. It's difficult country, but I know the route. We can be at the road in two hours, in time to catch a produce flat dead-heading for the coast."

"Why the coast?"

"I have a standing rendezvous arrangement with a man named Eridani. He has the contacts I need."

"For a man under house arrest, you do pretty well, Senator."

"I told you I have extraordinary methods of communication."

"So you did."

Down below, there was some activity now. A personnel carrier had cranked up and was taking on uniformed men. A squad was on its way down the drive on foot. You could hear a few shouts, but nobody seemed very excited— at least not from fifteen hundred yards away.

"Van Wouk's plans covered every eventuality except this one," the Senator said. "By slipping out of the net at this point, we side-step his entire apparatus."

"Not if we sit here too long talking about it."

"If you've caught your breath, let's get started."

Visibility wasn't too bad, once my eyes had adapted to the starlight. The Senator was a competent climber and seemed to know exactly where he was going. We topped the ridge and he pointed out a faint glow in the north that he said was Homeport, forty miles away. A copter went over, raking searchlights across the treetops half a mile away. IR gear might have found us at closer range; but there was an awful lot of virgin-forested hill country for us to be lost in.

The hike took ten minutes over the Senator's estimates, with no breaks. We came sliding down the angle of a steep cut onto a narrow pike that sliced through the rough country like a sabre wound. We moved on a few hundred yards north to a spot beside a gorge that offered better cover if we needed to get out of sight in a hurry. The Senator handed me a small silver flask and a square pill.

"Brandy," he said. "And a metabolic booster."

I tasted the brandy; it was the real stuff. "I get it," I said. "This is the deluxe prison break, American plan."

He laughed. "I've had plenty of time to prepare. It was obvious to me as much as three months ago that Van Wouk and the Council were up to something. I waited until I was sure."

"Are you sure you're sure? Maybe they know things you don't know they know."

"What are you getting at?"

"Maybe the route through the closet was a dummy. Maybe the phony window was a plant. Maybe they're watching you right now."

"I could have decided to go south just as easily, to the capital."

"But you had reasons for coming this way. Maybe they know the reasons."

"Are you just talking at random, Florin? Or . . . ?"

"If it was 'or', I wouldn't be talking."

He laughed again, not a loud or merry laugh, but still a laugh. "Where does that line of reasoning end, Florin? Everything is something other than what it seems, or what it seems to seem. You have to draw the line somewhere. I prefer to believe I'm thinking my own thoughts, and that they're as good as or better than anything Van Wouk has planned."

"What happens after you meet your pal Eridani?"

"He has access to broadcast facilities. A surprise Trideo appearance by me, informing the public of the situation, will tie their hands."

"Or play into them."

"Meaning?"

"Suppose you dreamed these aliens?"

"But I didn't. I told you I have proof of their presence, Florin."

"If you can imagine aliens, you can imagine proof."

"If you doubt my sanity, why are you here?"

"I agreed to help you, Senator, not believe all your ideas."

"Indeed? And your idea of helping me might be to lead me docilely to Van Wouk."

"You sent for me, Senator; it wasn't my idea." ·

"But you agreed to ally yourself with me."

"That's right."

"Then don't attempt to interfere with my plans."

"I'm just making conversation, Senator.

People do have illusions, you know. And they believe in them. What makes *you* immune?"

He started to snap off a sharp answer, but instead he shook his head and smiled. "I decline to tackle a paradox at this time of night." He broke off and cocked his head. I heard it too: turbines howling on a grade to the south, not far away.

"Here's our ride," I said. "Just as you predicted, Senator."

"It's common knowledge that this is a cargo artery; don't try to read anything mystical into it."

"I guess Van Wouk knows that, too."

"Hide in the ditch if you like. I'm flagging it."

"You hide: I'm the one with the bulletproof vest."

"What the hell," the Senator said abruptly, sounding a little out of character. "A man has to trust somebody." He strode into the center of the road and planted himself and waved the flat down as it came in view. We climbed on the back and settled down comfortably among some empty chicken crates.

* * *

The driver dropped us in the warehouse district a block from the waterfront, on a cracked sidewalk where a cold, gusty wind that smelled like dead fish and tarred hemp pushed grit and old newspapers ahead of it. Weak, morgue-colored light from a pole-lamp at the corner shone on storefronts with shaded windows like blinded eyes above them. There were a few people in sight, men in felt hats and women in cloches and bare legs and fur boots, bucking the wind. A boxy taxicab rolled past, splattering muddy water from the gutter.

"What is it, Florin?" the Senator said sharply.

"Nothing much," I said. "It doesn't look like what I expected."

"Were you expecting something in particular?"

"Don't count that one, Senator; it just slipped out. Where to now?"

"A place near here; there's a rendezvous arranged for every fourth hour until I arrive." He looked at a strap watch. "Less than half an hour now." We went past a closed tailor shop with dummies wearing double-breasted tuxes with dust on the shoulders, past a candy store with plates of fudge on paper doilies, a drugstore with bottles of colored water and a Dr. Pepper sign. I stopped him at the corner.

"Suppose we vary the route," I said, "just for the hell of it."

"Nonsense." He started through me but I didn't move.

"Humor me, Senator."

"Look here, Florin—your job is to carry out my orders, not to try to bully me!"

"Correction. I'm here to try to keep you alive. How I do that is my business."

He glared at me, then shrugged.

"Very well. It's two blocks west, one south."

We went along the dark street. All the other pedestrians seemed to be on the other side of the street, though I didn't see anyone cross to avoid us. A surprising number of women were tall and slim, and wore gray coats with squirrel collars. A Nile green open car with its side curtains buttoned up tight rolled slowly by. I picked a corner at random and turned in. A match flared halfway down the block. A green car was parked there, lights off, motor running, the off-side door hanging open. I saw that much in the flare of the match. The man who had struck it dropped it, stepped into the car. Its lights went on, dazzling at us from two nickle-plated bowls half the size of washtubs.

"Run for it!" the Senator blurted.

"Stand fast!" I said, and caught his arm, pushed him back into a doorway. The car gunned past, took the corner on two sidewalks. Its racketing died out along the dark street.

"Close," the Senator said in a strained voice. "Fast thinking, Florin."

"Uh-huh," I said. "Phony play. They wanted us to see them. Who were they, friends of yours?"

"What are you implying?"

"Not a thing, Senator. Just groping in the dark."

"Not nervous, are you, Florin?"

I gave him my best death-row grin. "Why should I be? You're the one they want to kill."

"Perhaps I exaggerated the dangers."

"Any idea why? The routine with the car, I mean."

"Coincidence," he said. "Stop reading deep significance into every incident, Florin."

He started past me and I stopped him. "Maybe I'd better go scout the area—alone."

"For God's sake, Florin—you'll be seeing

burglars under the bed next!"

"Sometimes they're there, Senator."

He made a disgusted sound. "I made a mistake in sending for you, Florin. You're not the man I was led to believe—" He broke off, listening to what he'd just said.

"Gets to you after a while, doesn't it, Senator?"

"What the devil does that mean?"

"I'm the man that took the job of guarding you, Senator. I take the job seriously—but you're not giving me much help."

He chewed his teeth and looked at me.

"Fire me and I'll walk away right now," I said. "But as long as I'm working for you we do it my way."

"You can't—" he started, but I waved that away.

"Name it, Senator."

"Damn it, man, can't you simply . . . go along?"

I looked at him.

"All right. We'll do it your way," he said between his teeth.

Something whispered behind my ear. The miniature voice said, *"Florin—there has been a slight hitch. You're to keep the subject away from the rendezvous for the present. Walk east; you'll receive further instructions shortly."*

"Well?" the Senator said.

"I changed my mind," I said. "Let's skip the meeting. You can make the next one in four hours."

"Damn it, man, every hour counts!"

"Only the ones while you're alive, Senator."

"All right, all right! What do you have in mind?"

"Suppose we walk east for a while."

He looked at me warily. "Florin—is there something you're not telling me?"

"I asked you first."

He snarled and pushed past me and headed east, and I followed. The blocks looked just like the ones we'd already walked along. A big green car with the top up cruised across an intersection half a block ahead. We kept going.

"All right, Florin," the little voice whispered. *"Stop at the next corner and wait."*

We came to the intersection and crossed. "You go ahead," I said. "I want to check something."

He gave me a disgusted look and strolled on fifty feet and stared into a dark window. I got out a cigarette and tamped the end and saw the green car round a corner two blocks down. I dropped the weed and faded back, sprinted toward the Senator.

"Now what?" he snarled, and put his back to the wall.

"In the alley—out of sight!" I snapped, and grabbed his arm.

"What for? What—"

"Hunch." I hustled him ahead, back into darkness and evil odors and things that crunched underfoot. I heard the purr of the big engine; it came closer, then stayed in one place and idled. A car door slammed. The car moved on, passed the alley mouth.

"Why, that's the same car. . . ." the Senator whispered.

"You know the owner?"

"Of course not. What is this, Florin?"

"Somebody's playing games. I get a feeling I don't like the rules."

"Can't you, for God's sake, speak plainly?"

"No plainer than I can think. Let's get out of here, Senator. That way." I pointed deeper into the alley. He grumbled but moved. We came out on a dark street that was wider but no more fragrant than the alley.

"Where are you leading me, Florin?" the Senator said in a voice that had gotten noticeably hoarser. "What are you getting me into?"

"I'm playing this one by ear," I said. "Let's find a quiet corner where we can talk—" I got that far with my reasonable proposal before the green car boomed out of a side street. It raked the curb, straightened out and roared down at us. I heard the Senator yell, heard glass tinkle, heard the *ba-ba-bam!* of a thirty caliber on full automatic, saw flame spurt and felt the sting of brick chips across my cheek. I was turning, grabbing the Senator and shoving him ahead of me, hearing the gun stutter again in the bellow of the big straight-eight that echoed and dwindled away and left us alone in a ringing silence bigger than a cathedral.

The Senator was leaning against the bricks, his back to me, folding slowly at the knees. I got to him and held him up and saw the big stain spreading on his side. Out in the street someone called cautiously. Feet clattered on pavement, coming our way. It was time to go. I got the Senator's arm over my shoulders; his feet fumbled at the bricks underfoot and some of his weight went off me. We did twenty drunken feet that way before I saw the door, set back in a deep recess on the left. It didn't look clean or inviting, but I lurched toward it and got the knob turned and we more or less fell into a dark little room with packing cases and scattered excelsior and odds and ends of wire and rope, barely visible in some dirty light leaking over the transom.

I settled the Senator on the floor and checked him and found two holes, low on his side, about six inches apart.

"How bad?" he whispered.

"Busted rib. The slug glanced off. You were lucky."

"You're hurt, too," he accused. I felt over my jaw, found some abraded skin that was bleeding a little.

"I take that back about your friends," I said. "Those were real bullets."

"They were trying to kill me!" He tried to sit up and I pressed him back.

"Don't sound so surprised. You told me that was the idea, remember?"

"Yes, but—" he stoppered it up. "They've gone out of their minds," he tried again, and let it go. "Florin, what are we going to do?"

"First, I'd better plug those holes." I peeled his shirt back and started to work.

"This chum you were supposed to meet: Eridani," I said. "Tell me about him."

"You were right. It was a trap. I can't go there now, I—"

"Hold it, Senator. I had my doubts about your story, but those slugs change things. This Eridani may be our out. How long have you known him?"

"Why—long enough, I suppose. A matter of years. I trusted him—"

"Any reason to tie him to the shooting?"

"Well . . . not specifically—but this whole thing has gone sour. I want to get clear of here, Florin, my life's not safe in this place; I—"

"Where will you go?"

"I don't know."

"Then maybe we'd better think about making that rendezvous."

"We can't go out there—into those streets!"

"We can't stay here."

"What the devil do you know about it? You're just—" He caught himself and sank back and glared at me.

"Sure; I'm the hired help. Why not let me work at what I was hired for? I'll check Eridani out alone. If it looks good, I'll bring him here—"

"No! I'm not staying alone!"

"It's the safest way."

He slumped. "I deserved that. I haven't borne up very well in the clutch, have I, Florin? Well, I told you violence wasn't my forte. But I'm all right now. I won't make a fool of myself again."

I finished my first-aid and wrapped a strip of shirt around him.

"Think you can walk?"

"Certainly." I helped him get to his feet. There was a faint *click!* behind my right ear and a voice the size of a Dutch half-dime said: *"All right, Florin; wait there for the next development."*

The Senator was busy buttoning his coat, grunting with pain at the movement. I felt back of my ear and found the gadget and pried it loose and ground it under my heel. A door across the room opened into a grimy hall that led to a glass door that let us out into the street.

No green Buicks were in sight; nobody shot at us. We kept to the shadows like a couple of mice caught outside the family hole and headed for the waterfront.

* * *

It was a mean-looking dive on a street only a little less shabby than the one where we'd been shot up. Two steps led down into dim brown light and the odors of booze and cigarettes. We took a booth at the back and ordered beer from an ex-heavyweight with broken-down arches and a face that had been hammered flat. He put two bleary glasses in front of us and went back behind the bar to brood. I had used my handkerchief to wipe the gore off my face, and with the coat folded the other way the Senator's stains didn't show; if our host noticed anything unusual for the neighborhood he was thoughtful enough not to mention it.

"He's late," the Senator said nervously. He was sitting on the side facing the door. "I don't like this, Florin. We're sitting ducks. They could fire through the window—"

"They could have done that any time. They didn't; maybe later we'll figure out why."

He wasn't listening; he was looking toward the door. I turned and saw a slim, dark-haired girl wrapped to the eyes in a red fox collar come down the two steps and look around. Her glance may have hesitated for a moment at our booth; or maybe it was just wishful thinking. She had a face like you see in dreams, and even then only at a distance. She went across the room and disappeared through a door at the back.

"Nice," I said. "On our side?"

"Who?"

"Don't overplay your hand, Senator," I said. "Nobody misses one like that."

He frowned at me. "See here, Florin, I don't care for your tone."

"Could it be there's something you're not telling me, Senator?"

"I've told you everything," he snapped. "This farce has gone far enough." He started to stand and froze that way, staring toward the windows. I turned my head and through the glass saw a Nile green Buick ease to a stop at the curb. The nearside door opened and a man stepped out. Under the brim of his dark hat I recognized the gray man. He seemed to see me through the windows and halted in midstride.

"You know him?" I snapped. The Senator didn't answer. His face was a trifle wavery around the edges. A high, singing noise was coming from somewhere in the middle distance. I tried to get my feet under me to stand, but couldn't seem to find them. The Senator was leaning over me, shouting something, but I couldn't make out the words. They ran together into a booming sound like a fast freight going through a tunnel, with me hanging onto

the side. Then my grip loosened and I fell off
and the train hurtled away into the dark, making mournful sounds that trailed away into
nothingness.

* * *

*I was lying on my back on hot sand, and the
sun was burning my face like a blast oven. Fire
ants were crawling over me, taking a bite here
and there, picking out a place to start lunch. I
tried to move, but my arms and legs were tied
down.*

"You're a damned coward," somebody was
saying.

"Damn you, I did all I could! It was all
coming apart on me!"

*The voices came from the sky. I tried to get
my eyelids up to see who was talking, but they
were tied down like the rest of me.*

"It's your own fault, Bardell," another voice
said. *This one reminded me of somebody.
Trait. Lenwell Trait, the name came from
somewhere a long way off, a long time ago. It
didn't sound like the name of anybody I'd
know.*

"My fault, hell! You were the masterminds,
the ones who knew what you were doing! I
went through hell, I tell you! You don't know
what it's like!"

"You quit—ran out! You ought to be shot!"

"Shut up—all of you!" *Big Nose talking. I
didn't know his name, or where I'd met him,
but I knew that voice.* "Lloyd, reset everything
for situation one. Bardell, get ready."

"Are you all crazy? I've had enough!"

"You're going back. You're a bungling in-

competent, but you're all we have. No arguments. The time for that's long past."

"You can't do it! I've lost confidence! I don't believe in the technique anymore! It would be murder!"

"Suicide," Big Nose said. "Unless you buck up and meet it. We're committed now. We can't back out."

"I need help—at least give me that! Things aren't breaking the way you said!"

"What about it, Lloyd?"

"All right, all right. For God's sake, settle it! I have my hands full!"

There was more talk, but another sound was drowning it.

The rising wind was hot as a blowtorch across my skin. A buzz saw started up and sliced its way across the sky; it split and darkness poured in like Niagara, swept away the voices, the ants, the desert, and me. . . .

* * *

I opened my eyes and the girl was sitting across from me, not wearing her fox skin now, looking at me with an anxious expression.

"Are you all right?" she said in a voice like doves cooing. Or like a spring breeze among the daffodils. Or like the gurgle of happy waters. Or maybe it was just a voice. Maybe I was slaphappy, coming out of it.

"Far from it," I said, using somebody else's voice by remote control. "I've got the damnedest urge to climb the chandelier and yodel the opening bars of *William Tell*. It's only my years of training that prevent me;

that and my rheumatism. How long was I out?"

She frowned. "You mean . . . ?"

"That's right, kid. Out. Cold. Doped. You know: unconscious."

"You were just sitting here. You looked a little strange, so I. . . .'

"They got him, huh?"

"Him? You mean your brother. He . . . just left."

"Which way? Did he go, that is. My drinking buddy, I mean. What makes you think he's my brother?"

"I . . . just assumed—"

"I don't suppose there's any point in asking where they took him, or why?"

"I don't know what you mean."

"This is where I'm supposed to work you over with my blackjack and get all your secrets. But frankly, honey, I'm not up to it."

I stood. That didn't feel at all good. I sat down again.

"You shouldn't exert yourself."

"What's it to you, doll?"

"Nothing—really. It's just. . . ." She let it go.

"Another time, maybe." I stood again. This time it worked a little better; but my head still felt like bagged gravel.

"Please wait!" she said, and put a hand on my arm.

"Another time I'd linger," I said, "but duty calls. Or something calls."

"You're hurt and sick—"

"Sorry, kid, I'm on my way. Sorry about no tip, but I seem to have left my change in my other suit. By the way, did you ever hear of the Lastrian Concord?"

She didn't answer, just shook her head. When I looked back from the door she was still watching me with those big lovely eyes. I let the door close between us and was back out in the street. A light snow was falling. In the thin layer of slush on the pavement I could see footprints leading back the way the Senator and I had come. I followed them, weaving a little, but still on the job.

* * *

The trail retraced the route the Senator and I had taken when we made our daring escape from the assassins, or whatever it was we had escaped from, if we had escaped. It ended at the spot where we had unloaded from the cargo flat. The tailor shop was still closed, but the second dummy from the left seemed to have an eye on me.

"Be my guest, buddy," I said. "We're two of a kind." He didn't answer, which suited me OK.

I felt as weak as a newborn squirrel and just about as smart. My wrists and ankles hurt. I wanted to lie down on something soft and wait for something nice to happen to me, but instead I moved along to a dark doorway and got comfortable in it and waited. I didn't know what I was waiting for. I thought about the girl back in the bar. She was nice to think about. I wondered if she'd been part of the dope-dream. I had an urge to go back and check, but just then a man stepped out of the alley-mouth across the street. He was in a dark overcoat and hat, but I knew the face. It was the scruffy redhead who had called at my hotel with the gray man.

He looked both ways along the street, then turned and set off at a brisk walk. I let him get to the corner, then followed. When I reached it, he was nowhere in sight. I kept going, passed a dark entry just in time to see the revolving door glide to a stop. I pushed through, was in a small lobby floored with black and white tiles, the small, rectangular unglazed kind, set in a pattern that zigged and zagged— just like my thoughts. The stairs led up to a landing; I could hear feet up above. They seemed to be in a hurry. I went up after them.

Two flights higher, the climb ended in a dark corridor. A faint greenish light was coming under a panel door at the far end. My feet made no sound at all on the Nile green carpet. No sounds came from behind the door. I didn't knock, just turned the knob and walked in.

There was a nice rug, a filing cabinet, a chair, a desk. And behind the desk, dressed in a snappy gray pinstripe, a cobra smiled at me.

Well, maybe not a cobra. A lizard. Pale violet, shading to powder blue, white at the throat. Smooth-scaled, glistening, round-snouted, with lidless eyes and a lipless mouth. Something not human. Something that leaned back in the chair and gave a careless wave of what was almost a hand and said, "Well, Mr. Florin—you've surprised us all." His voice was as light and dry as old rose petals.

I groped the Browning out into view and waved it at him. He lit up a cigarette and blew smoke through two small, noseless nostrils.

"Are you part of the first nightmare?" I said. "Or is this a double feature?"

He chuckled; a nice, friendly, relaxed chuckle such as you seldom hear from a reptile. Maybe he was all right at that.

"You're a most amusing fellow, Florin," he said. "But what are you attempting to accomplish? What do you seek in these ghostly rooms, these haunted corridors, eh?"

"You left out the phantom-ridden streets," I said. "I give up; what am I looking for?"

"Let me give you a word of friendly advice, Florin. Let it go. Stop seeking, stop probing. Let life flow past you. Accept what comes. You're Florin, a man of deeds, not philosophies. Accept what is."

"One at a time or all at once?" I raised the gun and aimed it at the middle of the smile.

"Tell me things," I said. "Anything at all. If I don't like it, I'll shoot."

The reptilian smile floated in a soft haze of cigarette smoke. A buzzing sound was coming out of the woodwork. I tried to say something, but there was no air in my lungs, only thick pink fog. I tried to squeeze the trigger, but it was welded in place, and I strained harder, and the buzzing got louder and the mist thickened and whirled around the little red eyes that gleamed now like two fading sparks far away across the sea and then winked out.

* * *

The girl was sitting across from me, wearing a close-fitting dark blue dress that shimmered like polished fish scales. She was looking at me with an anxious expression, like a bird-watcher watching a problem bird.

"No good," I said. "No bird watcher ever had eyes like those." The sound of my own voice startled me.

"Are you . . . all right now?" she said. Her voice was smooth as honey, as soft as a morning cloud, as sweet as music. Anyway, it was a nice voice. "Your friend left," she said, and looked worried.

I looked around. I was at the table in the beer joint, the same place I'd been the last time I swam up out of a Mickey. The Senator was nowhere in sight. Neither was the gray man or the Nile green car.

"Don't get the wrong idea," I said. "I'm not one of those habitual drunks. What makes you think he's my friend?"

"I . . . I just assumed—"

"How long was I out?"

"I'm not sure; I mean—you were just sitting here; you looked a little strange, so. . . ." Her voice trailed off.

I rubbed my temples; there was a light throbbing behind them that could become a heavy throbbing with very little encouragement.

"Did you ever get the feeling you'd been through a scene before?" I said. "I can almost guess your next line. You're going to suggest that I sit tight until I get to feeling better."

"I . . . think you should. You don't look well."

"I appreciate your interest, Miss—but why would you care?"

"Why wouldn't I? I'm a human being."

"That's more than I can say for some of the

folks I've been advised by lately. Say, you didn't see a fellow with a head like a garter snake? Only larger. His head, I mean."

"Please don't talk nonsense." She looked at me with an unreadable expression that I tried to read anyway.

"I knew you'd say that too. *Deja vu*, they call it. Or something. Have I come out of the smoke once, or twice? A question for the philosophers."

"I don't know what you're talking about," the girl said. "I thought you needed help. If I was wrong. . . ." She started to get up and I caught her hand and pulled her back.

"Don't rush off. You're my sole link with whatever you're my sole link with, if that makes any sense—or even if it doesn't."

She pulled against my grip, but not very hard. I let go and she didn't move.

"Maybe the Senator slipped me something," I said. "Or maybe he didn't. Maybe the gray man shot me with a dope dart. . . ."

"You've been shot?"

"At. They got the Senator, but it was just a graze. You wouldn't know who?"

She shook her head.

"Did you see the gray man? Or the green car?"

"No."

"But you saw the Senator. He was sitting with me when you came in. He pretended not to notice you. Why?"

"I have no idea."

"I'm his bodyguard," I said. "Or that's what they said. It turned out I was the finger. Dirty pool, don't you agree, Miss . . . ?"

"Regis. You're not making sense."

"I kind of don't like that, Miss Regis. I think maybe the Senator's lost confidence after what happened. Can't say I blame him. So maybe he ditched me; or maybe they got him. Either way, I don't care for it."

"Who is the Senator?"

"*The* Senator. A very big man. But no names. Not for the present. That's what the gray man said. I wish I knew which side he was on. I wish I knew which side *I* was on—or if there are any sides. How many sides to a ring-around-the-rosy, Miss Regis?"

She shook her head, just watching me.

"You'll have to overlook any little eccentricities I seem to demonstrate," I said. "I've been having a few mild hallucinations. Hard to tell which are which. You, for example. Why are you sitting here listening to me? You ought to be in full flight by now, yelling for the boys with the strap-down cots."

"I don't believe you're dangerous," she said calmly.

"Do you know me?"

"I never saw you before."

"What brought you out in the chill night air, to a place like this—alone?"

"I really can't say. It was . . . an impulse."

I nodded. "Swell. That clears that up. Any other points you'd like to cover before I go?"

"Please don't go—wherever it is you mean to go."

"Why not—except for those big blue eyes?" I got to my feet; my legs felt twelve feet long and the diameter of soda straws. I leaned on the table as if intentionally.

"I've got stuff to do, baby," I said. "I've got questions that want answers and answers looking for the right questions. And time's a-wasting." I tottered away, and she didn't call after me. I was a little sorry about that, but I kept going.

* * *

Outside I looked for tracks in the snow, but there wasn't any snow. In a way that was re-assuring; the snow was part of the dream. The street was still there; that was something. I turned right and headed the way I had gone the last time, or dreamed I had, or dreamed I'd dreamed I had, the time I met the fellow with the purple head. Meeting him had been a break. It helped me remember he wasn't really there. Whatever they'd fed me, it was potent stuff. I still felt woozy as a conventioneer discovering it's Tuesday morning in a strange town.

The streets were empty, even for the wee hours. No lights were on in the windows. No cars moved. Just the fitful wind and a feeling of mice scuttling behind the wainscoting. I made it back to the street where I'd made my debut in town a few hundred years—or maybe two hours—before. I turned the last corner and saw a man in a dark hat and overcoat standing in front of the tailor shop, looking into the window. I recognized him; it was Red, the rangy man who had paid the call at my hotel in company with the gray man. As prophecy, my dope-dream hadn't been too bad so far.

Then the Senator walked out of the alley

across the way. I eased back out of sight and
ran through the data. That confused me, so I
ran through it again, in the other direction.
That confused me still more.

"To hell with the data," I growled. "Let's get
back to essentials." I patted my gun and came
around the corner ready for action. They were
gone.

I strolled on up to the place where Red had
been standing, but I'm not enough of a tracker
to pick out the spoor of a leather sole on concrete. I looked up and down the street, saw nobody, heard nothing.

"All right, come on out," I called. "I know
you're there."

Nobody answered, which was just as well. I
went along to the corner. Nobody there. The
city looked as deserted as Pompeii—and as
full of ancient sin.

In the dream I had followed Red through a
door halfway down the block. Maybe that was
a clue. In the absence of any other, it would
have to do. I went along to the spot and found
a big glass door with a large number 13
painted on it in swooping gold characters. It
opened to a push, and I stepped into a foyer
with Nile green walls and a spiral staircase
and an odor like an abandoned library. Listening revealed a lot of stately silence. I went up
the carpeted steps, came out on a landing with
a gray door. I eased it open and saw the
scruffy man six feet away with his back to me.
He wasn't hiding; he was in the act of unlock-
ing the door; I had my gat in his left kidney
before he had time to turn around.

"Don't ever think I won't squeeze a few

rounds into your spine if it works out that way," I said in what I was using for a voice. It had a big, hollow ring to it, like a speech in an empty auditorium.

His eyes looked like mice caught outside their holes. His mouth sagged sideways like an overloaded pocket.

"Tell me things," I said. "Don't worry about getting it all in order. Just start. I'll tell you when to stop."

"You—can't be here," he said in a choked version of the high-pitched squeak.

"I know. Let's just pretend I am anyway. Where's the Senator?"

"You can forget the Senator now," he said, talking so fast his tongue couldn't keep up. "That's all over now."

"Been for a ride in a green Buick lately?" I said, and ground the gun in harder.

"I never meant to kill you; you'd have been phased back to Eta Level, I swear it!"

"That's a big load off my mind," I said. "Keep going."

"You have to believe me! When the operation's over, I can show you the tape—" He paused to gulp. "Look here; I can prove everything I'm saying. Just let me key the retriever, and—" He jammed the key in and turned it. I made a grab for him but all of a sudden the air was as thick as syrup and the same color, full of little whirly lights.

"You fool—you'll lose him!" somebody yelled. It was the Senator's voice but it was coming to me via satellite relay, backed by a massed chorus and a drum as big as the world, beating sixty beats a minute. I sucked

in some of the dead air and grabbed for Red
with a vague idea of holding on and going
where he went; but he turned to smoke that
spread out and washed up around me like
surf, and I took a breath to yell and the water
rose and covered me, and I sank down in a
graceful spiral while the light faded from
green through turquoise to indigo to black
like the dark side of Pluto.

* * *

She was sitting across from me, dressed in
a sissified white blouse and a powder blue
jacket. Her hair was a soft brown, and so were
her eyes. She was looking at me with an
anxious expression, like a mother hen watching her first egg hatch.

"Wrong." My voice sounded blurry in my
own ears. "A swan, maybe. But not a hen. And
definitely not a mother." I reached across the
table and caught her wrist. I was good at grabbing people's wrists. Holding on was another
matter. She didn't struggle.

"I . . . thought perhaps you needed help,"
she said in a breathless whisper.

"The thought does you credit," I looked
around the room. It was the same room it had
been the last time I ran through the scene. The
barman was still polishing the same glass;
there was the same odor of fried onions and
spilled wine, the same blackened beams, the
same tarnished copper pots beside the fireplace. Or were they the same? Maybe not. The
flames looked cheery and comforting, but if
they gave any warmth I couldn't feel it from
where I sat.

"The other man—your friend—went off and left you," the girl said. "You looked—"

"Sure—a little strange," I said. "Let's skip over the rest of the routine, honey. There's a deeper conversation that's been wanting us to have it."

"I don't know what you mean," she said in a small voice that still sounded like Gypsy guitars in the night.

"What's your name?" I said.

"Miss Regis. Curia Regis."

"And you already know mine, right?"

"Of course. I think perhaps you've made a mistake—"

"I had a wide choice of mistakes to make, and I made them all." I let go of her and rubbed my wrists, but it didn't help. I wanted to rub my ankles, but restrained the impulse. My chest hurt every time I breathed, but I breathed anyway.

"You can start by clearing up a point," I said. "Have we ever sat here before—at this table—in this room?"

"No—of course not."

"Why are you here?"

"Because of your message—of course." Her eyes searched mine for something she didn't seem to find.

"Tell me about my message."

"In the newspaper. The Personals column."

"What did it say?"

"Just—*I need you.* And your name."

"And you came—just like that."

"If you don't need me, I'll go away."

"Sit tight. Order a sandwich. Count to a million by hundreds. If I'm not back by then, start without me." I got a grip on the edge of the table and wrestled my feet under me. They were steady enough, but the room had a tendency to rock.

"Here I go again," I said. "Third time's the charm."

When I looked back from the door, the table was empty.

* * *

"Florin," I told myself, "there's something you're doing wrong; or something you're not doing right."

I looked up and down the street. A light snow was falling. There were no people in sight, no footprints on the sidewalk, no tire tracks in the street. I had the world to myself.

"I got doped," I said. "I'm having French fits coming out of it. But how many tries do I have to make before the big one? How do I know when it's for real?"

"It's a learning process," I said. "You're unconscious, thinking about it. Each time you take a wrong turning in your logic you get sent back to square one. Your subconscious is trying to tell you something."

"How about now?" I asked, cagy. "Am I really standing here having a friendly conversation with myself like any normal guy, or—"

I got that far with the question when the world disappeared.

Now, it's always a shock to the nervous system when the power fails, even when it's only a bridge lamp that goes off. But this time the sky went out, too. It was total, impenetrable black in every direction. I put out a hand and felt the wall beside me; with my nose an inch from it, I could sense it, but not see it.

"New rules, Florin," I said aloud, just to be hearing something. "But the same game."

I felt over the wall behind me, found the door I had just come out of. It was locked, frozen harder than a Nazi's Swiss account.

"No going back," I counseled myself. "That leaves forward, if you can call it forward. Back to the spot where the action is. You can do it by dead reckoning."

It wasn't much of an idea, but I didn't have a better one.

It took me half an hour, shuffling along with one hand on the wall and the other out in front, feeling the air. I stepped down curbs and up again on the other side, avoided falling over fireplugs, didn't get run over, all without a seeing-eye dog. I was proud of myself. Good work, Florin. If your enemies could see you now. . . .

That gave me a creepy sensation along the back of my neck. My being blind didn't mean anybody else was. Maybe they were watching me, tracking me every foot of the way, closing in for the kill.

I didn't know who I meant by "they." That made it worse. I had started off working for the Inner Council but had neglected to get the names. Then the Senator took over, and for a while we had worked out pretty well together, but then that went sour, too. There was a chance that he had given me the Mickey himself, but in the absence of proof he was still my client. If Van Wouk or someone else of the same name had grabbed him out from under my slumbering nose it was up to me to get him back, which meant I had to keep right on picking my way, counting the paces and the blocks, back to where I had last seen him and the scruffy man.

I was at the corner. I turned left and felt my way along to the glass door with the big 13. There wasn't any door. Maybe I'd counted wrong. Maybe somebody had come along and sealed it up just to confuse me. Maybe it hadn't been there in the first place.

I went on another few feet and stumbled into a revolving door; it revolved and palmed me into the blinding glare of a forty-watt bulb hanging on a kinked wire in a lobby that was either being built or torn down.

There was nothing pretty in sight, but it was nice to have my eyes back, even if all I was looking at was bare lath walls, a rough concrete floor, temporary wooden steps leading up.

"This time," I told myself, "you play it a little smoother. No blundering around with a gat in your fist; no pushing open strange doors and sticking your head in to see what they hit it with. Foxy all the way, that's the motto."

I went up. There was a landing covered with shavings and brick dust. A black fire door had the number 13 in heavy brass above it. With an ear pressed to it, I could make out the sound of voices. They seemed to be disagreeing about something. That suited me; I was in a mood to be disagreeable. I tried the knob; it turned, and I stepped through into a passage with a plastered wall on one side and obscure-glass cubicles on the other. The voices were coming from the third cubicle in line. I soft-footed along to it.

"... what do you mean, lost him?" Big Nose was saying.

"I tell you, there's a factor of unpredictability involved! I'm getting interference!" This in a thin, high-pitched tone.

"Get him back—before irreparable damage is done!"

"I don't understand it. The recovery was made in time. . . ."

"You see?" a voice that was not quite that of the Senator said. "I'm telling you I can't take many more shocks like the last one."

"Never mind what you can take! You knew what you were signing up for!"

"Did I? Not even the Professor knows what's going on!"

"Don't call me 'Professor,' Bardell!"

"Gentlemen—let's not lose sight of the objective! Everything else is secondary."

There was a rather long silence. I breathed through my mouth and tried to read minds through the door. Either I couldn't read minds or there was nobody there. I eased the door open. The room was empty, looked as though it had been empty for a long time. In the closet were three bent coat hangers and some brown paper on the shelf. That and a few dead flies. A connecting door into the next office had been boarded up. I checked the boards; something clicked and the wall glided back and ocher light blazed through. I palmed my toy gun and stepped through into a wide avenue of colored tiles.

I squinted up at the sky. The strange yellow light was the sun. It was midafternoon of a pleasant summer day. Not a snowstorm. A drop of water ran down my chin. I put the back of my hand against my face; the skin was as cold as frozen fish.

"Fake money, fake Senator, fake weather," I said. "Or maybe this is the fake. Maybe I'm in a big room with a sky-blue ceiling and an imitation sun."

"Could be," I agreed. *"The question remains —why?"*

"The Senator will know," I pointed out.

"Sure—but will he talk?"

"When I finish bouncing his phony head off this phony pavement he'll sing like three canaries," I stated with less confidence than I felt.

"You've got to catch him first."

"Nothing to it. He can't escape the eagle eye of Florin, the Master Sleuth—unless I happen to step on my shoelace and rupture my spleen."

"Do I detect a note of disillusionment? Not getting tired of your tricks, are you, Florin?"

"That's the trouble with tricks. They pall. God, how they pall."

"Try the park."

I was looking across the wide avenue at a stretch of downy-looking green grass set with tall, feathery trees. Beyond them tall, misty buildings loomed, gleaming white. A vehicle swung a corner and rolled toward me on high wheels. It was light, fragile-looking, like a buggy without a horse, painted a soft purple and decorated with curly corners and a complicated pattern in gold lines. A man and a woman sat in it, looking at each other while the buggy drove itself. They were both dressed in filmy white stuff with flecks of color here and there. The rubber tires made a soft whooshing sound against the tiles as it glided past.

"I knew Henry was planning a big surprise for '30, but I wasn't expecting this," I said, and realized I was not only talking aloud, I was waiting for an answer. Whatever it was the Senator had used to spike my beer had more side-effects than six months of hormone injections—perhaps including hallucinations involving purple carriages rolling down tile streets under a sun two sizes too big and three shades too yellow. It was time for me to curl up somewhere and sweat it out of my system. I headed for the biggest clump of flowering shrub in sight, rounded it, and almost collided with the Senator.

His head jerked. "You!" he said, not sounding pleased. "What are you doing *here!*"

"Sorry, I dozed off while you were talking," I said. "Rude of me. How's your busted rib feeling?"

"Florin—go back! Quickly! You have no business here! This is all wrong!"

"What is this place, Senator?"

He backed away. "I can't tell you. I can't even speak of it!"

"Sorry to be insistent," I said, and grabbed for him as he jumped back. He ducked aside and sprinted for it. I gave chase, using a pair of borrowed legs and towing a head the size of a blimp at the end of a hundred-foot cable.

It was a strange chase along the curving graveled path. We ran past fountains that threw tinkling jets of ink into green-crystal pools, past banked flowers like daubs of fluorescent paint, under the blue shadows of trees with bark like polished lacquer and foliage like antique lace. He ran hard, head down and legs pumping; I floated along behind, watching him get farther and farther away. Then he jumped a hedge, tripped, and was still rolling when I landed on him. He was a big boy and plenty strong, but he didn't know how to use it. A couple of solid hooks to the jaw took the shine off his eyes. I laid him out comfortably under what looked like a juniper except for the little crimson blossoms and worked on getting my wind back. After a while he blinked and sat up. He saw me and looked glum.

"You and I need to have a little talk," I said. "I'm two paradoxes and a miracle behind."

"You're a fool," he snarled. "You don't know what you're involving yourself in."

"But I'd like to," I said. "By the way, tell me again what the Lastrian Concord is."

He snorted. "I never heard of it."

"Too bad," I said. "I guess I imagined it. I saw this in the same place." I slid the flat gun I had taken from his safe into sight. "Maybe I'm imagining it, too."

"What does this mean, Florin?" the Senator said in a tight voice. "Are you selling me out, then?"

It was my turn to grin the lazy grin. "Nuts," I said. "Who do you think you're kidding, Senator—or whoever you are."

He looked astounded. "Why should I want to deceive you?"

"It was laid on with a trowel," I said. "The callers in the night, the fancy reception room, the hints of dark deeds in the offing. And the details were nice: fake official forms, fake money—maybe even a fake gun." I bounced it on my palm.

"It's a two-mm. needler," he said, sounding angry or maybe scared. "Be careful with it!"

"Yeah, the details were good," I went on. "It's just the big things that fit like a rent tuxedo. I went along to find out why."

"I'm out of it," the Senator said. "I wash my hands of the whole affair."

"What about the invasion?"

He looked at me and frowned.

"No invasion, huh?" I said. "Too bad. I kind of liked the invasion. It had possibilities. What then?"

His jaw muscles worked. "Aw, hell," he said, and made a face. "My name's Bardell. I'm an actor. I was hired to impersonate the Senator."

"Why?"

"Ask the man who hired me," he said in a nasty tone, and felt of his jaw.

"Hurts, huh?" I said. "I did that. I owed you a couple anyway for the beer. It was worth one without the Mickey."

"You're quite a fellow, aren't you? That dose should have held you until. . . ." He cut himself off. "Never mind. I can see we handled it wrong from the beginning."

"Tell me about the beginning." He started to get up and I stood over him and shook my head. "I never hit a man when he's down," I said. "Unless I have to. Talk it up, chum."

He looked at me and grinned. He laughed a short laugh. "Florin, the Man of Iron," he said. "Florin, the poor unsuspecting boob who lets himself be roped in with the old call to duty. They fixed you up with a costume and makeup and lines to say—plus a little gadget back of the ear to coach you through the rough spots. And what do you do? You kick a hole in it you could march a Shriners' band through."

"Looks like you've got all the good lines," I said.

"Don't misunderstand me, Florin," he said. "Hell, don't you get it yet?" He tapped the mastoid bulge behind his ear. "I've got the twin to it right here. I was roped in the same way you were."

"By who? Or 'whom'—if it means a lot to you."

"The Council."

"Keep going; you're doing fine."

"All right! They had plans; obviously they aren't working."

"Don't make me coax you, Bardell. I'm the guy who wants to be told things. Start tying it all together. I don't like all these loose ends."

"What I could tell you won't make you any happier."

"Try me."

He gave me a crafty look. "Let me ask you one instead, Florin: how did you get from your room—in a rather seedy hotel, as I recall —to Government House? For that matter, how did you get to the hotel?"

I thought back. I remembered the room. It was seedy, all right. I tried to recall the details of checking in, the face of the room clerk. Nothing. I must have let my poker face slip because Bardell grinned a savage grin.

"What about yesterday, Florin? How about your last case? Your old parents, the long happy days of your boyhood? Tell me about them."

"It must be the dope," I said, and my tongue felt thick.

"There seem to be a few small blank spots in the Florin total recall," the ex-Senator jeered.

"What's the name of your hometown, Florin?"

"Chicago," I said, pronouncing it like a word in a foreign language. The Senator looked puzzled. "Where's that?"

"Between New York and LA, unless you've moved it."

"Ellay? You mean . . . California? On Earth?"

"You guessed it," I said, and paused to moisten my lips with the dry sock I found where my tongue used to be.

"That explains a few things," he muttered. "Brace yourself, fellow. You're in for a shock."

"Go ahead," I said, "but remember my heart murmur."

"We're not on Earth. We're on Grayfell, the fourth planet of the Wolf 9 system, twenty-eight light years from Sol."

"It's a switch," I said, and my voice felt as hollow as a Christmas tree ornament. "We're not being invaded by an alien planet; we've invaded *them*."

"You don't have to take my word for it, Florin." A split lip blurred his voice a little; or something did. "Look around you. Do these look like Terran plants? Don't you notice the gravity is eighteen percent light, the air is oxygen-rich? Look at the sun; it's a diffuse yellow giant, four hundred million miles away."

"All right. My old mother, if I had an old mother, always told me to look the truth in the eye. You're not helping much. It was bad enough when I was chasing my tail back in Chi. Start making it all clear, Bardell. Somebody went to a lot of trouble, either to transport me to a place called Grayfell or to build a pretty convincing set. There'll be a reason for that. What is it?"

He looked at me the way a surgeon looks at a leg that has to come off.

"You don't know what you're doing. You're getting in out of your depth; matters aren't what they seem—"

"Don't tell me what they aren't, Bardell; tell me what they are."

"I can't do that." He had something in his hands, fiddling with it; something with shiny knobs and a crystalline loop at the top that was hard to look at. "I've been patient with you, Florin," he said, but his voice was sliding away from me, talking faster and faster like a runaway Victrola.

My head was throbbing worse than ever; my vision wasn't all it could have been. I made a grab for the blurry face in front of me; but it

slid back out of reach. I saw something glint
in the sunlight, and heard a voice from over
the hills saying, ". . . Sorry, Florin. . . ."

Then pink darkness exploded in my face
and I was back on that freight, riding it over a
cliff and down into an abyss filled with fading
thunder.

*   *   *

*"Mr. Florin," the feather-light voice was say-
ing, "you're creating something of a problem
for us all."*

*I opened my eyes and the chap with the
snake's head smiled his lipless smile at me and
puffed pink smoke from his noseless nostrils
and glittered his lidless eyes. He was lounging
in a deck chair, wearing an open jacket made
of orange toweling, and a pair of yellow shorts,
the color of which reminded me of something
that I couldn't quite get a grip on.*

*"That's something," I said, and sat down in
a camp chair. There was a table between us
with a blue and white umbrella over it. There
was a stretch of white sand behind the terrace
that looked like the seashore except that there
wasn't any sea. I tried not to look at his glistening silver-violet thighs, the ribby pale gray
chest with tiny crimson flecks, the finger-thin
toes in the wide-strapped sandals. He saw me
not looking and made a soft clucking sound
that seemed to be laughter.*

*"Forgive me," he said. "I find this curiosity
of yours amazing. I suspect that in the
moment of your dissolution, you'd crane your
neck to discover the nature of the solvent."*

"It's just a harmless eccentricity," I said,

"like your taste in clothes."

"You pride yourself on your self-control," he said, not quite as genially as before. *"But what if your equanimity is presented with anomalies too great to be assimilated? What then, eh?"* He raised a hand and snapped his fingers. Fire billowed up around him; his smile rippled in the heat shimmer as gusts of flame whipped toward me. I sat tight, partly from paralysis and partly because I didn't believe it. He snapped his fingers again and green water was all around us, the sun dazzling on the surface ten feet above. A small fish came nosing between us, and he waved it away negligently and snapped his fingers again. Snow was falling. A thick layer of it covered the table, capped his head. His breath was a plume of ice crystals.

"Neat," I said. *"Are you any good at card tricks?"*

He waved the ice away and put his fingertips together.

"You're not impressed," he said matter-of-factly. *"The manipulation of the Universe implies nothing to you?"*

I faked a yawn. Then it wasn't a fake. *"The Universe?"* I said. *"Or my eyeballs?"*

"Umm. You're a surprising creature, Florin. What is it you want? What motivates you?"

"Who's asking?"

"You may call me Diss."

"That's not what I asked you."

"Just consider that . . . there are other interested parties than those you traditionally know. You act on a larger stage than you hitherto suspected. You should therefore con-

duct yourself with circumspection."

I yawned again. "I'm tired," I said. "I'm behind on sleep, on food, on love—on everything except mysterious phonies who drop large hints that big affairs are in the offing and that my best bet is to play along and keep my nose clean. Who are you, Diss? What are you? Do you really look like Alexander the croc, or is that just my bilious outlook?"

"I am a representative of certain powers active in the Cosmos. My appearance is of no importance. The fact of my existence is enough."

"Bardell said something about an invasion."

"A word reflecting a primitive view of reality."

"What are you invading? Earth—or Grayfell?"

I had the pleasure of seeing his head jerk.

"What do you know of Grayfell, Mr. Florin?"

"You know—in the Wolf 9 group, twenty-eight lights from old Chicago." I smiled a big happy smile. He frowned and reached almost casually for something on the table. I started to get up fast, and a flashbulb as big as the sky winked and folded down on blackness blacker than the inside of a sealed paint can. I lunged across the table, and my fingers brushed something as hot as a cook-stove, as slippery as raw liver. I heard an excited hiss and grabbed again and got a grip on something small and hard and complicated that resisted and then came free. There was an angry yell, a sense of words being shouted faster than I could follow, a blinding explosion—

She was sitting across the table from me, wrapped in a threadbare old cloth coat with a ratty squirrel skin collar. Her eyes looked into mine with a searching expression.

"Don't tell me," I said, sounding groggy even to me. "I was sitting here with my eyes crossed, singing old sea chanteys to myself in colloquial Amharic; so you sat down to see if I was all right. Good girl. I'm not all right. I'm a long way from all right. I'm about as far from all right as you can get and still count your own marbles."

She started to say something but I cut her off: "Let's not run through the rest of the lines; let's skip ahead to where you tell me I'm in danger, and I go charging out into the night to get my head bent some more."

"I don't know what you mean."

"I mean it seems we sat and talked like this before. We looked at each other in the same way then—"

"That's an old popular song."

"It seems to be. Everything seems to be something. Usually what it isn't. What are you?" I reached across and took her hand. It was cool and smooth and didn't move when my fingers closed around it. I said, "Listen carefully, Currie. I know your name because you told it to me. Sitting right where you're sitting now. . . ." I paused to take a look around the room. It was done in pine paneling with varnish that was black with age and lack of laundering. A sign on the wall invited me to drink Manru beer.

". . . or almost. You said you came in answer to my ad—"

"You mean your telephone call."

"OK, make it a phone call. Or a carrier pigeon. That's not important. At least I don't think it's important. Maybe I'm wrong. Who knows? Do you?"

"Florin—you're not making sense. You told me on the telephone that it was urgent."

"And you came running—in the middle of the night."

"Of course I did."

"Who are you, Miss Regis?"

She looked at me with eyes as big and tragic as the cave where Floyd Collins was trapped.

"Florin," she whispered. "Don't you remember me? I'm your wife."

I leered at her. "Oh, yeah? Last time we talked you said we'd never met."

"I knew you'd been working too hard. It was too much—for anyone—"

"Ever heard of a place called Grayfell?" I cut into her routine.

"Of course. Our summer place at Wolf Lake."

"Sure. Silly of me. Twenty-eight miles from —where?"

"Chicago."

"One other point: among our close-knit circle of friends, does there happen to be a fellow with a purple head?"

She almost smiled. "You mean poor old Sid?"

"That's Diss spelled backward. Only with one S. Better make a note of that. Maybe it's important."

"Poor Florin," she started, but I waved that away.

"Let's marshall our facts," I said. "Maybe we don't have any facts, but let's marshall them anyway. Fact number one, a couple of hours ago I woke out of a sound sleep and found two men in my room. They gave me a pitch that smelled plenty fishy, but I went along. They took me to a committee of VIP's who told me the Senator was subject to delusions; that they'd arrange to make his delusions real; and I was to enter into his fantasy with him. But I have a feeling the fantasy with had already started. Big Nose was part of it. But I didn't know that then. That was a couple of hours ago.

"Since then, I've been asking myself just how much I know about their boss—the 'Senator.' That one comes up blank too. Senator who? I don't even know the man's name. That strikes me as odd. How does it strike you?"

"Florin—you're raving—"

"I'm just starting, baby. Wait till I really get going. Fact number two, the Senator may or may not be someone else of the same name, got me? Possibly an actor named Bardell. Does the name ring a bell?"

"You mean Lance Bardell, the Trideo star?"

"Trideo . . . now that's an interesting word. But let's skip it for now. As I was saying, this Senator fellow is kind of an inconsistent player. First it was a murder plot. Then we had alien invaders. Next, he was an actor, a kidnap victim, or maybe a planted spy—I can't quite remember which. But I went along, followed him to a tavern, where he fed me something that put me out like two runners at third. When I woke up you were there."

She just looked at me with those big, wide, hurt eyes.

"I won't ask the old one about what a nice girl like you was doing in a place like this," I said. "Or maybe I will. What was a nice girl like you doing in a place like this?"

"Now you're mocking me. Why must you be cruel, Florin? I only want to help."

"Back to the facts. How far did I get? Fact number three? That was where I hotfooted it on somebody's backtrail and found a missing door. Or didn't find it."

"Does that really matter now—?"

"You're not paying attention. First there was a door, then there wasn't. Doesn't that seem odd to you? Or am I confused?"

"You make a joke of everything."

"Baby, after considerable thought I've reached the conclusion that the only conceivable legitimate answer to the Universe as constituted is a peal of hysterical laughter. But I digress."

"This isn't a joke, Florin. It's deadly serious."

"I remember once waking up in the middle of the night with the phone ringing. I groped around in the dark and picked it up and got it in position and all of a sudden I was asking myself a question: *Is this right? Do you really talk to an inanimate object?*"

"Florin, please stop—"

"But I was telling you about the door that wasn't there. I settled down to wait. My old associate, the gray man, came out of an alley and I followed him. He led me to a room with nobody in it, not even him."

"I don't understand—"

"Me, too, kid. But let me get back to my story. I want to see how it turns out. Where was I? Oh, yes—all alone with some bent coat hangers. So I prowled around until I found somebody to talk to. He turned out to be the fellow with a head like a garter snake."

"Florin—"

I held up a hand. "No interruptions, please. I'm learning plenty, just listening to me talk. For example, I just said he looked like a garter snake. The first time I saw him it was a cobra I thought of. Maybe I'm licking my neurosis. If I can work him down to a harmless angleworm maybe I can live with that. The funny thing is, he was like you in some ways."

She tried to smile. She was humoring me now. "Oh? In what way?"

"He advised me to stop asking questions and drift with the current. I promptly blacked out. And guess what? I was back here—with you—again."

"Go on."

"Aha—I'm getting your attention at last. That was the second time we met—but you don't remember."

"No—I don't remember."

"Sure. You warned me I was in trouble and I went out and ran around the block looking for it, and found enough to end up back here. It made me feel kind of like one of those rubber balls they tie to ping pong rackets."

"That was . . . our third meeting, then."

"Now you're catching on, girl. Stay with me. From here on it gets complicated. I still had a yen to see my old boss, the Senator. This time there was a trick door. I went through it and suddenly it was a summer afternoon in a place with eighteen percent light gravity, too much sun, and trees like lace underwear. The Senator was there. We were just beginning to get somewhere when he pulled a swifty and knocked me colder than a plate of Army eggs."

She waited, watching my face.

"That was when I saw Snake Head the second time. Diss, he said his name was. Wanted me to smarten up and play by the rules. Said he was a big shot—but he blew his cool when I mentioned Grayfell. He turned out the lights and I heard voices and passed out. . . ."

"And now—you're here."

"When I wake up you're always there to greet me. It's enough to make a man look forward to a tire-iron on the head. Except that I don't exactly wake up. First I'm *there*—then I'm here."

"You spoke of *dejà vu*—the already seen," she said in a brisk, case-worker tone. "There's a theory that it results from a momentary distraction; when your attention returns to your surroundings you have a sense of having been there before. And of course you have—a split second earlier."

"Nice theory. Of course it doesn't explain how I know your name. But I'm forgetting: you're my wife."

"Yes."

"Where did we meet?"

"Why, we met. . . ." Her face became as still as a pond at dawn. The tip of her tongue came out and reassured itself that her upper lip was still there.

"I don't know," she said in a voice you could have printed on the head of a pin.

"Welcome to the group. Do I begin to interest you in my problem, Miss Regis?"

"But—why?" She grabbed a finger and started twisting it. "What does it mean?"

"Who says it means anything? Maybe it's all a game, played for someone else's amusement."

"No—I can't believe that; I won't!" She said this in a shocked gasp.

"But we can refuse to play."

"That's what you've been doing, isn't it, Florin? Has it helped you?"

I grunted. "There's a certain satisfaction in messing up their plans—if they're there and they have plans."

"Please, Florin—don't drop back into that brittle, cynical pose! It isn't like you—not really."

"How would you know?"

"Some things one simply knows."

"And some things one finds out. I've picked up a few items I don't think they intended me to know."

"Go on." Her eyes held on mine. They were a pellucid green with flecks of gold swimming in their depths.

"Maybe I wasn't supposed to see the purple money with 'Lastrian Concord' printed across it," I said. "Or maybe it was another plant.

But then Red stuck his head up. I can't figure that. He ran when he saw me. After that I listened in on a conversation I'm pretty sure I wasn't intended to hear. Big voices, talking in the sky, arguing about things going wrong. Maybe they meant me. Or maybe I dreamed it. The Senator was there, and Big Nose. They talked about situation one. Not much help there."

"Go on, Florin."

"Then you stepped into the picture. I don't know why, but I have a feeling you're not part of Big Nose's plans."

"I'm not, Florin! Please believe me! I'm not part of anything—that I know of," she finished in a whisper.

"Then there's Grayfell," I said. "Magic gates into other worlds don't fit any world-picture of mine. Bardell was surprised to see me there. And when I squeezed him he told me things I don't think Big Nose wanted me to know. Or maybe not. Maybe I'm being led every foot of the way. Maybe there are coils within coils, traps within traps—"

"Florin! Stop! You have to believe in something! You have to have a starting point! You mustn't begin to doubt yourself!"

"Yeah. *Cogito ergo sum.* I've always got that to fall back on. I wonder what a polyplex computer's first thought is when they shoot the juice to it?"

"Is that what they expect you to say, Florin? Is that the role they want you to act out?"

I shook my head. "How much of myself can I peel away and have anything left? If the itch I've got to get my hands on the Senator isn't my own, I'm no judge of compulsions."

"Florin — can't you just — forget the Senator? Forget all of it, come home with me?"

"Not now, baby," I said, and felt myself start to smile. "Probably not before, and definitely not now. Because they goofed."

She waited; she knew there was more. I opened the hand that I had been holding in a tight fist for the past quarter hour and looked at the gadget I was holding. It was small, intricate, with bulges and perforations and points of brilliance that scintillated in the dim light; a manufactured article, and manufactured by an industry that was a long way from human.

"I took it away from Snake Head," I said. "That means Snake Head is real—at least as real as you and me."

"What is it?"

"Evidence. I don't know what of. I want to show it to people and see what happens. I can hardly wait. I've got a feeling they won't like it, and that alone will be worth the price of admission."

"Where will you go?"

"Back where they don't want me to."

"Don't do it, Florin! Please!"

"Sorry. No turning back for the Man of Iron. Straight ahead into the brick wall, that's my style."

"Then I'm going with you."

"You always let me go before. What's different now?"

"I don't know anything about all that. Shall we go?"

"It's a switch," I said. "Maybe it's a good omen."

Outside, the chilly wind was blowing in the empty street. She hugged herself, a chore I'd have been glad to do for her.

"Florin—it's so bleak—so lonely. . . ."

"Not with you along, doll." I took her arm; I could feel her shivering as we started off.

* * *

The tailor shop was still there, and the candy store; but now there was a vacant lot between them, full of dry weed-stalks and rusty cans and broken bottles.

"Tsk," I said. "No attention to details." I led the way to the corner and along to where the revolving door had been. It was gone. In its place was a tattoo parlor with a display like a retired Buchenwald guard might have on his den wall. But no door. Not even a place where a door could have been. This started my head hurting again. On the third throb, a voice the size of a cricket rubbed its wing cases together inside my ear and said, *"All right, Florin. Wait there for the next development."*

"What is it?" the girl said.

"Nothing: just a twinge from my sciatica," I said, and felt back of my ear. No little pink chip seemed to be there. I checked the other side. OK. So now I was hearing voices without the aid of hardware. It wasn't an unheard-of-trick: lots of psychotics could do it.

We went along to an archway that opened on a musty arcade full of cobwebs and damp air. I tried the first door I came to and stepped into a room I'd seen before.

The thick rug was gone, the heavy drapes were missing, the plaster walls were cracked and blotched with age. Newspapers that looked as if someone had slept in them were scattered across the floor. The only furniture was the collapsing steel frame of what might have been a leather lounge. But the door to the safe, somewhat corroded but still intact, hung half open, just as it had the last time I'd been here.

"Do you know this place?" Miss Regis whispered.

"It's my old pal the ex-Senator's private hideaway. The only trouble is, it's sixty miles from here, in a big house with lots of lawn and fence and a full set of security men. Either that, or I had a ride on a cargo flat that drove in circles for three hours."

I looked in the safe; there was nothing there but some dust and a torn envelope with a purple postage stamp, addressed to *Occupant, Suite 13*. I checked the fake window, the one the Senator had opened like a door for our midnight escape; but if there was a latch there I couldn't find it.

"It seems the Senator moved out and took all his clues with him," I said. "A dirty trick, but maybe I know a dirtier one." I went to the closet and felt over the back wall.

"He told me the official escape route was here," I told the girl. "Maybe he was lying, but—" The chunk of wall I was pushing on pivoted sideways and cool air blew in from the darkness beyond.

"Aha," I said. "Predictability is the test of any theory; now all we need is a theory." I had

the gun the Senator had called a 2-mm.
needler in my hand. I poked it out ahead of me
and stepped through into a narrow passage
with another door at the end. It was locked,
but a well-placed kick splintered wood and it
bounced open. Outside was a standard-model
dark alley with empty apple crates and
battered galvanized garbage cans and clumps
of weed between weathered bricks. A high
board fence barred the way to the left.

"Well, well," I said. "It seems to me I've
been here before, too. Last time there was
some shooting, but I don't see any spent slugs
lying around. And they've added a fence."

"This is all wrong," the girl said. "I have a
good sense of direction; there can't be anything like this here. We should be in the
middle of the building now, not outside!"

"I couldn't agree with you more, pet." I
went toward the street where the car had
rolled past the last time, spraying lead. This
time everything was quiet; much too quiet.
The street looked all right, except that instead
of the buildings across the way, there was just
a featureless gray. Not a fog, exactly; solider
than that, but less tangible.

"Florin, I'm afraid," the girl said, sounding
brave.

"Smart girl," I said. "Let's look around."

I picked a direction and started off. We
turned a couple of corners. There was a sort
of syrupy haze hanging over everything, blur-
ring details. The sidewalk seemed to be
running uphill now. We were in an alley,
cluttered with the usual assortment of
slopped-over garbage cans, defunct orange

crates, dead cats, and drifted paper—for the first five yards. After that the bricks were clean, the way unimpeded. There was enough filtered light from the street to show me a high board fence that closed the space between buildings.

"It looks like the same fence," Miss Regis said.

"But the other side," I felt of the boards; they were just boards.

"It stinks," I said. "Topologically speaking."

"What does that mean?"

"There are relationships of surfaces that aren't modified by distortion of the surface. But we've seen two faces of the same plane—and we haven't turned enough corners. Somebody's getting careless; we're pressing them harder than they like. That makes me want to press harder."

"Why? Why not just go back—"

"Aren't *you* a little curious, Miss Regis? Aren't you a little tired of the man at the other end of the string, pulling whenever he feels like it? Wouldn't you like to squeeze back?"

"What are we going to do?"

"Funny," I said. "It could have been a brick wall or concrete—or armor plate. But it's just pine planks. It's almost an invitation to tear it down." I put my gat away and stooped to examine the bottom edges of the boards. There was room to get a hand under them. I heaved and wood resisted and then splintered and broke away. I threw the pieces aside and stepped through into the conference room, looking just as I'd seen it last, fancy spiral chandelier and all.

"We're getting closer to home," I said. I went around the long table to the door I had entered the room by last time and pulled it open.

I was back in my hotel room, complete with blotched wallpaper, chipped enamel washbowl, broken roller shade, and sprung mattress. The door I had come through was the one that had had the bathroom behind it in an earlier incarnation.

"No wonder the boys came in so nice," I said. "I've been feeling kind of bad about not hearing the door. But it never opened."

"What is this place?" Miss Regis said, and came close to me.

"It's where it all started, and I do mean started. As the Senator pointed out, my life story begins here. Before this—nothing. No home, no past. Just a lot of unexamined preconceptions that are due for examination." I took a step toward the hall door and it burst open and the scruffy man came through it holding the biggest hogleg .44 I ever saw, aimed right between my eyes. The hole in the end looked wide enough to drive a small truck through, or maybe even a large one. No words were needed to tell me that the time for words wasn't now. I went sideways as the gun roared and exploded plaster from the wall behind the spot where I'd been standing. Red shouted something, and the girl cried out and I worked hard to get my feet under me and get turned around, but the floor seemed to be swinging up at me like the deck of a sinking liner. I held on and watched the ceiling swing past, then another wall; nothing spectacular, just a nice easy procession. Red sailed by, and the girl, moving faster now, sliding by. I heard her call: "Florin—come back!"

It took a long time for the words to push through the gray fog where my brains used to be. *Come back*, she'd said. It was a thought, at that. I'd had the ride before, but maybe I didn't have to go again—not if I fought back. The world was spinning like bathwater getting ready for that last long dive down the drain, and somehow suddenly I knew that if I went with it, this time it was for real.

There was nothing to hold onto, but I held on anyway.

I felt pressure against one side of me. That would do for a floor. I swung it around under me and built walls and a roof and held them in place by sheer willpower, and the roaring faded and the world slowed to a stop and I opened my eyes and was lying on my back in the middle of the world's biggest parking lot.

A dead flat sugar-white expanse of concrete marked off by blue lines into fifty-foot squares ran all the way to the horizon. That was all there was. No buildings, no trees, no people. The sky was a pale fluorescent azure, without clouds, without an identifiable source of light.

Voices came out of the sky.

"... *now! Follow emergency procedures, damn you!*" That in Big Nose's bell-shaped tones.

"*I'm trying ... but—*" Lard Face speaking.

"*This is no time to blunder, you cretin!*"

"*I can't ... it won't. ...*"

"*Here—get out of my way!*"

"*I tell you, I threw in the wipe circuit! Nothing happened. It's . . . He's. . . .*"

"*He what? Don't talk like a fool! He's got nothing to do with it! I control this experiment!*"

Hysterical tittering. "*Do you? Do you really? Are you sure? Are you sure we haven't been taken, had, gulled—*"

"*Damn you, kill the power! All the way back!*"

"*I did—or tried to. Nothing happened!*"

"*Close down, damn you!*" Big Nose's voice rose to a scream. At the same time the pain in my wrists and ankles and the ache in my chest rose to a crescendo, like bands of fire cutting me into pieces; and suddenly thunder rolled and the sky cracked and fell, showering me with sharp-edged fragments that turned to smoke and blew away and I was lying strapped down on my back looking up at the rectangular grid of a glare-ceiling, in a small green-walled room, and the man I had known as Big Nose was bending over me.

"Well, I'll be damned," he said. "He's alive after all."

* * *

A man with gray hair and a matching face, dressed in a white smock, and a scruffy man in a scruffy coverall came over and looked at me. Somebody finally got around to unstrapping me, unclamping something from my head. I sat up and felt dizzy and they handed me a cup of stuff that tasted terrible but seemed to be the right prescription. The dizziness went away, leaving me with nothing worse than a queasy stomach, a mouth that a family of moles had nested in, a dull headache, and an ache in my wrists and my ankles that wasn't so dull. The gray man—Dr. Eridani was his name, I remembered, the way you remember things you haven't thought about for a long time—smeared some salve over the raw spots. The rest of them were busy looking at the dials on a big console that filled up most of one wall, and muttering together.

"Where's the Senator?" I said. My thoughts seemed to be moving slowly, like heavy animals in deep mud.

Big Nose looked up from his work and frowned.

"He's just kidding," the scruffy man said. His name was Lenwell Trait, and he was a lab assistant. I didn't quite remember how I knew that, but I knew.

Big Nose—Van Wouk to his intimates—came over and looked at me without any visible affection.

"Look here, Bardell," he said, "I don't know what kind of ideas you're getting, but forget them. We have a legal agreement, signed and witnessed. You went into this with your eyes open, you'll get what's coming to you, not a penny more, and that's final!"

"*You're* giving him ideas," Eridani said quietly. Trait handed me a cup of coffee.

"Bardell's not getting any ideas," he said, and grinned a sly grin at me. "He knows better than that."

"Bardell's an actor," I said. My voice

sounded weak and old.

"You're a stumblebum we picked out of a gutter and gave an opportunity to," Van Wouk growled. "Like all your kind, you now imagine you're in a position to exert pressure. Well, it won't work. Your health hasn't suffered, so don't start whining."

"Don't kid me, Doc," I said, firing from the hip. "What about the wipe circuits? How about Eta Level? Everything jake all down the line?"

That shut them up for a couple seconds.

"Where did you pick up those terms?" Lard Face asked me.

"A little lizard told me," I said, and suddenly felt too tired to bother with games. "Forget it; I was just ribbing you. You wouldn't have a drink handy?"

Trait went off and came back in a minute with a flask of rye. I took a couple ounces from the neck and things started to seem a little brighter.

"Something was said about payment," I said.

"One hundred dollars," Big Nose snapped. "Not bad for an hour or two of a rummy's time."

"I had a feeling it was longer," I said. "No damage, eh? How about amnesia?"

"Uh-uh," Trait said lazily. "You know better, Bardell."

"Get him out of here," Van Wouk said. "I'm sick of the sight of him. Here." He grabbed at his pocket and brought out a wallet and extracted some worn currency and pushed it at me. I counted the spots.

"A hundred is right," I said. "But that was the straight dope about the amnesia. I'm a little confused, gents. I remember you boys. . . ." I looked at them, remembering. "But I kind of don't remember our deal—"

"Get him out!" Van Wouk yelled.

"I'm going," I told Trait. He had hold of my arm, twisting it, moving me toward the door. "You don't have to get tough."

He walked me out into the corridor, green tile like the room, along it to steps that went up with light at the top.

"Just between pals," I said, "what happened to me in there?"

"Nothing, chum. A little scientific experiment, that's all."

"Then how come I don't remember it? Hell, I don't even know where I live. What town is this?"

"Chicago, chum. And you don't live no place. You just kind of get by."

Double doors that opened out onto concrete steps. There was lawn and trees that looked familiar in the dark.

"The Senator's Summer Retreat," I said. "Only no searchlights."

"You can't count on them politicos," Trait said. "Take my advice and don't squeeze it, Bardell. You got your century, even if maybe your marbles is scrambled a little, but hell, they wasn't in too good shape when you come in. I'd watch that off-brand Muscatel if I was you, chum."

"The Lastrian Concord," I said. "Diss. Miss Regis. None of that happened, huh?"

"You had like a nightmare. You damn near

blew all the tubes in old Pickle-puss' pet Frankenstein. Go tank up and sleep it off and you'll be good as new."

We were down the steps now, and he turned me and pointed me toward the gate.

"By the way, what color do you call those tiles?" I said.

"Nile green. Why?"

"Just curious," I said, and did a half-turn and rammed the old stiff-finger jab to the breastbone and doubled him over like peeling a banana. I held him up and pried my hundred out of his left hand that I'd felt making the touch, and then checked his hip and got thirty more, just for carfare.

"So long, Red," I said. "I never cottoned to you much anyway." I left him there and beat it by a back route out the side gate.

* * *

It was cold in town that winter. I headed for the waterfront with the idea of making an early start on my bender. With a hundred and thirty to blow at $2.79 per fifth, that was a lot of Muscatel. I tried to work out just how much, and got to about fifteen gallons and happened to catch sight of myself in a window I was passing.

At least I guessed it was me. I hardly knew me. My eyes stared back from the dark glass like a pair of prisoners doing life in solitary. My face looked left out in the weather, worn out, caved in. There was gray stubble a quarter of an inch long on my jaw, wild grayish locks on my head. My Adam's apple bobbed like a yo-yo when I swallowed. I stuck my tongue out; it didn't look good either.

"You're in bad shape, old man," I told the stranger in the glass. "Maybe fifteen gallons of rotgut isn't what you need."

I stood there and stared at the reflection staring at me and waited for the little voice to pipe up and remind me how good the old heartwarmer was, how it slid down so nice and tongue-filling and hit bottom and burned its way out, taking the ache out of bones and the strain out of joints, bringing comfort to the body and ease to the mind.

But it didn't. Or if it did I didn't hear it. I was feeling my heart thump with a dull, sick thump, working too hard just to keep going. I listened to the wheeze and grunt of my lungs trying to suck in enough air, felt the tremors that wobbled my knees like base viol strings, the sour, drained feel of unhealthy muscles, the sag of dying skin, the sick weight of neglected organs.

"What's happened to me?" I asked the old man in the glass. He didn't answer, just touched his withered lips with a gray tongue.

"You look as scared as I feel, Pop," I said. "By the way, do I know your name?"

Big Nose called you Bardell.

"Yeah. Bardell. I . . . used to be an actor." I tried the idea on for size. It fit like a second-hand coffin.

"They hauled me in off the street," I told myself. *"The white-coat boys, Van Wouk and the rest. They needed a guinea pig. I volunteered."*

"So they said. And before that—what?"

"I don't remember so good. Must be the

Muscatel, old man. It's rotted your brain. My brain. Our brain."

"So—what are we going to do about it?"

I thought of booze and felt a stir of seasickness. *"No more booze,"* I said. *"Definitely no more booze. Maybe a doctor. But not like Eridani. Food, maybe. Sleep. How long since you slept in a bed, old man?"*

I couldn't remember that, either. I was good and scared now. It's a lonely feeling not to know who you are, where you are. I looked along the street. If I'd ever seen it before, I didn't know when. But I knew, without knowing how I knew, that the waterfront was *that* way; and a block of old frame houses with *Room to Let—Day, Week, Year* signs in the windows was *that* way.

"That's it," I said. My voice was as cracked and worn as a thrown-away work shoe. "A clean bed, a night's sleep. Tomorrow you'll feel better. You'll remember, then."

"Sure. Everything will be jake—mañana."

"Thanks, pal; you've been a big help." I waved to the old man in the glass and he waved back as I turned and started off; not toward the waterfront.

* * *

The old woman didn't like my looks, for which I didn't blame her, but she liked my ten-dollar bills. She puffed her way up two flights and to the back, threw open the door of a bare, ugly high-ceilinged little room with a black floor showing around a bald rug, a brass single bed, a chiffonier with washstand. It was the kind of room that would be an icebox in winter and a steam bath in summer. Rusty springs squeaked with an ill-tempered sound as I sat down on the threadbare chenille. I said, "I'll take it."

"Bathtub at the end of the hall," my new landlady said. "You got to bathe off 'fore you go to laying in my beds."

For an extra buck she supplied a yellowish-white towel and a washcloth with a thin spot in the middle, as stiff as a currycomb, and an only slightly used bar of coral-colored soap that smelled like formaldehyde. The feel of eleven dollars in cash must have gone to her head, because she went along and started pipes clanking and spurting brownish water into the tub. She even wished me a good night, and handed me an old safety razor before she went away.

I soaked for a while, which felt good in spite of the rusty patch right where my *glutei maximi* rested. Afterward I raked at my whiskers and went on to trim a few of the drake's tails curling around my neck.

"Nice work, old timer," I told the face in the mirror. "You'll make a good-looking corpse yet."

Back in the room, I slid in between the sheets which felt like starched burlap and smelled like chlorine, curled myself around a couple of broken springs that were poking up through the cotton padding, and sailed off someplace where age and sickness and human frailty don't exist, where the skies are pink all day, and the soft voices of those we love tell us what great guys we are, forever and ever, amen.

I felt better in the morning, but not good. When I started to get dressed I noticed the goaty smell coming from my clothes. There were heavy feet in the hall just then, and I stuck my head out and entrusted my landlady with another ten-spot and the commission of buying me some new BVDs and socks. What she brought back weren't new, but they were clean and there was nine dollars change.

I turned down her offer of breakfast (seventy-five cents) and bought an apple at a fruit stand. There were plenty of sartorial emporia in the neighborhood specializing in mismatched pinstripes and shirts with darned elbows, all with the same dusty look, as if the owners had died and been buried in them. I selected a snazzy pinkish-tan double-breasted coat and a pair of greenish-black slacks which were thick and solid if not stylish, a couple of shirts, formerly white, a pair of cracked high-top shoes made for some-body's grandpa, and a snappy red and green tie that probably belonged to a regiment of Swiss Marines. The ensemble wasn't what anyone would call tasteful, but it was clean and warm, and mothballs smell better than goats any day.

After that I gave a lucky barber a crack at my locks. He trimmed me back to an early Johnny Weissmuller length, and said, "That's a switch. I seen black hair with gray roots, but never before visey-versey."

"It's my diet," I said. "I just went on dis-tilled carrot juice and virgin duck eggs, boiled in pure spring water."

He made a note of that on the back of an

envelope, threw in a free shave that hit the spots I'd missed the evening before, and offered me a chance in what he called a lottery.

"I'm doing you a favor," he said, getting confidential. "This here is the hottest game in town." He showed me a purple ticket to prove it. If fancy engraving was any indication, I was onto something. I paid my buck and tucked it away. As I left he was looking at me over the cash register, grinning a lipless grin and glittering his eyes in a way that reminded me of something I couldn't put a finger on.

I sat in the park after that and breathed fresh air and watched the people pass. None of them looked at me. I bought my dinner at a grocery store, making a point of including lettuce and carrots and other wholesome items. I ate in my room, without much appetite.

Two weeks went by that way, at the end of which I had drunk no booze, had gained five pounds, lost the stomachache, and was broke. I spent the last day looking for work, but there seemed to be a shortage of job opportunities for applicants of indefinite age and uncertain abilities. My landlady seemed uneager to extend any credit. We parted with expressions of mutual regret, and I went and sat in the park a little longer than was my custom, right through dinner time, as a matter of fact.

It got cold when the sun went down. The lights were still on in the Public Library across the way. The librarian gave me a sharp look but said nothing. I found a quiet corner and settled down to enjoy as much of the warmth as possible before closing time. There's something soothing about the quiet stacks, and the heavy old yellow oak chairs and the smell of dusty paper and bindings; even the whispers and the soft footsteps.

The footsteps stopped, and a chair scraped gently, being pulled out. Cloth rustled. I kept my eyes shut and tried to look like an old gent who'd came in to browse through the bound volumes of *Harper's* and just happened to doze off in mid-1931; but I could hear soft breathing, and feel eyes on me.

I opened mine and she was sitting across the table from me, looking young and tragic and a bit threadbare, and she said, "Are you all right?"

* * *

"Don't disappear, lady," I said. "Don't turn into smoke and vanish. Don't even get up and walk away. Just sit there and let me get my pulse back down into the low nineties."

She blushed a little and frowned.

"I . . . thought perhaps you were ill," she said, all prim and proper and ready to say all the magic words that made her a conforming member of the current establishment.

"Sure. What about the fellow I came in with? Isn't that the way the next line goes?"

"I haven't any idea what you mean. No one came in with you—not that I saw. And—"

"How long have you been watching me?"

This time she really blushed. "Why, the very idea—"

I reached across and took her hand. It was

soft as the first breath of spring, as smooth as
ancient brandy, as warm as mother love. My
hand closing around it felt like a hawk's talon
getting a grip on a baby chick. I let go, but she
hadn't moved.

"Let's skip over all the ritual responses," I
said. "Something pretty strange is happening;
you know it and I know it, right?"

The blush went away and left her pale, her
eyes clinging to mine as if maybe I knew the
secret that would save a life.

"You . . . you *know?*" she whispered.

"Maybe not, Miss, but I've got a strong sus-
picion."

It was the wrong word; she tensed up and
her lips got stiff and righteous.

"Well! It was merely a Christian impulse—"

"Balls," I said. "Pardon my crudeness, if it
is crudeness. You sat down here, you spoke to
me. Why?"

"I told you—"

"I know. Now tell me the real reason."

She looked at the end of my nose, my left
ear, finally my eyes. "I . . . had a dream," she
said.

"A bar," I said. "On the shabby side. A fat
bartender. A booth, on the right of the door as
you come in."

"My God," she said, like somebody who
never takes the name of her deity in vain.

"Me too," I said. "What's your name?"

"Regis. Miss Regis." She stopped, as if she'd
said too much.

"Go ahead, Miss Regis."

"In the dream I was someone who was

needed," she said, not really talking to me now, but to someone inside herself maybe, someone who hadn't had a whole lot of attention in the past. "I was important—not in the sense of rank and titles, but because I'd been entrusted with something of importance. I had a duty to perform, a sense of . . . of honor to live up to."

I had sense enough not to say anything while she thought about it, remembering how it had been.

"The call came in the middle of the night, the secret message I'd been waiting for. I was ready. I knew there was great danger, but that was unimportant. I knew what to do. I got up, dressed, went to the appointed place. And . . . you were there." She looked at me then. "You were younger, bigger, stronger. But it was you. I'm certain of that."

"Go on."

"I had to warn you. There was danger—I don't know what sort of danger. You were going to face it, alone."

"You asked me not to go," I said. "But you knew I had to go away."

She nodded. "And . . . you went. I wanted to cry out, to run after you—but . . . instead, I woke up." She smiled uncertainly. "I tried to tell myself it was just a foolish dream. And yet —I knew it wasn't. I knew it was important."

"So you came back."

"We walked through cold, empty streets. We entered a building. Nothing was as it seemed. We went through room after room, searching for . . . something. We came to a wall. You broke it down. We were in a big

room with a strange, elaborate chandelier,
like a place where kings and ambassadors
might sign treaties. And the next room was a
flophouse."

"Oh, I don't know," I said, "I've seen
worse."

"Then a man burst in," she went on, ignor-
ing me. "He had a gun. He aimed it at you
and . . . shot you down at my feet." The tragic
look was back, a look to break a stone heart
down into gravel.

"Not quite," I said. "I'm here. I'm alive. It
didn't really happen. None of it. We dreamed
it—together."

"But—how?"

"I was in an experiment. A human guinea
pig. Big machines, hooked to my head. They
made me dream, crazy stuff, all mixed up.
Somehow, you got mixed into my dream. And
the funny thing is—I don't think they know
it."

"Who are they—the people you're talking
about?"

I waved a hand. "At the university. The lab.
Some bigdomes, doctors, physicists. I don't
know. The kind of guys who spend their time
in little rooms full of radio tubes and dials,
making marks on a clipboard."

"How did you happen to be taking part in
their tests?"

I shook my head. "That's all a little vague. I
think I was on the sauce pretty heavy, for a
long time."

"Where's your family, your home? Won't
they be worried about you?"

"Don't waste your sympathy, Miss Regis. I

don't have any."

"Nonsense," she said, "no human being exists in a vacuum." But she let it go at that. "You mentioned a university." She tried a new tack. "What university was it?"

"How many you got in your town, lady?"

"Please don't talk like a hobo. You don't have to, you know."

"Apologies, Miss Regis. The one over that way." I jerked a thumb over my shoulder. "Nice grounds, big trees. You must have noticed it, if you live here."

"I've lived here all my life. There's no university in this town."

"OK, so maybe it's a research lab; a government project."

"There's nothing like that. Not here, Mr. Florin."

"Three blocks from where we're sitting," I said. "Maybe four. Ten acres if it's an inch."

"Are you sure it wasn't part of the dream?"

"I've been living on their money for the last two weeks."

"Can you lead me there?"

"Why?"

She stared at me. "Because we can't just drop it, can we?"

"I guess it can't hurt to take a look," I said. "Maybe I can touch 'em for a new stake."

She followed me out into the light, trailed by the disapproving eyes of the elderly virgin at the front desk. It took us ten minutes to do the three blocks to where I had left the university grounds two weeks before. A block away I knew something was wrong with my calculations. The stores and gas stations and pawnshops along the way looked all right, but where the high red brick wall should have been there was an abandoned warehouse: an acre or so of warped siding and broken glass.

Miss Regis didn't say any of the things she could have. She came along quietly while I retraced the route. I found a familiar pawnshop with a dummy in the window wearing a dusty tux, the candy shop with the dusty fudge, the street where my ex-boardinghouse was. But when we got back to the university, it was still a warehouse.

"The neighborhood's still here," I said. "All that's missing is the college campus. Kind of big to mislay, but at my age a man tends to get careless."

"Are you sure you walked all the way from —wherever you were—to the rooming house? Maybe you took a cab, or—"

"Uh-uh. No cab, no bus, no trolley, not even a bicycle. Shanks' mare. I don't remember much, maybe, but what I remember I remember good. The way I felt I couldn't have walked over a quarter of a mile. Let's face it, Miss Regis. Somebody swiped the university and left this dump in its place, maybe for a reason. My trick is to figure the reason."

"Mr. Florin—it's late. You're tired. Perhaps it would be better if you rested now. Tomorrow we can meet after work, perhaps. . . ." Her voice trailed off.

"Sure," I said. "Good idea, Miss Regis. Sorry to have wasted your time. You were right all along. No university, no scientists, no dream machine. But the hundred bucks was real. Let's leave it at that. Good night, and thanks for your company."

She stood there looking undecided. "Where will you go?"

"Who knows, Miss Regis? The world is a big place, especially when you aren't tied down by any arbitrary limitations. Grayfell, maybe. It's a nice place, with eighteen percent light gravity and plenty of O_2 and a big yellow sun, a couple hundred lights from here."

"Who told you about Grayfell?" she whispered.

"Bardell. He was an actor. Not a very good one. Funny thing, Big Nose thought I was him. Can you figure it?"

"Grayfell was our summer place," she said, sounding puzzled.

"Don't tell me: at the lake, twenty-eight miles from here.

"Where did you get that idea?"

"All right—you tell me."

"Grayfell is in Wisconsin—near Chicago."

"Stop me if I'm singing off-key—but isn't this Chicago?"

"Why—no. Of course not. It's Wolfton, Kansas."

"I knew there was something unfamiliar about the place."

"How could you have been here for weeks, as you said, without knowing that?"

"The question never arose. Of course, my social contacts were limited."

She looked at me and I could almost hear her thinking over all the things she might say. What she came up with was, "Where will you sleep tonight?"

"I feel like walking," I said. "A night of contemplation under the stars."

"Come home with me. I have room for you."

"Thanks, Miss Regis. You're a nice kid—too nice to get mixed up in my private war with the universe."

"What are you *really* going to do?" she whispered.

I tilted my head toward the warehouse. "Poke my nose in there."

She looked earnest and businesslike. "Yes, of course, we'll have to."

"Not you. Me."

"Both of us. After all ..." she gave me a glimpse of a smile like an angel's sigh. "It's my dream too."

"I keep forgetting," I said. "Let's go."

* * *

The doors were locked, but I found a loose board and pried it free and we slid into big dark gloom and dust and cobwebs and the flutter of bats' wings, or of something that fluttered. Maybe it was my heart.

"There's nothing here," Miss Regis said. "It's just an old abandoned building."

"Correction: it's a place that looks like an old abandoned building. Maybe that's window dressing. Maybe if you scratch the dust you'll find shiny paint underneath."

She made a mark on the wall with her finger. Under the dust there was more dust.

"Proves nothing," I said. "For that matter nothing proves anything. If you can dream a thing you can dream it's real."

"You think you're dreaming now?"

"That's the question, isn't it, Miss Regis?

How do you know when you're alive and awake?"

"Dreams aren't like this; they're vague and fuzzy around the edges. They're two-dimensional."

"I remember once thinking about dreams while I was walking up a hill in a college town in the fall. I could feel the dry leaves crunching under my shoes, and the pull of gravity at my legs; I could smell leaves burning somewhere, and feel the bite of the nippy autumn air, and I thought: 'Dreams aren't like reality. Reality is *real*. All the senses are involved, everything is in color and dimension.'" I paused for effect. "Then I woke up."

She shivered. "Then you can never be sure. A dream within a dream within a dream. I'm dreaming you—or you're dreaming me. We can never know—really."

"Maybe there's a message in that for us. Maybe we should be looking for truths that are true awake or asleep. Permanent things."

"What things?"

"Loyalty," I said. "Courage. Like you. Here with me, now."

She said, "Don't be silly," but she sounded pleased. I could barely see her face in the gloom.

"What do we do now? Go back?" she said.

"Let's look around first. Who knows? Maybe it's a game of blindman's buff and we're only a inch from winning." I felt my way forward across the littered floor, over scraps of board and paper and cardboard and tangles of baling wire. A rickety door was set in the far wall. It opened into a dark passage no neater than the big room.

"We should have brought a flashlight," Miss Regis said.

"Or a squad car full of cops," I said. "Look —or maybe you'd better not." But she was beside me, staring at what I was staring at. It was the Senator, lying on his back, with his head smashed like an egg. I felt the girl go rigid, and then relax and laugh, a shaky laugh, but a laugh for all that.

"You frightened me," she said, and went past me and looked down at the body sprawled on its back in its dusty tuxedo.

"It's only a dummy," she said.

I looked closer and saw the paint peeling from the wooden face.

"It looks..." Miss Regis gave me a troubled look. "It looks like you, Mr. Florin."

"Not me; the Senator," I said. "Maybe they're trying to tell me something."

"Who is the senator?"

"The man I was hired to protect. I did my usual swell job, as you can see."

"Was he ... part of the experiment?"

"Or it was part of him. Who knows?" I stepped over the imitation corpse and went on along the passage. It seemed too long to fit inside the building. There were no doors or intersecting corridors for a hundred yards, but there was one at the end, with a line of light under it.

"Always another door," I said. The knob turned, the door opened on a room I had seen before. Behind me Miss Regis gasped. Dim moonlight shone through tall windows on damask walls, oriental carpets. I went across the deep pile to the long mahogany table and pulled out a chair. It felt heavy and smooth, the way a heavy, smooth chair ought to feel. The chandelier caught my eye. For some reason it was hard to look at. The lines of cut-crystal facets spiraled up and up and around in a pattern that wove and rewove itself endlessly.

"Mr. Florin—why would such a room as this be here—in this derelict building?"

"It's not."

"What do you mean?"

"Don't you remember your last visit?"

"Is it really the same room? Is all this really just a dream?"

"It wasn't a dream then and it isn't a dream now. I don't know what it is, but at some level it's *happening*."

Miss Regis had paused, her head tilted alertly.

"There's someone near," she whispered. "I can hear them talking."

I got up and soft-footed it over and put my ear to the door. There were two voices, both familiar, one high-pitched, one as resonant as a commercial for a funeral parlor.

". . . getting out now," the latter was saying. "I want no part of the responsibility. You've all lost whatever sense you had."

"You can't," Trait's voice said, sounding like a cop turning down a speeder's alibi. "We'll recover him, never fear. It's only a matter of time."

"What if he dies?"

"He won't. And if he should—we're covered. You've been given assurances on that point."

"I don't believe them."

"You're not going anywhere, Bardell."

"Get out of my way, Len."

"Put the bag down, Bardell."

"I'm warning you—"

Someone hit a cast-iron stove with a ball-peen hammer. Someone made a gargling sound. Someone dropped a hundred-pound bag of potatoes on the floor. I threw the door open and slammed through into my old original bedroom and almost collided with the Senator, standing over Trait's body with a smoking gun in his hand.

* * *

He looked at me and his mouth came open but no words came out. I lifted the gun from his hand and sniffed it, just to be doing something. It smelled like a gun.

"I never liked him either," I said. "Where are you off to?"

"I didn't mean to kill him," he said. "It was an accident."

"Don't sweat it, Senator. Maybe this one doesn't count."

I squatted beside Trait and went through his pockets. I didn't like doing it but I did it anyway. I could have saved myself the trouble. They were empty. I looked at his face, gray-green now, not pretty.

"Tell me about it," I said to the Senator—the ex-Senator—Bardell: whoever he was.

"I thought he had a gun. He's crazy enough to use it. I shot first."

"Skip on to who you are and who Trait is and what you were doing here, and where

here is. And, oh yeah—what it's got to do with me."

He gave me a sharp glance with something that might have been hope in it.

"You don't remember?"

I cocked his gun and aimed it at his vest. "There seem to be a few blanks. Start filling them."

"I hardly know where to begin. What *do* you remember?"

"Tell me about the Lastrian Concord."

He shook his head and frowned. "Look here, I swear to you—"

"Skip it. What about Eridani?"

"Oh." He licked his lips and looked disappointed. "Very well. You know what I was up against there. It wasn't as though I had a great deal of choice—"

"What were you up against?"

"He threatened to wipe me. Otherwise, I'd never have—"

"Start further back."

"Well—Eridani approached me on the seventeenth. His story was that my services were needed in a professional capacity. I needed the work, frankly. Once I'd seen the situation, they couldn't afford to let me go—or so they said."

I turned to Miss Regis. "Has he said anything yet?"

She shook her head. "I think he's playing for time. Who is he?"

"An actor named Bardell."

"My God," Bardell said. "If you know that, you know—" He cut himself off. "How did you find out?"

"You told me."

"Never."

"In the park," I said, "on Grayfell."

His face fell apart like a dropped pie. "But you're not supposed—" he said in a strangled voice, and turned and lunged for the window. I put a round past him without slowing him; he hit the opening like a runaway egg truck and went through in a cloud of smashed mullion and glass splinters. I got there in time to hear his fading scream and the impact far, far below.

Miss Regis made a shocked sound. I felt over the metal frame, touched a spot that clicked. The whole window, dribbling glass chips, swung into the room like a gate. Behind it was a plain gray wall.

"If a phony man jumps out a phony window," I said, "is it suicide or just a harmless prank?"

"It's a nightmare," the girl said. "But I can't wake up." Her eyes were wide and frightened.

I wet my lips, which felt like blotting paper, and thought of two or three smart remarks, and said, "I've got a hunch this wasn't part of their plan. I don't know what the plan is, or who planned it, or why, but things aren't going just the way they were supposed to. That means they aren't as smart as they think they are—or that we're smarter. That gives us a kind of edge, maybe. Check?"

"We're going in circles," she said. "We're like blind people in a maze. We stumble on, deeper and deeper—"

"Sometimes when you're going in circles you're skirting the edge of something. If we get deep enough we'll break through, maybe."

"Into what?"

"Funny—I would have said '*out* of what'." I stuck my head inside the gray-walled passage, scarcely eighteen inches deep. It might have been the one the Senator and I had used for our fake escape from the fake Senatorial mansion, or its twin.

"Call it, Miss Regis," I said, "Shall we go on —or go back?"

"Back—to what?"

"Not losing faith in Wolfton, Kansas, are you?"

"Did I ever really live there?" she whispered. "A mousy little woman in a drab little town, working in an insurance office with varnished doors and creaky floors and wooden filing cabinets, typing up reports on an old open-frame LC Smith, going home at night to a dreary little room, dreaming impossible dreams—"

"And waking up and living them. I wish I could answer that, Miss Regis. Maybe the answer's in there." I nodded toward the dark and narrow way behind the dummy window.

"Are we probing into dark tunnels in a fantastic building?" she said. "Or are the tunnels in our minds?"

"Maybe our minds are the tunnels. Maybe we're thoughts in the minds of the gods, burrowing our way through the infinite solidity of the Universe. And maybe we're a couple of cuckoos chirping in the dark to cheer each other up. If so, we're doing a bad job of it. Come on, girl. Let's go exploring. We might stumble out the other end into the pink sunshine on the white sugar beach beside the popcorn sea." I stepped through and turned to give her a hand, but there was something in the way, something invisible and hard, like clean plate glass. She spoke, but no sound came through the barrier. I hit it with my shoulder and something splintered, maybe my shoulder, but I plowed on through the enveloping folds of darkness and stumbled out into noise and a blaze of light.

* * *

I was in a vast, high-ceilinged hall that went on and on into the misty distance. On one side was a formal garden beyond a high glass wall, on the other huge panels like airline arrivals boards covered with lines of luminous print that winked and changed as I looked at them. Down the center of the hall white plastic desks were ranked, and behind each desk was a man, or almost a man, in a white uniform and a pillbox cap with a chin strap, and soft brown hair covering every square inch of exposed skin except the pink palms of the long-fingered hands, and the face from eyebrows to receding chin. There were lines of men and women in assorted costumes queued up in front of each desk, and I was in one of the lines.

The customer in front of me—a dazzling female in a tiny jeweled sarong and a lot of smooth, golden suntan—picked up her papers and disappeared behind a white screen. That made me number one.

"Right; Florin, Florin . . . yes, here we are," the monkey man said in clipped Oxonian tones, and gave me a bright-eyed look that included a row of big square yellow teeth. "Welcome back. How did it go this trip?"

"Like Halloween in the bughouse," I said. "Don't bother telling me who you are, or what. I wouldn't believe a word of it. Just tell me what this is."

"Oh—oh, a nine-oh-two," he said, and poked a button and white walls sprang up on all four sides of us, making a cozy cubicle with just him and me inside.

"What did you do with the girl?" I said, and tried to watch all four walls at once.

"All right, Florin, just take it easy, lad. You're an IDMS operative just returning from an official mission into Locus C 992A4." He pursed his wide, thin monkey-lips at me, frowning. "Frankly, I'm surprised to encounter an amnesiacal fugue syndrome cropping up in a field agent of your experience. How far back have you blanked?"

I felt in my pocket for the Senator's gun. It wasn't there. Neither was the 2-mm. needler. I found a ball-point pen that I didn't remember owning. On impulse I pointed it at the ape-man behind the desk. He looked startled and one hand stole toward the row of buttons on his desktop. It stopped when I jabbed the pen at him.

"Talk it up, Slim," I said. "Don't bother with the rehearsed pitch. I want her and then I want out—all the way out."

"Be calm, Florin," he said steadily. "Nothing's to be gained by hasty action, no matter what you imagine the situation to be. Won't you take a seat so that we can get to the bottom of this?"

"I'm tired of the game," I said. "I've been flim-flammed, gulled, hoodwinked, and had; no hard feelings, but I want the girl back. Now."

"I can't help you there, Florin. As you see, there's no girl here."

"On the count of three, I fire. One . . . two . . . ." I paused to take a new breath, but someone had pumped all the air out of the room and substituted chalk dust. It hung as a white haze between me and the monkey-man. My fingers dropped the pen and my knees folded without any help from me and I was sitting on the edge of a chair like a nervous interviewee for a secretarial job, listening to him talk through a filter from his position on the other side of the desk, half a mile away across unexplored country.

"What's happening to you is a recognized hazard of the profession," he was telling me. "You've been well briefed on the symptoms, but of course if the fugue becomes well advanced before you notice something's amiss, you can of course slip too far; hence, no doubt, your auto-recaller returned you here to HQ. Let me assure you you're perfectly safe now, and in a very short time will again be in full command of your faculties—"

"Where's Miss Regis, damn you, Monkey-puss?" I snarled, but it came out sounding like a drunk trying to order his tenth Martini.

"You were dispatched on assignment to observe an experimental machine detected in operation at the Locus," he went on calmly. "A primitive apparatus, but it was causing certain minor probability anomalies in the Net. Apparently you were caught up in the field of the device and overwhelmed. Naturally, this created a rather nasty stress system, ego-gestalt-wise; a confusing experience, I don't doubt. I want you now to make an effort to recognize that what you've been through was entirely subjective, with no real-world referential basis."

"Oh, yeah?" I managed to say well enough to cut into his rhetoric. "Then where'd I get the gun?"

"It's IDMS issue, of course."

"Wrong, chum. It's a ball-point pen. Where's the girl?"

"There is no girl."

"You're a liar, Hairy-face," I tried to get my legs under me and succeeded and lunged across the desk and hit sheet ice that shattered into a fiery cascade that tinkled down around me like a shower of cut gems that rose higher and higher, and I drew a breath to yell and smelled pipe smoke, the kind that's half orange peel and soaked in honey. I snorted it out of my nose and blinked and the air cleared and Big Nose was sitting across the desk from me, smiling comfortably.

"Now, now, lad, don't panic," he said soothingly. "You're a bit confused, coming out of the ether, nothing more."

I looked down at myself. I was wearing a long-sleeved sweater, corduroy knickers, argyle stockings and worn sneakers, and my shanks were thin, skinny adolescent teen-age shanks. I stood and he jerked the pipe out of his mouth and pointed the stem at me and said, "You behave, boy, or I'll report this entire matter to your mother!"

There was a window behind him. I ran around his desk and ducked under his grab and pulled the Venetian blind aside and was looking out at wide campus lawns and trees and walks under a yellow summer sun.

"I'll see you expelled from this institution!" Big Nose yelled.

"What did you do with her?" I yelled back, and threw myself at him with no higher ambition in life than to get my fingers into the soft fat under his chin, but he faded back before me and I clawed my way through a syrupy substance full of little bright lights and stumbled out into a room with curved walls covered with dials and winking lights, and a gray man in a form-fitting green uniform put out a hand and said, "Are you all right now, Captain?"

I looked past him. Lard Face sat before a round ground-glass screen, squinting at wiggly green lines; the bird man was next to him, tapping keys like a grocer adding up a week's supplies for a family of twelve. Trait looked over his shoulder and grinned a crooked grin and winked.

"We've just passed a field-inversion screen, Captain," the gray man was saying. "Possibly you're a bit disoriented for the moment; it sometimes has that effect. . . ?"

"Where's Miss Regis?" I said, and pushed his hand away, noticing as I did that I had a fancy ring on my index finger, a complicated spiral of diamond chips. On impulse I made a fist, ring out, and pushed it at him.

"Ever see that before?" I said—and surprised myself. I'd never seen it before either—but my gesture suggested itself to me as a cagey thing to do.

The gray man's eyes bugged and he shied violently. "Put that thing away!" he gasped.

"Why should I, Eridani?"

All heads in sight jerked around when I called his name. Trait came out of his chair clawing for the gun at his hip; the gray man spun to face him just in time for a beam of green light to lance out from where Lard Face sat and bore a hole through his back. He went down coughing blood and smoke, and everyone was around me, all talking at once.

"How did you spot him, Captain?" the bird man said. "How did you know he was a spy?" Big Nose loomed up then, barking orders, clearing the mob.

"Come with me, Captain," he said. "As ship's medical officer I'm ordering you to your quarters."

I let him walk me past the door, and then turned and rammed the fist with the ring into his paunch.

"Bring her back, Van Wouk," I said.

"What . . .!" he coughed, half bent and looking up at me. "What . . . ? Why . . . ? Who . . . ?"

"When, where, and how. Yeah," I admitted. "There are a lot of questions a guy could ask. The difference is you know some of the answers and I don't know any. Start supplying me."

He just kept gasping and looking at me as if

I'd gone too far round the bend to catch sight of any longer.

But Trait stepped up jabbering fast: "Why did you strike him, Captain? We're all loyal! You know that! Can't you see what we're doing is for your benefit? Just tell us what you want—"

"What's my name?"

"Captain Florin of Security Ship 43; you've been temporarily incapacitated."

"Where am I?"

"On the command deck; the ship is nearing Grayfell in the Wolf System."

"What's this ring?" It had suddenly begun to burn my finger. In fact the glow of fire at my hand had already taken over top billing in my attention. I looked at it with care for the first time, while Trait's voice in explanation died to a buzzing in my ears. Somehow the ring was hard to look at. There were loops of what looked like miniature neon tubing, and curious twisted planes of polished metal, and rods and wires that seemed to go out of focus as I tried to trace their connections. At the center a glowing point pulsated like something alive; fire darted through the tubes and sparkled along the wires. I made a fierce gesture to pull it off my finger.

But my finger rippled and waved as if a sheet of iridescent water had come between my eyes and them. I stepped back and found the plate glass of the haberdashery stiff and unbroken at my back. Trait, Eridani, and the others still stood around me but the dust on their tuxedos showed they hadn't conversed or shaken hands or clapped each other on the back for a long long time. I turned and bumped a dummy I hadn't seen and it fell down.

I bent to look at the shattered head and found it was the Senator—again. I looked up, recognized the echoing dust-draped passage in the abandoned warehouse.

"Damn you, Florin," said a familiar voice. Bardell was getting up off the floor, rubbing his face.

"That slap in the puss wasn't in the script," he whined. "When I hired on for the good of the republic and a pair of cees they said nothing about a belaboring by the beneficiary of the project."

I grabbed him by the collar. "Cough it up. Who are you? What are you? What am I?"

"We'll give you all the information you require," said a voice behind me. I whirled and saw Lard Face and the full complement of henchmen alighting from the Nile green Buick, tommy guns at the ready. I wished for an instant of time I had the ring again—then didn't know why I wished it. I advanced to meet them. The bullets rattled around me like horizontal hail and I reached out with the idea I'd take somebody with me wherever I was going.

But I made the trip alone. The Buick shimmered and slid away. The street was gone. I turned and was standing in a desert and the lizard man was leaning against a rock ten feet away, dressed all in pink and smiling at me lazily.

* * *

"Well," he said. "At last. I was beginning to fear you'd never tread the maze to its conclusion."

I took a deep breath of hot, dry air that had a faint smell of eucalyptus, or of something that smelled like eucalyptus, and had a look around. Sand, a few pebbles, rocks, plenty of stone, all well-worn by time and the patient elements. No signs of life, not even a cactus.

"A swell place to visit," I said. "But I wouldn't want to die here."

"No need for any talk of dying," Diss said in his ashes-of-roses voice. "The only danger that existed was to your sanity, and it seems to me you've handled that quite nicely. In fact, you showed unexpected resourcefulness. I was quite surprised, actually."

"That relieves my mind a whole lot," I said. "What do you do now, stick a gold star in my book?"

"Now," he said briskly, "we can begin to deal." He twinkled his little red eyes expectantly at me.

"That's my cue to ask you what kind of deal," I said. "OK—what kind of deal?"

"There's only one kind of deal, wherever in the Universe one happens to be. There's something you need, and something I need. We exchange."

"Sounds simple. What do I need?"

"Information, of course."

"What's your end of it?"

He shifted position and waved a lean lilac-colored hand. "There's a service you can perform for me."

"Let's start with the information."

"Certainly. What first? The Senator?"

"He's not a Senator; he's an actor named Bardell."

"Bardell is Bardell," the lilac lizard stated. "The Senator . . . is the Senator."

"If that's a sample, I don't think we're going to get together."

"You," the lizard man said with the air of one enjoying himself, "are the victim of a plot."

"I knew it all along."

"Now, Florin, don't discount what I tell you in advance." He produced a long cigarette holder from under his pink vest, fitted a brown cigarette to it and tucked it in a corner of a mouth that was made for catching flies on the wing. He puffed and pale smoke filtered out his noseholes.

"That doesn't make you any easier to believe," I said. "If this pitch is supposed to convince me, you're going at it all wrong."

"Oh, I'm not interested in convincing you of anything in particular. I feel the facts will speak for themselves—"

"Where's Miss Regis?"

Diss frowned; even his cigarette holder drooped.

"Who?"

"The girl. A nice, quiet little lady, not like the rest of the inmates of this menagerie. She was trying to help me; I don't know why."

Diss was shaking his head. "No," he said judiciously. "Really, Florin, it's time you began to distinguish the actual players from the simulacra. There is no young lady involved."

I took a step toward him and he recoiled slightly.

"Dear me," he said, sounding amused, "surely it's not necessary for me to point out that I'm not susceptible to any hasty, violent impulses on your part." He curved the smile at me. "I'm not precisely an ally, Florin, but I mean you no harm—and as I've said, you can be of service to me. Wouldn't it be best if we simply explore matters in a rational way and seek an accommodation?"

"Go ahead," I said. "I'm too tired to argue."

"Ah, there's a clever chap. Now, the plot: A benign plot, you understand, but a plot nonetheless. A plot, to be brief, to restore you to sanity."

"Late reports from the front indicate it's not working. You may not believe this, but at this very moment I'm imagining I'm having a heart-to-heart with a fatherly salamander."

Diss opened his mouth and made some hissing sounds that I guessed were supposed to be laughter.

"It must be confusing for you at this point, I concede; however, remember to apply the simple criterion: facts are facts, however revealed. And if my revelations illuminate the situation—why then, if I'm not real I'm as good as, eh?"

"I've also got a headache," I said. "You just got to where they were saving my sanity. How about mentioning who 'they' are, and why they're interested in unscrambling my wits, if I've got any."

"They . . . are the Research Council, a high-level governmental group—of which you were

—or are—Chairman."

"You must have the wrong pigeon, Diss.
The only research I do is into who pulled the
trigger or pushed the breadknife, as the case
may be."

He waved that away. "A transparent rationalization. Your own common sense must tell
you that it's necessary now to widen the scope
of your self-concept. Would I waste my time
interviewing an obscure private eye, with or
without his wits about him?"

"I pass. Keep talking."

"Your last project as Chairman was the development of a device for the study of dreams,
an apparatus designed to search the subconscious for operative symbols, and concretize
and externalize them, making the unconscious mental activities available for study.
You insisted on being the first test subject. Unfortunately, due to fatigue and stress
factors, you were unequal to the experience.
Your mind embraced this new avenue of
escape; you slipped away into a fantasy world
of your own devising."

"I'm disappointed in me; I'd have thought I
could devise something that was more fun
than being chased, run away from, shot at,
slugged, and generally scared to death."

"Indeed?" Diss chuckled, like a safety valve
letting off a little extra pressure. "Know thy-
self, Florin. You're a scientist, a theoretician,
not a doer of deeds. You welcomed the opportunity to shed responsibility in a simpler
world of brute law, of kill or be killed. But
your loyal henchmen, naturally enough, were
far from content with this turn of events. It

was necessary that they bring you back from your dream-world. You had escaped into the *persona* of a legendary character of Old Earth —Florin by name. Van Wouk countered this move by setting you a task—in your chosen guise, of course—and thereupon introducing difficulties into your path, with the object of rendering your refuge untenable. Matters proceeded as planned—to a point. You entered the fantasy, accepted the charge. Abruptly, things went awry. Unplanned elements cropped up, complicating affairs. Van Wouk attempted to abort the treatment, but found himself unable to do so. Matters had been taken out of his hands. He was no longer in control of the dream machine." He paused for the question. I asked it.

"*You* were now in charge, of course," he said. "Rather than acting as a passive receiver of the impulses fed to your brain, you seized on them and wove them into a new fabric, closer to your needs: specifically, the need to cling to your chosen role."

"Why don't I remember any of this? And what do you mean, 'Old Earth'?"

"You still don't remember, eh?" Diss said. "A portion of your mind has carefully blanked out the evidence of the situation you found insupportable. By supplying the data from another source, I am in effect outflanking your own mental defenses. As for Old Earth— it's the name given to a minor world thought by some to be the original home of humanity."

"I guess this is where I say I thought humanity only had one home."

"Oh, of course—Earth was the setting you

chose for yourself, as appropriate to your role as Florin, the Man of Steel. But by now you must be ready to accept the thesis that such a stage is a trifle too small to contain both you and—myself." He gave me the lipless smile.

"Not to mention Grayfell—and the monkey man."

Diss made his hissing laughter again. "Van Wouk was growing desperate. He intended to pacify you by offering you an alternate avenue of rational escape, an acceptable alibi to seize on: that you were a secret agent, suffering from a brainwashing during which you had gained certain false impressions; but you carried his gambit on to a *reductio ad absurdum*, discrediting it. He then attempted to overawe you with authority, convince you you were delirious, emerging from anesthetic —and again you twisted his charade into absurdity. He tried again, closer to home, thrusting you into the role of an authority figure broken by overwork—and a third time you used his strength against him, reaching out, in fact, to attack and nearly destroy him. It was at that point that I felt it essential to step in—both to save your sanity and to prevent a wider tragedy."

"I see; just a selfless individual, out to do a little good in the big bad imaginary world."

"Not quite." He tipped the ashes from his cigarette. "I mentioned that there was a service you could perform for me."

"I guess you'll tell me what it is, whether I coax you or not."

"The dream machine," he said, "is a most ingenious device; *too* ingenious, I fear. You're to be congratulated, my dear Florin, on your achievement. But it won't do, you know. It will have to be shut down—permanently."

I scratched my jaw, which I discovered hadn't been shaved for quite a while, which might have been a clue to something, but at the moment I didn't stop to chase it down.

"Picture the problems which would be created," Diss went on, "if a band of untutored aborigines on some remote ocean isle accidentally stumbled on a means of generating powerful radio waves. Some incidental by-product, perhaps, of an improved anti-devil charm. In all innocence they could well disrupt planetary communications, interfere with satellite operations, wreak havoc with Trideo, and open and close carport doors on the other side of the planet."

"It doesn't sound all bad. But I get the point."

"The dream machine, unhappily, has such side-effects. Unwittingly, when you and your Council set it in operation, you created repercussions in the probability fabric that extend half across the galaxy. This is, of course, an intolerable situation. Yet, galactic law closely restricts direct interventions. Candidly, my present activities in confronting you in a semicorporeal state border on the illegal. But I judged that the circumstances warranted a slight bending of regulations."

"What does semicorporeal mean?"

"Only that I'm not actually here—no more than you."

"Where are you?"

"In the transmission cubicle of my transport, on station some two light-years from Sol. While you, of course, are occupying the dream machine in your own laboratory."

"Why the exotic Saharan background?"

"Oh, you see a desert, do you? You're supplying it from your own fund of imagery, of course. I merely dialed a neutral setting."

I looked at the desert behind him; it looked as real as a desert ever looked. He gave me time for that idea to soak through.

"I'll now intervene in the operation of the machine," he said, "to bring you back to consciousness—and sanity. In return—you will destroy the machine, including all notes and diagrams. Agreed?"

"Suppose I don't?"

"Then it will inevitably be shut down by other means, less soothing to your planetary pride."

"Just like that, eh? What if I don't believe you?"

"That's of course your option."

"I'll still know how to rebuild it—if what you say is true."

"So you will. But if you should be so unwise as to attempt to do so—or to allow any other to do so—you'll find yourself back here— quite alone. So—what do you say?"

"No deal," I said.

"Oh, come now, Florin. Surely you place some value on life and sanity?"

"I don't like blind deals. Maybe this is all happening, and maybe it isn't. Maybe you can do what you say and maybe you can't. Maybe I'm a great inventor—and maybe I'm swinging from the chandelier by my tail. You'll have to show me."

Diss jammed his cigarette out angrily, shredded the weed into the wind, and tucked the holder away.

"Look here, Florin. I've been most patient with you, considerate. I could have taken violent steps at once; I refrained. Now you seek to blackmail me—"

"Put up or shut up, Diss."

"You're a stubborn man, Florin—most stubborn!" He folded his lean arms and drummed his fingers on his biceps. "If I return you to your normal base-line in full possession of your senses and you see that matters are as I described—will you *then* destroy the machine?"

"I'll make the decision when I get there."

"Bah! You're incorrigible! I don't know why I waste time with you! But I'm a benign being. I'll go along. But I warn you—"

"Don't. It would blight our beautiful friendship."

He made an impatient gesture and turned and I got a brief, ghostly impression of vertical panels and lines of light; Diss made quick motions with his hands, and the light faded, changed quality; the distant horizon rushed closer, blanked out the sky. There was an instant of total darkness, and a sound like a series of doors slamming, far away. Ideas, names, faces rushed into my mind like water filling a bucket.

Then the lights came up slowly.

I was lying on my back in a room thirty feet on a side, ceiled with glare-panels, floored in patterned tiles, walled with complex apparatus. Big Nose stood by a console that winked and flared with emergency signals that bleeped and shrilled in strident alarm. Beside him, the gray man in a white smock bent over a smaller panel, jabbing at switches. Bardell was stretched out on the next cot, snoring.

I made a sound and Big Nose whirled and stared at me. His mouth worked, but no words came out.

"You can unstrap me now, Doctor Van Wouk," I said. "I'm no longer violent."

* * *

Half an hour had passed, as half hours are wont to do. The lard-faced man—Dr. Wollf as he was known to his intimates—had un-snapped the contacts, clucked over my wrists and ankles where the straps had cut in, and smeared some salve over the raw spots. The gray man—Dr. Eridani—had hurried out and come back with hot coffee laced with some-thing that restored the glow to my cheeks, if not to my pride. The others—Trait, Tomey, Hyde, Jonas, et al. (the names were there, ready in my memory, along with a lot of other things) gathered around and took turns telling me how worried they'd been. The only one who hung back and sulked was Bardell. Eridani had administered a hypo that had brought him out of his doze yelling; they had calmed him down, but he still seemed to be nursing a grudge.

"My God, Jim," Van Wouk said to me, "we thought for a while we'd lost you."

"Nevertheless I'm here," I said. "Give me a

report, the whole thing, from the beginning."

"Well . . ." He ran his fat fingers through his thinning hair. "As you know—"

"Assume I know nothing," I said. "My memory's been affected. I'm still hazy."

"Of course, Jim. Why, then, on completion of SAVE—the Symbolic Abstractor and Visual Elaborator, that is to say—you authorized an operational test, with yourself as subject. I objected, but—"

"Stick to the substantive, Doctor."

"Of course, sir. Ah, an operational test was initiated, with you as subject. You were placed under light hypnosis and the electrodes positioned. Calibration proceeded normally. The program was introduced, the integrator energized. Almost at once, power demand jumped tenfold. Feedback protection devices were activated without result. I tried various control and damping measures in an effort to regain control, to no avail. I reluctantly ordered an abort, and cut all power— but you remained in a deep coma, failing to respond to the recall signals. It was as though you were drawing power from some other source, fantastic though that seems.

"In desperation, I tried corrective reprogramming, to no avail. Then—out of a clear sky—you snapped out of it."

"Any idea why?"

"None. It was as though an external vector had been introduced. Neural potentials that had been running sky-high—at full emergency stimulus level—suddenly dropped back to rest state. The next moment—you were with us again."

I tipped my head toward Bardell, who was sitting across the room, nursing a cup of coffee and looking resentful. "What does he do?"

"Why, that's Bardell. Temporary employee; he was used as an ancillary vector in the mock-ups during the test. A sort of, ah, bit player, you might say."

"All part of the dream machinery, eh?"

"The. . . ? Oh, yes, a very appropriate nickname, Jim."

"How does it work?"

He stared at me. "You mean. . . ?"

"Just pretend I've forgotten."

"Yes. Why, then, ah, it's simply a matter of first monitoring the dream mechanism, then stimulating the visual, olfactory, and auditory cortex in accordance with previously determined symbolic coding to create the desired, eh, hallucinatory experiences. The program mock-ups occupy the adjacent bay—"

"Show me."

"Why . . . certainly, Jim. Just this way." He walked across to a blank wall and pushed a button and a plain gray panel slid back on two walls of a shabby hotel room, complete with brass bed and broken windows.

He noticed me looking at the latter and chuckled insincerely. "You grew rather violent a time or two, Jim—"

"Have you always called me Jim?" I cut in.

"I—" He stopped and glittered his eyes at me; his jowls quivered a little. "I beg your pardon, Doctor," he said stiffly. "I suppose during these tense hours I've allowed protocol to lapse, somewhat."

"Just asking," I said. "Show me the rest."

He led the way through the conference room—not nearly so plush, in a good light— the street scenes—cardboard and plaster— the boardinghouse; all just shabby, hastily built sets, that wouldn't fool a blind man.

"All that was required," Van Wouk explained importantly, "was a triggering stimulus; you supplied the rest from your subconscious."

The series of sets ended at a heavy fire door, locked.

"Our premises end here," Van Wouk said. "Another agency has that space."

The route back led through the warehouse scene. I poked a toe at the broken dummy that looked like Bardell.

"What was this for?"

He seemed to notice it with surprise. "That? Oh, we hoped at first to make use of mannikins; but we soon determined that human actors were necessary." He gave me a twitch of his jowels. "A human being is a rather complex device, not easy to simulate."

"How does all this get into the picture? If I was strapped down in the next room—"

"Oh, that was only at the end. After you, er, ran out of control. We began with you in an ambulatory state, under light narcosis."

"How long since this test began?"

Van Wouk looked at a big watch expensively strapped to his fat hairy wrist.

"Nearly eight hours," he said, and wagged his head in sympathy for himself. "A trying eight hours, Jim—ah, sir, that is."

"And now what, Doctor?"

"Now? Why, an analysis of the tapes, determination of just what it was that went wrong, corrective action, and then—new tests, I would assume."

"I'd have to authorize that, of course."

"Naturally, sir."

"What would you think of suspending testing?"

Van Wouk pulled at his lower lip; he cocked an eye at me. "That's for you to determine, of course, sir," he murmured, "if you're convinced there's danger—"

"Maybe we ought to smash the machine," I said.

"Hmmm. Perhaps you're right."

In the next room, voices were raised excitedly.

". . . I don't know what you're trying to pull now," Bardell was yelling, "but I won't stand for it! Unlock this door, damn you! I'm leaving here, right now!"

We went back in. Bardell was at the hall door, wrenching at the knob, his face pink from exertion. Eridani was fluttering around him; Trait was at the side door, rattling the knob. He looked up at Van Wouk.

"Some joker has locked this from the outside," he said. He went across to Bardell, shouldered the bigger man aside, twisted the knob, then stepped back and gave the door a kick at latch height. It looked as if it hurt his toe, if not the door.

"Here—what the devil are you doing, Trait!" Van Wouk went to the door and tried it, turned and looked at me with a disturbed expression.

"Do you know—" he started, then changed his tack. "Some error," he said. "Somehow, I suppose, the security system has become engaged."

"You won't get away with this," Bardell shouted. He grabbed up a metal chair and crashed it against the door; it bounced off, one leg bent. Van Wouk brushed past me into the room we had just come out of, hurried to the broken window and swung the frame out and recoiled.

"Is this your doing?" he said in a choked voice. I went across and looked at what he was looking at: solid concrete, filling the space where the passage had been.

"That's right," I said. "While you were watching Red kick the door I ordered up two yards of ready-mix and had it poured in here. Sorry, I forgot to scratch my initials in it."

He snarled and ducked around me, ran back into the green-tiled lab. Eridani and Trait and the others were in a huddle; Bardell was against the wall at the far side, watching everybody. I went to the door he had tried first and pounded on it; it gave back a solid *thunk!* that suggested an armored bunker.

"No phone in here?" I asked.

"No, nothing," Eridani said quickly. "Special isolation arrangements—"

"Got a pry bar?"

"Here—a locking bar from the filing cabinet." Trait hefted the four-foot length of one-inch steel as if he might be thinking about using it on my head; but he went to the door, jimmied the flat end in between door and jamb, and heaved. Wood splintered; the door popped wide.

Solid concrete filled the opening.

Trait staggered back as if he were the one who'd been hit with the bar. Bardell let out a yelp and scuttled sideways to a corner.

"You plan to kill me," he yelled. "I'm on to you now—but it won't work—" He broke off, his eyes fixed on me. "You," he said. "They'll get you, too; you're no safer than I am! Maybe together we can—"

Van Wouk whirled on him. "You damned fool! Don't appeal to *him* for help! We're all his victims! He's the one who's responsible for this! It's *his* doing!"

"Liar!" Bardell yelled, and swung back to me. "You're the one they were out to get! They tricked you into the dream machine! They intended to drive you insane—certifiably insane! It was the only way to eliminate you without killing you—"

Trait reached him then, slammed a hard-looking fist into his stomach, straightened him up with a left hook. It didn't knock him out, but it shut him up. He sagged against the wall, his mouth open.

"All right!" Van Wouk said, his voice a little high, a trifle shaky. He swallowed hard and lowered his head as if I were a brick wall and he was going to ram me.

"Call it off," he snapped. "Whatever it is you're up to—call it off!"

"Let's you and him make me," I said.

"I told you," Eridani said. "We were tampering with forces we couldn't control. I warned you he was taking over!"

"He's taking over nothing," Van Wouk snapped, and groped inside his coat and brought out a flat gun with a familiar look.

"Call it off, Florin," he snapped. "Or I'll kill you like a snake, I swear it!"

"I thought Florin was folklore," I said. "And your needler won't work; I jimmied it."

He gave a start and aimed the gun off-side. It went *bzzaap!* and something screamed past my knees as I went low and took him just under the belt-line and slammed him back and down across the slick floor and into the wall. His head hit pretty hard; he went limp and I scooped up the gun and came up facing them before they had gotten more than half-way to me.

"Fun's over," I said. "Back, all of you." I jerked a thumb at the connecting door. "Through there."

Bardell advanced, blubbering.

"Listen to me, Florin, you're making a mistake, I was on your side all along, I warned you, remember? I tried to help, did all I could—"

"Shut up," Trait snapped, and he did. "Florin, somehow you've managed to take over the dream machine, and use it against us. I don't claim to know how; I'm just the fellow who follows the wiring diagrams. But Eridani's right: you're tinkering with forces that are too big for you. All right, so you've walled us up in concrete. You've showed what you can do. But you're caught too! The air will start getting foul in a matter of minutes; in a couple of hours, we'll be dead—all of us! So back down now, before it goes too far, before it runs away with you! Get us out of this and I swear we'll make an accommodation with you! We were wrong—"

"Shut up, you damned fool!" Van Wouk yelled. "You'd blabber your guts to *him*? We don't need him! Smash the machine!"

I squeezed a careless burst at the door at his feet; he leaped and yelped and a red patch appeared on his shin.

"Next one's higher," I said.

"Rush him!" Van Wouk squealed, but he didn't move; I raised my sights and was squeezing when he broke and scuttled for it. Trait backed to the indicated door. Eridani, looking pale but calm, started to make a pitch but I chipped the door frame beside him and he faded back.

"Bardell, you know how to rig the dream machine?" I said.

"Y-yes, certainly, but—"

"I'm going back," I said. "You're going to help me." I went to the door the others had disappeared through, closed it and shot the heavy barrel bolt, came back and sat in a chair beside the control panel.

"Florin—are you sure?" Bardell said shakily. "I mean—wouldn't it be better if we did as they said? Disabled the infernal machine?"

"Listen carefully, Bardell," I said. "One wrong move and no more sweet you. Got it? Now start things moving."

He tottered to the board, flipped keys and punched buttons as if he knew what he was doing. A row of red lights went on.

"It's hot," he said, as if he hated saying it.

I picked up the gadget with the wires attached. There was a power pack that went into my pocket. The rest clipped to my collar just under my right ear, with a little pink chip in the ear itself.

"What program?" Bardell asked in a quivery voice.

"No program. Just fire me up and let me run free."

"It might kill you! What if you die—?"

"Then I made a mistake. Now, Bardell."

He nodded, and reached for a switch. Something jabbed inside my head. I felt dizzy, and wondered if maybe this time I'd made my last mistake. The ceiling went past, then a wall, then Bardell, looking sad and worried. The floor drifted into view, another wall, then the ceiling again, nothing spectacular, just a nice gentle processing. Bardell's mouth was moving now, but I didn't hear any words. Then I speeded up and everything blurred and I shot off into space and burned up like a meteorite in the atmosphere, leaving a tiny ember that glowed red, then cooled and went out, slowly, lingeringly, reluctantly, amid a clamor of forgotten voices reminding me of blasted hopes and vain regrets that dwindled in their turn and faded into nothingness.

* * *

I opened my eyes and she was sitting across the table from me, dressed in a form-fitting gray outfit with bits of silver and scarlet braid on the shoulders. The table was smooth and white and not perfectly flat, like a slab of hand-carved ivory. The walls behind her were in many shades of russet and gold and tawny, textured like the bark of a Shaggy-man tree. There were sounds in the air that weren't music, but were soothing for all that. She looked at me with compassion and put a hand over mine and said, "Was it bad, Florin?"

"Bad enough, Miss Regis. Glad to see you looking so well. How did you get from there to here?"

She shook her head. "Oh, Florin—I'm afraid for you. Are you sure what you're doing is the right thing?"

"Miss Regis, I'm winging it. I wouldn't tell anyone else that. Funny thing, but I trust you. I don't know why. Who are you, anyway?"

She looked from one of my eyes to the other, as if I were hiding somewhere behind them. "You're not joking, are you? *You really don't know.*"

"I really don't. We've met before: in a beer joint, in a library. Now here. What is this place?"

"It's the Temple of Concord. We came here together, Florin, hoping to find peace and understanding. You've been under narco-meditation for many hours. Seeker Eridani let you come with me—but I sensed you weren't really yourself." Her hand held mine tighter. "Was it a mistake, Florin? Have they hurt you?"

"I'm fine, my dear," I said, and patted her hand. "Just a little mixed up. And every time I try to unmix myself, I step off another ledge in the dark. Sometimes it's Big Nose and his boys, sometimes Diss, the lilac lizard, and now and then it's you. I have a kind of line on

Van Wouk, and Diss explained himself more or less plausibly, once you accept the impossible. But you don't fit in. You aren't part of the pattern. You aren't trying to sell me anything. Maybe that would tell me something if I just knew how to listen."

"We shouldn't have come here," she whispered. "Let's leave now, Florin. We won't go any further with it. It was a forlorn hope—"

"That's the best kind, Miss Regis."

"Can't you call me Curia?"

"I can't leave here now, Curia. I don't know why, but that's what the little bird called instinct tells me. What I have to do is break down a few doors, peek into a few dark places, intrude in some sanctuaries, unveil a couple of veiled mysteries. Where should I start?"

She got paler as I spoke. She shook her head and her grip on my hand was almost painful. "No, Florin! You can't! Don't even speak of it!"

"It has to be that way. Just point me in the right direction and stand back."

"Come with me—now. Please, Florin!"

"I can't. And I can't explain why. I could talk about dummies with bashed heads and Nile green Buicks and little voices back of the ear, but it would take too long, and wouldn't mean anything anyway. See, I'm learning? All I know is I've got to keep pushing. I don't really have any evidence, but somehow I sense I'm rocking something on its foundations. Maybe the next push will bring it down with a smash. Maybe I'll be caught in the wreckage, but that doesn't seem so important." I stood, feeling weak in the knees and with a faint, distant buzzing in my skull.

"I see I can't stop you," Miss Regis said. All the life had gone out of her voice. Her clutch on my hand loosened and I took it back. She stared ahead, not looking at me.

"Through there," she said, and lifted a hand to point at the big carved bronze door across the room. "Along the corridor to the black door at the end. It's the Inner Chamber. No one but the anointed can enter there." She still didn't look at me. She blinked and a tear ran down the curve of her cheek.

"So long, Miss Regis," I said. She didn't answer.

* * *

The door was big and black and lumpy with sculptured cherubs and devils and vindictive-looking old men with beards and haloes, plus a few sportive angels hovering about the crowd. I fingered the worn spot at one side and it swung back with a soft hiss on a room walled with green tiles. Van Wouk, Eridani, Trait and the rest were grouped around a chair beside the panel with all the dials. No lights were lit on the board now. The door behind them that led to the stage sets was open. Bardell lay on the floor, breathing through his mouth rather noisily. The dummy with the bashed head was seated in the chair.

I said, "Ahem," and they all turned around as if they were mounted on swivels.

"Mother of God," Wolff said, and made a magic sign in the air. Van Wouk made a sound that wasn't speech. Eridani flared his nostrils. Trait cursed and reached for his hip.

"Naughty, naughty," I said. "Try anything cute and I'll turn you into an ugly redhead with a bad complexion."

"This has got to stop, Florin," Van Wouk blustered, but weakly. "We can't go on this way any longer!"

I sidestepped and glanced at the door I had just come through. It was just an ordinary door, splintered around the lock, with a blank surface of ordinary concrete behind it.

"I agree," I said. "In fact, we can't go as far as we've gone, but you notice I didn't let that slow me down. Now, who wants to spill the beans? Erdani? Wolff?"

"The truth?" Van Wouk made a noise that might have been a laugh being strangled at birth. "Who knows what the truth is? Who knows anything? Do you, Florin? If so, you have the advantage over us, I assure you!"

"The machine must be disabled, put out of action once and for all," Eridani said in a cold voice. "I assume you see that now, Florin?"

"Not yet," I said. "What's the matter with Bardell?"

"He fell down and bumped his head," Trait said in a nasty tone.

"Wake him up so he can join the party."

"Forget him, he's unimportant, merely a hired flunky," Van Wouk spoke up. "We're the ones who're in a position to deal with you."

"Who taught him to operate the dream machine?"

"What? No one. He knows nothing about it."

Bardell groaned and rolled over. At my insistence, Eridani and Trait helped him up and walked him up and down the room until he threw them off and rubbed at his face and looked around at the company assembled.

"They tried to kill me," he said in a voice like broken bottles. "I told you they wanted to kill me, and—"

"Quiet, Bardell," I said. "I'm about to try an experiment. You can help."

"What do you mean?" Van Wouk blurted. "You, and this . . . this—"

"Yeah. I admit Bardell doesn't have a lot going for him; but you boys don't seem to like him. That makes him a pal. How about it, Bardell? Will you throw in with me, or ride it down in flames with Van Wouk and company?"

Bardell looked from them to me and back again. "Now, wait just a minute, Florin—"

"The waiting's over. Now we act. Are you in, or out?"

"What are you going to do?"

"Make up your mind."

He gnawed his lip; he twitched. He opened his mouth to speak, he hesitated.

Trait laughed. "You picked a poor stick to lean on, Florin," he said. "That's not a man, it's a bowl full of jelly."

"All right, I'll help you," Bardell said quite calmly, and walked over to stand beside me.

"Trait, will you never learn to keep your stupid mouth shut?" Eridani said in a tone stamped out of cold rolled steel.

"Sure, be tricky," I said. "It adds to the game." I waved a hand. "Back against the

wall, all of you." They obeyed, in spite of no
guns in sight.

"Bardell, fire up the dream machine."

"But—you're not linked to it."

"Just get the circuits hot. I'll take it from
there."

"I demand you tell us what you intend
doing!" Van Wouk growled.

"Easy," I said. "Up to now I've just been
along for the ride. Now I'm taking the wheel."

"Meaning?"

"Somebody along the line dropped hints
that I was responsible for the certain
anomalies. The old 'monsters-from-the-id'
idea. According to that theory I've been the
prime mover as well as the prime victim—un-
consciously. I'm moving the action over to the
conscious area. The next trick you see will be
on purpose."

Eridani and Van Wouk made simultaneous
inarticulate noises; Trait pushed away from
the wall and stopped, poised. Bardell called,
"Activated!"

"Don't do it, Florin!" Van Wouk barked.
"Can't you see the terrible danger inherent—"
He got that far before Eridani and Trait
charged me, heads down, legs pumping. I
stood where I was and pictured a knee-high
brick wall across the room, between them and
me.

And it was there.

Trait hit it in full stride, did a forward flip
and slammed the deck on his back like a body
falling off a roof. Eridani checked, skidded,
hands out in front, his mouth in a tight little
moue of anticipated pain; he smacked the

bricks and tumbled over mewing like a stepped-on cat.

"For the love of God!" Van Wouk blurted and tried to crawl up the wall behind him. Eridani bleated like a sheep, mooed like a soprano cow, rolling around and clutching his shins. Bardell clucked like a chicken in the throes of an epileptic seizure. Trait just lay where he was, as inert as a dead horse.

"That'll be all from the menagerie for the present," I said, and pictured them not there anymore. They weren't.

"Now we're getting somewhere," I said, and imagined the side wall of the room out of existence.

It disappeared obediently, leaving a porous surface of concrete in its place.

"Go away, concrete," I wished; but it stayed put. I threw away the other three walls and the roof and the floor, furniture and all, exposing rough concrete on all six sides of me, glowing faintly with an eerie, violet glow.

I tried again, harder. Nothing.

"OK," I said aloud, and my words hit the blind walls and fell dead. "Let's try a little concentrated effort." I picked a spot on the wall and told myself it wasn't there. Maybe it got a little hazy; but it didn't go away. I narrowed my focus down to a spot the size of a dime. The violet glow dimmed there; nothing else. I tightened down to a pinpoint, threw everything I had at it—

Zigzag cracks ran across the concrete, radiating from the target. A large chunk fell, letting in gray light and curling tendrils of fog. The rest of the wall collapsed like damp pastry, almost soundlessly. I picked my way across the soft debris, into swirling mist. A light gleamed ahead, a fuzzy puffball in the gloom. As I came closer, it resolved itself into a streetlight, an old-fashioned carbide lamp in a wrought-iron cage on a tall cast-iron pole. I stopped under it and listened. Someone was coming. A moment later Diss, the mauve monster, strolled into view, dapper in black evening dress.

"Well, well," he said, somehow not sounding as casual as he might have. "And how did you get *here?*"

"I didn't," I said. "You're in your cubbyhold, two lights from Sol, and I'm driving matched nightmares down that ol' Street of Dreams, remember?"

He trotted out a light chuckle for my benefit and put it away again, almost unused. "You failed to fulfill our agreement," he said in a tone that suggested feelings that were hurt, but not fatally.

"Maybe it slipped my mind. I've learned a few tricks since then, Diss. Like this." I turned the lamppost into a tree and set the crown afire. The flames leaped up into the night, crackling merrily. Diss hardly twitched an eyebrow—or the place where an eyebrow would be if he had an eyebrow.

"What you're doing," he said over the roar of fire, "is dangerous. Far too dangerous to be tolerated. I've told you—"

"Uh-huh, you told me," I said. "Who are you, Diss? What team do you play on?"

The shadows danced on his face as the fire burned itself out. "That's a matter of no concern to you," he said in the sharp tone of one who wants to stop a line of argument before it gets started. "You're a petty creature, involved in great affairs. Out of compassion, I've offered you guidance; ignore it at your peril!"

"The next line is, you're giving me one more chance, right, Diss? What if I turn you down?"

"Don't be an utter fool, Florin! Go back to where you belong and destroy the apparatus that's precipitated you into your present difficulties."

"Why should I? Just for the sake of your little red eyes?"

"You owe me a debt, Florin! They thrust you into their machine as a guinea pig, a puppet, responsive to their wishes. How do you suppose it was that you threw off their control? By your own unaided efforts?" He smiled his contempt at the thought. "Do you have a lottery ticket in your pocket, dear fellow? No matter—I know you do. I planted it there, I believe the expression is. In actuality it's an extraordinarily complex printed circuit, keyed to your control rhythms. I gave it to you to help you regain your freedom of action so that I could deal with you as an equal. So you see, you owe me something, eh?"

"You'll have to spell it out better than that, Diss. I'm just a small-town boy, remember? Or so you've been telling me."

Diss made an exasperated gesture. "By sheer good luck you have it in your power to preserve your world's innocence, hopefully until a time in the far future when you'll be capable of a confrontation with the Galactic Power! Don't throw that chance away out of some misguided sense of pique, some atavistic simian curiosity—"

"You know too much about my little backwater world, Diss. That worries me. Lies always worry me, especially when there seems to be no good reason for them. What are you really after?"

"That's enough, Florin! I've been patient with you—far more patient than you deserve! You'll return now to your prime locus and carry out the destruction of the dream machine!"

"If it's all that important, why haven't you smashed it yourself, a long time ago?"

"Reasons of policy have restrained me; but now my patience runs thin—"

"Fooey. I don't believe you. You're bluffing, Diss."

"Bah, I'll waste no more time on you!" He started to turn away—and banged his nose on a stone wall I'd thrown up in his path.

"You fool! You unspeakable fool! Is this the reward I get for my restraint, for my desire to spare you suffering?"

"Right now I'm suffering most from curiosity. Tell me things, Diss. Start anywhere, I'm not particular anymore."

He scuttled off to the right; I planted another wall in front of him. He doubled back and I hemmed him in on the third side. He screeched in frustration—I thought.

"Get on with the exposé, Diss," I said, "before I yield to my yen to practice some more of my magic tricks."

"Magic! You use the word sardonically, but I assure you that there are forces in the Universe that would make turning princesses into pumpkins seem as routine as winking an eye!"

"Talk, Diss. If I don't like what I hear, I turn you into a mouse pulling a coach and go for a ride, got it? You can start now." I was still in charge, but somehow I had a feeling he wasn't as worried as he had been a few seconds before. I tried to spot my blunder while he edged past me toward the open side of the space I had walked in.

"You're a child—an idiot child with a new toy," he shrilled at me. "I order you—I *command* you to cease this inane harassment at once—" He jumped for freedom and I slammed a fourth wall across to close us both in and he turned and grinned at me like a sculpture peering down from the top of Notre Dame and placed his thumb between his noseholes and waggled his fingers and disappeared just like the pumpkin coach, without even a puff of purple smoke to mark the spot where he'd been standing.

"Suckered," I told myself, and watched the light fade as the walls I'd trapped myself inside of moved closer. They were rough-poured concrete with the form-marks plain on them, still slightly green, but hard for all that. I had my back against one and was pushing at another with everything I had, but it wasn't enough, and they came together and squashed me flat, spreading me out as thin as the wax on a gum wrapper, as thin as the gold on a Gideon bible, as thin as a politician's ethics. Somewhere along the line I lost consciousness.

. . . and came to strapped in a gimbaled chair suspended high before the face of a gigantic illuminated grid where patterns of light winked and flashed in sequences too fast for the eye to follow.

"Hold on, Florin," the Senator's voice called from somewhere above and to my right. I was groggy, but I managed to swivel my head far enough to see him, perched in a chair like mine, gripping the arms and leaning forward, his eyes on the big board.

"You held them," he called. "You've won us some time! Maybe there's still hope!"

* * *

I was as weak as yesterday's tea bag. He got me down and helped me to a cot and shot something cool into my arm and broke something pungent under my nose and after a while I felt better. I sat up and looked around. It was a big, empty room with smooth ivory walls, curved like the inside of an observatory, occupied by the lighted grid and banks of controls and not much else. Two round ports looked out on the black loneliness of deep space.

Bardell sat down on a stool he had brought over and said, "You held them off, Florin. I was going under; you took over the board just in time. That was as close as they've come. Next time . . ." He looked at me, level-eyed, firm-jawed. "Next time nothing will stop them."

I sat up.

"Where are Van Wouk and Trait and the rest of the cast?"

"You ordered them back, Florin. Don't you remember? There's just you and me now, manning the mind-grid."

"Your name's Bardell?" I asked him. He looked surprised.

"Yes—of course, Florin."

"I seem to have a slight touch of total amnesia. You'd better give me a little fill-in on where I am and what's going on."

Bardell looked disconcerted for a moment, then smoothed his face.

"A certain amount of disorientation is normal after a session on the grid," he said heartily. "You'll soon be yourself again." He gave me a tense smile. "You're at Grayfell Station, in retrograde orbit twenty-eight parsecs from Imperial Center. We're manning the grid against the Diss attack."

I looked across at the glistening curve of wall, imagined it blushing a deep pink. Nothing happened.

"What is it?" Bardell turned to look the way I was looking.

"Nothing. Just clearing away the fog. I dreamed I was having an argument with a lizard—"

"The Diss are reptilian in appearance, you know."

"I thought the name belonged to just one lilac lizard," I said. "He wanted me to wreck the dream machine—"

Bardell started to say something, broke off, looked at me a bit warily.

"Don't worry, I turned down the idea," I said. "I don't know why. Just to be contrary, maybe. He seemed a little too insistent."

Bardell gave a short sample of a laugh. "I should think so! If they'd managed to subvert you—Florin himself—it would have been the end."

"Tell me about this enemy you say we're fighting."

"We don't know where they come from; they appeared a few years ago out of nowhere, attacking the worlds of the Empire—vicious mind-attacks that turn a man into a shambling zombie, without meaning or direction. There are billions of the devils, unimpressive individually, but potent *en masse*. They possess a degree of group consciousness that enables them to combine their intellectual energies for brief periods. It's in that way that they hurl their attacks against us. We fight back by way of the grid—an artificial means of joining a multitude of minds in a single gestalt. Few human brains can stand the strain of controlling the weapon: yours, mine, Van Wouk's, and the others'. We make up the slim ranks of the Mind Corps, manning the Deep Space Grid Stations, fighting humanity's battles for her." He snorted, a tired, cynical ghost of a laugh. "For which we receive scant thanks—or even awareness. They don't know the war is going on, the vast mass of our fellowmen. They don't understand the kind of attack they're under. How can you explain a light symphony to a blind man? Oh, they accept the indications of the instruments; they can see for themselves some of the results of the Diss attack. But only intellectually. Emotionally they suspect us of being charlatans, self-styled heroes, fighting our lonely battles in our imaginations. Only a handful even bother to link up now when the call goes out. That's why we're losing, Florin. If the entire race would recognize the threat, join together to pour their mental energies into the grid system—we'd neutralize the Diss at a stroke!"

"Van Wouk and the rest," I said, "how did they feel about it?"

Bardell looked at me sharply. "I see it's coming back to you. They were losing heart. They'd had enough. They spoke of peace terms; you wouldn't hear of it. You called them traitors and sent them home."

"And how do you feel, Bardell?"

He hesitated before answering, like a man trying words on for size.

"I stood by you last time," he said. "Now— I can see it's hopeless. We don't have the strength, Florin; we don't have the backing of our own kind—and we can't do it alone." As he spoke he got more excited. "If we go on the grid again it means death. Worse than death: destruction of our minds! And for what? They'll overwhelm us, we know that; we'll be swept aside as if we weren't here, and the Diss will move into Human Space—whether we fight or not. If we recognize that fact now, face it—and evacuate the station before it's too late—we can still save our own sanity!"

"What about the rest of the population?"

"They aren't lifting a finger to help us," Bardell said flatly. "They go about their petty pursuits, business as usual. Our appeals don't touch them. They don't care. *They don't care, Florin!* And why should we?"

"How do you know we'll lose?"

"Wasn't this last assault proof enough for you?" He was on his feet, his eyes a little wild, his diction not quite so precise. "It was only a routine probe, tapping for a weak spot in the station line—but it almost broke through! You know what that means! Right now they're gathering their power for an all-out assault on our station—on you and me, Florin. Our minds can't stand against them. We're doomed! Unless...." He broke off and looked sideways at me.

"Go ahead, Bardell. Get it off your chest."

He drew a breath and let it out. "Unless we act swiftly. We don't know how long the present respite will last. We have to move before they do. They caught me short last time—" He broke off. "That is, before we had time to discuss the matter they were on us—but now—"

"I thought you volunteered to stay."

"I could have gone with the others. Obviously, I didn't."

"So you stayed—but not to fight, eh? You had other plans—but they hit before you were ready. Ready for what, Bardell?"

He tried a shaky laugh. "Well, you're recovering your old sharpness, I see, Florin. Yes, I had a reason for staying—and the reason wasn't suicide. With their Mind Corps credentials and priorities Van Wouk, Eridani, and the others can be well on their way toward the hinterlands by now. But what will that avail them, when the Diss advance—as they will—in five years or ten? They're fleeing in panic, Florin—but not me. Not us. We have an alternative."

"Spell it out."

"The grid." His eyes went to the high, wide, glittering construction that filled and dominated the white-walled room. "We can use the energies of the grid for something other than futile efforts to shield a mob of ingrates, Florin."

"Tell me about it."

"I've studied it," he said, talking fast now, spilling the beans. "I've experimented during extended lulls. The grid is a fantastic device, Florin, capable of things the designers never dreamed of! It can transmit matter—including men—instantaneously—across the Galaxy!"

"Wouldn't we feel a little lonely there?"

"Not just ourselves, Florin; whatever we choose goes with us. We can take our pick of the human-occupied worlds, transfer to it whatever we like—*whom*ever we like—and shift the entire planet into a stable orbit around a congenial sun a hundred thousand light years from the Diss threat. It will be generations before they penetrate that far—and perhaps in that time we can ready a new and better defense against them."

"Aren't you afraid the population of the planet in question might resent being ripped untimely from the bosom of the Empire?"

Bardell grinned a fierce grin. "What does it matter what those sybarites think? Not that it has to be Grayfell, of course; naturally, you'll have a say in the matter." He gave me a smile to reassure me, but refrained from patting me on the head. "As for any potential hostile actions by the ingrates we've saved, it will be simple enough to arrange matters so that we'll be quite invulnerable from them. We'll have vast powers, Florin, unassailable powers."

"Why not take an unoccupied planet?"

"And live like savages? No, thank you. I've no taste for hewing down jungles and opening stasispacks. Nor do I wish to live in solitude. We want cities, parks, dining places, gracious avenues, cultivated gardens. We want people around us, Florin. There are so many services that only a human servant can provide."

"I see you've given this a lot of thought, Bardell. Are you sure the grid can handle it?"

"Certainly. We simply send the emergency signal via trans-L; when the still-active units have linked, one single, well-directed pulse—and it's done."

"How many still-active units are there?"

"Less than half a billion in the entire sector," he said with a curl of his well-chiseled lip. "Still, it's sufficient—for a single pulse."

"Why a single pulse?"

His smile was a bit grim this time. "First, because the instantaneous peak demand will drain the contributing units dry in a fractional hemiquaver of time—and secondly, the discharge energies will melt the grid to slag in a matter of moments."

"So all we have to do is reduce to idiocy half a billion people who still trust in us, and

destroy the station they entrusted us with,
and we're home free."

"Well—those are rather emotional terms—
but essentially, yes."

"I can't help wondering, Bardell, why
you're letting me in on the deal."

He spread his hands and smiled benignly.
"Why not? After all, we're friends, associates;
I've always respected you...." His smile
widened, became self-indulgent. "Your
talents, that is, if not always your judgment."

"Help me up," I said.

He jumped forward and put a hand under
my elbow and I came up fast and drove a
straight right-hand punch to his solar plexus
with all the power in my body behind it. He
made an ugly sound and jackknifed past me
and hit on his face.

"My judgment is still off," I said. "I'm
staying."

Just then the alarm went off. Even through
his agony, Bardell heard it. He rolled to his
side, still curled like a worm on a griddle, and
gasped out: "Florin ... quickly ... it's our ...
last chance...." He was still talking as I
turned back to the battle board to do what I
could before the end.

* * *

The knowledge was all there, crowding into
the forefront of my mind; all I had to do was
let my body respond automatically: my hands
going out to touch the coding keys, punching
in the sequences that summoned up the power
of the grid; then walking to the chair, seating
myself, strapping in, tripping the action sta-

tion sequence. The chair rose swiftly to its position at the focal point. I felt the first preliminary vibrations strike the grid and saw the lights flash across it in response, felt the energies pouring into my brain, filling it, felt my mind reaching out for contact, while around me the curving bone-white walls faded and dissolved. I had one last fleeting image of the tiny mote that was the station, alone in intersteller space—and myself, alone inside it. Then it was gone, lost in the immensity behind me. And out of the darkness ahead, Diss appeared. I saw him at a great distance, a gigantic figure striding toward me, dinosaurian, magnificent, irresistible, light glinting from his polished purple scale-armor, from his flashing violet eyes. He halted, towering against a backdrop of stars.

"Florin!" his voice boomed out, filling all space the way an organ fills a cathedral. "We meet again, then! I thought last time you'd had your fill of dueling."

I didn't answer him. I picked a spot on the pale curve of his exposed belly and thought a hole in it, or tried to. Diss didn't seem to notice.

"It's still not too late for an accommodation," he thundered. "I can, of course, wipe you out of existence, as Bardell so rightly warned you. But I have no vindictiveness toward you, no wish to injure you. Bardell lied when he painted me as a villain, determined to eat away the minds of your kind." He laughed, a gargantuan laugh. "Why would I wish to commit any such atrocity? What would I gain from that?"

I narrowed down the scope of my target, concentrated everything I had at it. Diss raised a Herculean hand and scratched idly at the spot.

"I admire your spirit, of course—standing alone, defending your forlorn cause. You see, I am not without emotion. But I can't allow such sentimental considerations to stand in the way of my duty. I asked you once, on a gentlemanly basis, to destroy the dream machine. Well, you didn't do it. Instead you're persisting in your prying, turned up a few more small facts—but to what end? Very well, the machine is not quite so innocent as I painted it; your role not quite so minor as that of a delegate representing a trivial planet in your Galactic Parliament. But is anything changed—except in scale? The Galactic Consensus is old, Florin—older than your infant race. It can no more tolerate your chaos-producing expansionism than a human body can tolerate cancer cells. As the body marshals its defenses to destroy the malignancy, so we marshal whatever force is needed to contain you. That's all we intend, Florin: to restrict you to your own sector of space, put an end to your disturbments. Surely you see the wisdom now of bowing to the inevitable?"

I didn't answer, concentrating on my attack. He fingered the spot absently and frowned.

"Withdraw from the grid, Florin. Use the method Bardell proposed to destroy the apparatus; I have no objection if you skip nimbly across the Galaxy with whatever loot you choose; I assure you, you'll be allowed to dwell in peaceful obscurity thereafter—" He broke off and put a hand over his belly. "Florin," he bellowed. "What are you—" He screeched suddenly and clawed at himself.

"Treacher! Under cover of parley, you attacked me—" He broke off to beat at the bright purple flames that were licking up around him, curling and blackening the bright scales. Suddenly he looked a lot smaller, as if my whole perspective on him had changed. He wasn't a giant across the plain now, just a man-sized reptile capering in front of me, squealing in fury more than pain, I thought.

"Whee," I said. "This is easy—and a lot more fun that having it done to me."

"Stop," he cried, in a tone that was half an octave higher than the one he'd been using. "I confess I've been misleading you! I'll tell you the truth now—but stop, before it's too late for all of us!"

I lowered the heat. "Start talking, Diss," I said.

"What I told you before was true, in the main," he yelped. "I merely distorted certain elements. I see now that was a mistake. My only intention was to avoid complicating matters, settle the affair as quickly and simply as possible. But I misjudged you." He gave me a wild-eyed reptilian look, while the smoke from the damped-down blaze curled about his narrow head. "You are not an easy being to manipulate, Florin.

"As I told you, you voluntarily entered the environment simulator—the dream machine —but not for the purpose of testing as I said.

It was for treatment. You're an important human, Florin. They needed you, you see. You were hypnoed, your superficial memories suppressed, new conditioning taped into your brain—conditioning matching your imagined role. The intention was to manipulate your hallucinations in such a way as to render them an untenable escape, and thus to force you back to rationality."

"It sounds kind of familiar," I said. "Except it was the Senator who was off the rails."

Diss looked disconcerted. "But haven't you understood yet?" he said. "You are the Senator."

* * *

"It's really quite amusing," Diss said. "You escaped into the *persona* of the legendary Florin, whereupon Van Wouk arranged for you to be engaged—as Florin, the Man of Steel —as bodyguard to the Senator. He set you to guard yourself, thereby presenting you with an insoluble paradox."

"That sounds like a dirty trick. Why didn't it work?"

"With commendable ingenuity, your beleaguered imagination produced a Senator who was yourself, and who was yet not yourself. In due course, as the pressure to recognize yourself mounted, you explained him away by calling him an actor. This was, however, merely begging the question. It left unanswered the more threatening mystery of the identity of the real Senator—yourself. You became obsessed with the need to find and confront him. Van Wouk and his group, monitoring your fantasy, attempted, without success, to remove Bardell from the scene. In the end they presented you with his corpse—a measure of desperation. But you—or your subconscious—were equal to the challenge. You could not, of course, accept your own removal from the board. You transformed the dead impostor into a lifeless puppet, and went on to confront your bugaboo yet again—whereupon you promptly drove him to apparently destroy himself. But even then you were dissatisfied; you saw through the deception, and persevered—to the discomfiture of the Galactic Community."

"So you stepped in and gave me pieces of the story and sent me back to wreck the gizmo you call the dream machine."

"Which you failed to do. I hope that now you realize you can never rid yourself of yourself, Florin; your nemesis whom you pursue, and who pursues you—whom you've sworn to protect, but must attack—or is it the other way round?" He glittered his eyes at me, regaining his confidence.

"Try as you will, Florin, you're doomed forever to walk where you would have flown, to crawl where you would have run—dragging always the intolerable but inescapable burden of yourself."

"Very poetic," I said. "Why didn't you tell me I was the Senator to begin with? Why the story about an experiment?"

"I was unsure how you'd accept the news that you had been declared insane," he said, rather tartly. "Now, having seen your monumental ego in action, I'm not so inhibited."

"Just that, huh? You make it all so simple and sweet. And I don't remember any of it because part of the treatment was to blank out my memory, eh? And the joker in the deck was that we were playing with a loaded gun, and you're the nice policeman who came along to take it away. You know what, Diss? You're a nice fellow, and I like you, but I think you're lying."

"What, me lie? That's preposterous. Now, I mean. Before, of course, when I hadn't yet fully assessed your capabilities—"

"Don't bother, Diss. You've developed what they used to call a credibility gap. As polite a way as they could think up for calling a man a damned liar. Why do you want the dream machine smashed?"

"I've already explained—"

"I know. And I didn't believe you. Try again."

"That's absurd! What I've told you is absolutely factual!"

"You don't like me playing around with this substitute reality we're making do with, do you, Diss?" I pictured us boxed in by walls. We were. I turned the walls into backdrops painted to represent the green-tiled lab. Then I made the pictures real. Diss hissed and backed against the big console, where every light in sight was lit up now. I could see the lettering on them: *Emergency Overload*. Somehow, the lizard man looked smaller in this context; a rather pathetic little lizard in an out-of-style stiff collar and string tie.

"What do you want, Florin?" he whispered. *"What do you want?"*

"I don't know," I said, and put a pale blue Persian carpet on the floor. It clashed with the walls. I changed it to pale green. Diss screeched and danced as if the floor had gotten hot under him.

"No more! *No more!*" he hissed.

"Ready to give up?" I said. "Before I change this dump into a Playboy club, complete with cold-blooded bunnies with armor-plated bosoms?"

"Y-you can't!" His voice had now developed a quaver to go with the soprano pitch.

"I'm getting reckless, Diss. I don't care if school keeps or not. I want to see something give at the seams." I took away the green tiles and put flowered wallpaper in their place. I added a window with a view across a landscape that, somewhat to my surprise, was a yellow desert, stretching farther than any desert had a right to stretch. I looked at Diss and he was dressed in a skin-tight, golden uniform, with sparkling insignias and silver braid and rainbow-colored medals and polished boots and sharp-looking spurs and he held a quirt in his right hand that he *whap!*ped against his armored shin in a gesture of impatience. Somehow the outfit made him look smaller than ever.

"Very well, Florin, since you leave me no choice, I now inform you that I am a Chief-Inspector of Galactic Security Forces and that you are under arrest." He yanked a large and elaborate handgun from the bejeweled holster at his lean hip and pointed it at me, left-handed.

"Will you come quietly?" he chirped, "or

will I be forced to place you in ambulatory coma?"

"I've already been there," I said, and shot the gun out of his hand with a nickle-plated double-action .44 caliber revolver. He whipped a saber out of a sheath I hadn't noticed and aimed a vicious cut at my head. I got my cutlass up in time, and metal clanged on metal and Diss staggered back, whipped out a bamboo tube and propelled a curare-tipped dart in my direction. I ducked under it and he produced a flame-thrower and flame bellowed and spurted at me, licking harmlessly off my asbestos suit until I hosed it out, sputtering and smoking, with a big brass nozzle.

Diss was scarcely two feet high now; he lobbed a grenade at me, and I bounced it back off a garbage-can lid; the detonation knocked him back against the control panel. All the red lights went to green, and a strident alarm bell began to clang. Diss jumped up and on the chart-table, no longer wearing his natty gold threads. His hide was a dull purplish-gray. He chittered like an enraged squirrel and threw a thunderbolt that exploded harmlessly, with a crash like a falling cliff, filling the air with the reek of ozone and scorched plastic. A foot high now, Diss danced in fury, shook his fist, and launched a nuclear rocket. I watched it come across the room toward me, and leaned aside, gave it a nudge as it passed; it flipped end-for-end and streaked back toward its owner. He dove over the side—he was about six inches long now—and the whole room blew up in my face. Luckily, I was wearing my full-spectrum invulnerable armor, so no harm came to me. I waded through the ruins and out into yellow sunlight filled with boiling dust. The dust settled and a small pale-violet lizard coiled on a rock just before me uttered a supersonic hiss and spat a stream of venom at my eyes. That annoyed me. I raised my gigantic flyswatter to crush the grasshopper-sized lizard, and he uttered a piercing minia-ture shriek and ducked into a crack in the rock, and I jammed my crowbar in after him and levered and cracks opened all across the stone.

"Florin! I surrender! I yield utterly! Only stop now!" His eyes glittered like red sparks from the depths of the cleft. I laughed at him and jammed the pry-bar in deeper.

"Florin, I confess I tampered with the dream machine! Van Wouk and the others had nothing to do with it! They're unwitting dupes, nothing more. When I came upon you in a vulnerable state—your mind open to me like a broached mollusk—I couldn't resist the temptation to meddle! I thought to frighten you, make you amenable to my wishes—but instead you seized on my own sources of energy and added them to your own. As a result, you've acquired powers I never dreamed of—fantastic powers! You'll rend the very fabric of the Cosmos if you go on!"

"Swell; it could stand a little rending." I heaved hard on the bar and felt something give, deep inside the rock, as if the planetary crust was readjusting along a fault line. I heard Diss screech.

"Florin—I've been a fool, an utter fool! I see

now that all along you've been drawing on another source, one I never suspected! The woman—Miss Regis—she's linked to you by a bond of such power as could shift Galaxies in their courses!"

"Yeah, the kid likes me; that's what makes the world go round. . . ." I levered again, and heard boulders rumble. Diss gave a shriek.

"Florin—what avails victory if you leave only ruins behind you?"

He was just a cricket chirping in a desert. I levered again and the whole gigantic boulder split with a noise like thunder and fell apart carrying the earth and the sky with it, exposing the velvet blackness of absolute nothingness.

* * *

"Nice," I called into the emptiness, "but a trifle stark for my taste. Let there be light!"

And there was light.

And I saw that it was good, and I divided the light from the darkness. It still looked a little empty, so I added a firmament, and divided the waters under it from the waters above it. That gave me an ocean with a lot of wet clouds looking down on it.

"Kind of monotonous," I said. "Let the waters be gathered together off to the side and let's see a little dry land around here."

And it was so.

"Better," I said. "But still dead looking. Let there be life."

Slime spread across the water and elaborated into seaweed and clumps floated ashore and lodged there and put out new shoots and crawled up on the bare rocks and sunned itself; and the earth brought forth grass and herbs yielding seeds, and fruit trees and lawns and jungles and flower boxes and herbaceous borders and moss and celery and a lot of other green stuff.

"Too static," I announced. "Let's have some animals."

And the earth brought forth whales and cattle and fowl and creeping things, and they splashed and mooed and clucked and crept, livening things up a little, but not enough.

"The trouble is, it's too quiet," I pointed out to me. "Nothing's happening."

The earth trembled underfoot and the ground heaved and the top of a mountain blew off and lava belched out and set the forested slopes afire, and the black clouds of smoke and pumice came rolling down on me. I coughed and changed my mind and everything was peaceful again.

"What I meant was something pleasant," I said, "like a gorgeous sunset, with music."

The sky jerked and the sun sank in the south in a glory of purple and green and pink, while chords boomed down from an unseen source in the sky, or inside my head. After it had set I cranked it back up and set it again a few times. Something about it didn't seem quite right. Then I noticed it was the same each time. I varied it and ran through half a dozen more dusks before I acknowledged that there was still a certain sameness to the spectacle.

"It's hard work, making up a new one each time," I conceded. "It gives me a headache.

How about just the concert, without the light show?"

I played through what I could remember of the various symphonies, laments, concerti, ballads, madrigals, and singing commercials. After a while I ran out. I tried to make up one of my own, but nothing came. That was an area I would have to look into—later. Right now I wanted fun.

"Skiing," I specified. "Healthful exercise in the open air, the thrill of speed!" I was rushing down a slope, out of control, went head over insteps and broke both legs.

"Not like that," I complained, reassembling myself. "No falling down."

I whizzed down the slope, gripped in a sort of invisible padded frame that wrenched me this way and that, insulating me from all shocks.

"Talk about taking a bath in your BVDs," I cried, "I might as well be watching it on TV."

I tried surfing, riding the waves in like the rabbit at a dogtrack, locked to the rails. The surf was all around, but it had nothing to do with me.

"No good. You have to learn how—and that's hard work. Skydiving, maybe?" I gripped the open door frame and stepped out. Wind screamed past me as I hung motionless, watching a pastel-toned tapestry a few feet below grow steadily larger. Suddenly it turned into trees and fields rushing up at me; I grabbed for the ring, yanked—

The jolt almost broke my back. I spun dizzily, swinging like the pendulum of a grandfather clock, and slammed into solid rock.

. . . I was being dragged by the chute. I managed to unbuckle the harness and crawl under a bush to recuperate.

"There's tricks to every trade," I reminded myself, "Including being God. What's the point in doing something if I don't enjoy it?" That started me thinking about what I did enjoy.

"It's all yours, old man," I pointed out. "How about a million dollars to start with?"

The bills were neatly stacked, in bundles of $1,000, in tens, twenties, fifties, and hundreds. There were quite a lot of them.

"That's not quite it. What good is money per se? It's what you can buy with it. Like for example, a brand-new 1936 Auburn boat-tailed Speedster, with green leather upholstery."

It was there, parked on the drive. It smelled good. The doors had a nice slam. I cranked up, gunned it up to 50 along the road that I caused to appear in front of it. I went faster and faster: 90 . . . 110 . . . 200. . . . After a while I got tired of buffeting wind and dust in my eyes, and eliminated them. That left the roar and the jouncing.

"You're earthbound," I accused. So I added wings and a prop and was climbing steeply in my Gee Bee Sportster, the wind whipping back past my face bearing a heartening reek of castor oil and high octane. But quite suddenly the stubby racer whip-stalled and crashed in a ploughed field near Peoria. There wasn't enough left of me to pick up with a spoon. I got it together and was in a T-33, going straight up as smooth as silk. 30,000 feet . . . 40,000 feet . . . 50,000 feet. I leveled off and did snap rolls and loops and chandelles and started getting airsick. I sailed between heaped clouds, and got sicker. I came in low over the fence, holding her off for a perfect touchdown and barely made it before I urped.

The trouble is, chum, wherever you go, you're still stuck with yourself. How about a quieter pastime?

I produced a desert isle, furnished it with orchids and palm trees, a gentle breeze, white surf edging the blue lagoon. I built a house of red padauk wood and glass and rough stone high on the side of the central mountain, and set it about with tropical gardens and ponds and a waterfall, and strolled out on my patio to take my ease beside my pool with a tall drink ready to hand. The drink gave me an appetite. I summoned up a table groaning under roast fowl and cold melon and chocolate eclairs and white wine. I ate for a long time; when my appetite began to flag, I whipped it along with shrimp and roast beef and chef salad and fresh pineapple and rice with chicken and sweet-and-sour pork and cold beer. I felt urpy again.

I took a nap in my nine-foot square bed with silken sheets. After fourteen hours' sleep it wasn't comfortable anymore. I ate again, hot dogs and jelly doughnuts this time. It was very filling. I went for a dip in the lagoon. The water was cold and I cut my foot on the coral. Then I got a cramp, luckily in shallow water so that I didn't actually drown. Drowning, I decided, was one of the most unpleasant ways to go.

I limped back up and sat on the beach and thought about my 5,000-tape automatic music system, my 10,000-book library, my antique gun and coin collections, my closets full of hand-woven suits and hand-tooled shoes, my polo ponies, my yacht—

"Nuts," I said. "I get seasick, and don't know how to ride. And what can you do with old coins but look at them? And it'll take me forty years to get through the books. And—"

I suddenly felt tired. But I didn't want to sleep. Or eat. Or swim. Or anything.

"What good is it?" I wanted to know, "if you're alone? If there's nobody to show off to, or share it with, or impress, or have envy me? Or even play games with?" I addressed these poignant queries to the sky, but nobody answered, because I had neglected to put anybody up there for the purpose. I thought about doing it, but it seemed like too much effort.

"The trouble with this place is no people," I admitted glumly. "Let there be Man," I said, and created Him in my own image.

"It was Van Wouk's scheme," he said. "Once you'd decided to go ahead with the simulator project he said it was only justice that you should be the one to test it. I swear I didn't know he planned to drop you. I was just along for the ride, I was victimized as much as you—"

"My mistake," I said. "Go back where you came from." He disappeared without a backward glance.

"What I really want," I said, "is strangers.

People I never saw before, people who won't start in telling me all the things I did wrong."

A small band of Neanderthals emerged from a copse, so intent on turning over logs looking for succulent grubs that they didn't see me at first. Then an old boy with grizzled hair all over him spotted me and barked like a dog and they all ran away.

"I had in mind something a bit more sophisticated," I carped. "Let's have a town, with streets and shops and places where a fellow can get in out of the rain."

The town was there, a straggle of mud-and-wattle huts, bleak under leaden skies. I ordered sunshine, and it broke through the clouds and I made a few improvements in the village, not many or important, just enough to make it homey, and it was Lower Manhattan on a bright afternoon. The Neanderthals were still there, shaved and wearing clothes, many of them driving cabs, others jostling me on the sidewalk. I went into a bar and took a table on the right side, facing the door, as if I were expecting someone. A fat waitress in a soiled dress two sizes too small came over and sneered at me and fetched her pencil down from behind an ear like a bagel.

I said, "Skip it," and waved the whole thing away and pictured a cozy little fire on the beach with people sitting around it cross-legged, toasting weiners and marshmallows.

"Ah, the simple life," I said, and moved up to join them and they looked up and a big fellow with a mat of black hair on his chest stood up and said, "Beat it, Jack. Private party."

"I just want to join the fun," I said. "Look, I brought my own weenie."

A girl screamed and Blackie came in fast throwing lefts and rights most of which I deftly intercepted with my chin. I went down on my back and got a mouthful of calloused foot before I whisked the little group out of existence. I spat sand and tried to appreciate the solitude and the quiet slap of the surf and the big moon hanging over the water and might have been making some headway when an insect sank his fangs into that spot under the shoulder blades, the one you can't reach. I eliminated animal life for the moment, and paused for thought.

"I've been going about it wrong. What I want is a spot I fit into; a spot where life is simpler and sweeter, and has a place for me. What better spot than my own past?"

I let my thoughts slide back down the trail to the memory of a little frame schoolhouse on a dirt road on a summer day, long ago. I was there, eight years old, wearing knickers and sneakers and a shirt and tie, sitting at a desk with an inkwell full of dried ink, and covered with carved initials, my hands folded, waiting for the bell to ring. It did, and I jumped up and ran outside into the glorious sunshine of youth and a kid three sizes bigger, with bristly red hair and little eyes like a pig grabbed me by the hair and scrubbed his knuckles rapidly back and forth across my scalp and threw me down and jumped on me, and I felt my nose start to bleed.

So I wrapped him in chains and dropped a seventeen-ton trip-hammer on him and was alone again.

"That was all wrong," I said. "That wasn't the idea at all. That wasn't facing real life, with all its joys and sorrows. That was a cop-out. To mean anything, the other guy has to have a chance; it has to be man to man, the free interplay of personality, that's what makes for the rich, full life."

I made myself six feet three and magnificently muscled, with crisp golden curls and a square jaw, and Pig Eyes came out of an alley with a length of pipe and smashed the side of my head in. I dressed myself in armor with a steel helmet and he came up behind me and slipped a dirk in through the chink where my gorget joined my *epauliere*. I threw the armor away and slipped into my black belt and went into a *neko-ashi-dashi* stance and ducked his slash and he shot me through the left eye.

I blanked it all out and was back on the beach, just me and the skeeters.

"That's enough acting on impulse," I told myself sternly. "Hand-to-hand combat isn't really your idea of fun; if you lose, it's unpleasant; and if you always win, why bother?"

I didn't have a good answer for that one. That encouraged me so I went on: "What you really want is companionship, not rivalry. Just the warmth of human society on a non-competitive basis."

At once, I was the center of a throng. They weren't doing anything much, just thronging. Warm, panting bodies, pressed close to me. I could smell them. That was perfectly normal, bodies do have smells. Someone stepped on my foot and said, "Excuse me." Somebody else stepped on my other foot and didn't say excuse me. A man fell down and died. Nobody paid any attention. I might not have either, except that the man was me. I cleared the stage and sat on the curb and watched the sad city sunlight shine down on the scrap paper blowing along the sidewalk. It was a dead, dirty city. On impulse, I cleaned it up, even to removing the grime from the building fronts.

That made it a dead, clean city.

"The ultimate in human companionship," I thought to myself, "is that of a desirable and affectionate female of nubile years and willing disposition."

Accordingly, I was in my penthouse apartment, the hi-fi turned low, the wine chilled, and she was reclining at ease on the commodious and cushion-scattered chaise longue. She was tall, shapely, with abundant reddish-brown hair, smooth skin, large eyes, a small nose. I poured. She wrinkled her nose at the wine and yawned. She had nice teeth.

"Golly, haven't you got any groovy records?" she asked. Her voice was high, thin, and self-indulgent.

"What would you prefer?" I asked.

"I dunno. Something catchy." She yawned again and looked at the heavy emerald and diamond bracelet on her wrist.

"Come on, really," she said. "How much did it cost?"

"I got it free. I have a pal in the business. It's a demonstrator."

She took it off and threw it on the inch-thick rug. "I've got this terrible headache," she whined. "Call me a cab."

"That shows what you really think of the kind of girls who go with penthouses and hi-fi," I told myself, dismissing her with a wave of my hand. "What you really want is a home girl, sweet and innocent and unassuming."

I came up the steps of the little white cottage with the candle in the window and she met me at the door with a plate of cookies. She chattered about her garden and her sewing and her cooking as we dined on corn bread and black-eyed peas with lumps of country ham in it. Afterward she washed and I dried. Then she tatted while I sat by the fire and oiled harness or something of the sort. After a while she said, "Well, good night," and left the room quietly. I waited five minutes and followed. She was just turning back the patchwork quilt; she was wearing a thick woolen nightgown, and her hair was in braids.

"Take it off," I said. She did. I looked at her. She looked like a woman.

"Uh, let's go to bed," I said. We did.

"Don't you have anything to say?" I wanted to know.

"What shall I say?"

"What's your name?"

"You didn't give me one."

"You're Charity. Where are you from, Charity?"

"You didn't say."

"You're from near Dotham. How old are you?"

"Forty-one minutes."

"Nonsense! You're at least, ah, twenty-three. You've lived a full, happy life, and now

you're here with me, the culmination of all
your dreams."

"Yes."

"Is that all you have to say? Aren't you
happy? Or sad? Don't you have any ideas of
your own?"

"Of course. My name is Charity, and I'm
twenty-three, and I'm here with you—"

"What would you do if I hit you? Suppose I
set the house on fire? What if I said I was
going to cut your throat?"

"Whatever you say."

I got a good grip on my head and
suppressed a yell of fury.

"Wait a minute, Charity—this is all wrong. I
didn't mean you to be an automaton, just
mouthing what I put in your head. Be a real,
live woman. React to me—"

She grabbed the covers up to her chin and
screamed.

I sat in the kitchen alone and drank a glass
of cold milk and sighed a lot.

"Let's think this thing through," I suggested. "You can make it any way you want it.
But you're trying to do it too fast; you're
taking too many shortcuts. The trick is to
start slowly, build up the details, make it
real."

So I thought up a small Midwestern city,
with wide brick streets of roomy old frame
houses under big trees with shady yards and
gardens that weren't showplaces, just the
comfortable kind where you can swing in a
hammock and walk on the grass and pick the
flowers without feeling like you're vandaliz-
ing a set piece.

I walked along the street, taking it all in, getting the feel of it. It was autumn, and someone was burning leaves somewhere. I climbed the hill, breathing the tangy evening air, being alive. The sound of a piano softly played floated down across the lawn of the big brick house at the top of the hill. Purity Atwater lived there. She was only seventeen, and the prettiest girl in town. I had an impulse to turn in right then, but I kept going.

"You're a stranger in town," I said. "You have to establish yourself, not just barge in. You have to meet her in the socially accepted way, impress her folks, buy her a soda, take her to the movies. Give her time. Make it real."

A room at the Y costs fifty cents. I slept well. The next morning I applied for work at only three places before I landed a job at two dollars a day at Siegal's Hardware and Feed. Mr. Siegal was favorably impressed with my frank, open countenance, polite and respectful manner, and apparent eagerness for hard work.

After three months, I was raised to $2.25 per day, and took over the bookkeeping. In my room at the boardinghouse I kept a canary and a shelf of inspirational volumes. I attended divine service regularly, and contributed one dime per week to the collection plate. I took a night class in advanced accountancy, sent away for Charles Atlas' course, and allowed my muscles to grow no more than could be accounted for by dynamic tension.

In December I met Purity. I was shoveling

snow from her father's walk when she emerged from the big house looking charming in furs. She gave me a smile. I treasured it for a week, and schemed to be present at a party attended by her. I dipped punch for the guests. She smiled at me again. She approved of my bronzed good looks, my curly hair, my engaging grin, my puppylike clumsiness. I asked her to the movies. She accepted. On the third date I held her hand briefly. On the tenth I kissed her cheek. Eighteen months later, while I was still kissing her cheek, she left town with the trumpeter from a jazz band I had taken her to hear.

Nothing daunted, I tried again. Hope Berman was the second prettiest girl in town. I wooed her via the same route, jumped ahead to kisses on the lips after only twenty-one dates, and was promptly called to an interview with Mr. Berman. He inquired as to my intentions. Her brothers, large men all, also seemed interested. A position with Berman and Sons, Clothiers, was hinted at. Hope giggled. I fled.

Later in my room I criticized myself sternly. I was ruined in Pottsville: word was all over town that I was a trifler. I took my back wages, minus some vague deductions and with a resentful speech from Mr. Siegal about ingrates and grasshoppers, and traveled by train to St. Louis. There I met and paid court to Faith, a winsome lass who worked as a secretary in the office of a lawyer whose name was painted on a second-story window on a side street a few blocks from the more affluent business section. We went to the movies, took long streetcar rides, visited museums, had picnics. I noticed that she perspired moderately in warm weather, had several expensive cavities, was ignorant of many matters, and was a very ordinary lay. And afterward she cried and chattered of marriage.

Omaha was a nicer town. I holed up at the Railroad Men's Y there for a week and thought it through. It was apparent I was still acting too hastily. I wasn't employing my powers correctly. I had exchanged the loneliness of God for the loneliness of Man, a pettier loneliness but no less poignant. The trick was, I saw, to combine the highest skills of each status, to live a human life, nudged here and there in the desired direction.

Inspired, I repaired at once to the maternity ward of the nearest hospital, and was born at 3:27 A.M. on a Friday, a healthy, seven-pound boy whom my parents named Melvin. I ate over four hundred pounds of Pablum before my first taste of meat and potatoes. Afterward I had a stomach-ache. In due course I learned to say bye-bye, walk, and pull tablecloths off tables in order to hear the crash of crockery. I entered kindergarten, and played sand blocks in the band, sometimes doubling in a triangle, which was chrome-plated and had a red string. I mastered shoetying, pantsbuttoning, and eventually rollerskating and falling off my bike. In Junior High I used my twenty cents lunch money for a mayonnaise sandwich, an RC Cola half of which I squirted at the ceiling and my classmates, and an O Henry. I read many dull books by Louisa May

Alcott and G. A. Henty, and picked out Patience Froomwall as my intended.

She was a charming redhead with freckles. I took her to proms, picking her up in my first car, one of the early Fords, with a body hand-built from planks. After graduation, I went away to college, maintaining our relationship via mail. In the summers we saw a lot of each other in a nonanatomical sense.

I received my degree in business administration, secured a post with the power company, married Patience, and fathered two nippers. They grew up, following much the same pattern as I had, which occasioned some speculation on my part as to how much divine intervention had had to do with my remarkable success. Patience grew less and less like her name, gained weight, developed an interest in church work and gardens and a profound antipathy for everyone else doing church work and gardening.

I worked very hard at all this, never yielding to the temptation to take shortcuts, or to improve my lot by turning Patience into a movie starlet or converting our modest six-roomer into a palatial estate in Devon. The hardest part was sweating through a full sixty seconds of subjective time in every minute, sixty minutes every hour. . . .

After fifty years of conscientious effort I ended up with a workbench in the garage.

At the local tavern, I drank four Scotches and pondered my dilemma. After five Scotches I became melancholy. After six I became defiant. After seven, angry. At this point the landlord was so injudicious as to suggest that I had had enough. I left in high dudgeon, pausing only long enough to throw a fire bomb through the front window. It made a lovely blaze. I went along the street fire-bombing the beauty parlor, the Christian Science Reading Room, the optometrist, the drugstore, the auto parts house, the Income Tax Prepared Here place.

"You're all phonies," I yelled. "All liars, cheats, fakes!"

The crowd which had gathered labored and brought forth a policeman, who shot me and three innocent bystanders. This annoyed me even in my exhilarated mood. I tarred and feathered the officious fellow, then proceeded to blow up the courthouse, the bank, the various churches, the supermarket, and the automobile agency. They burned splendidly.

I rejoiced to see the false temples going up in smoke, and toyed briefly with the idea of setting up my own religion, but at once found myself perplexed with questions of dogma, miracles, fund drives, canonicals, tax-free real estate, nunneries, and inquisitions, and shelved the idea.

All Omaha was blazing nicely now; I moved on other cities, eliminating the dross that had clogged our lives. Pausing to chat with a few survivors in the expectation of overhearing expressions of joy and relief at the lifting of the burden of civilization, and praise of the new-found freedom to rebuild a sensible world, I was dismayed to see they seemed more intent on tending their wounds, competing in the pursuit of small game, and looting TV sets and cash than in philosophy.

By now the glow of the Scotch was fading. I saw I had been hasty. I quickly re-established order, placing needful authority in the hands of outstanding Liberals. Since there was still a vociferous body of reactionaries creating unrest and interfering with the establishment of total social justice, it was necessary to designate certain personnel to keep order, dressing them in uniform garments, for ease of identification.

Alas, mild policies failed to convince the wreckers that the People meant business and were not to be robbed of the fruits of their hard-won victory over the bloodsuckers. Sterner measures were of necessity resorted to. Still the stubborn Fascists took advantage of their freedom to agitate, make inflammatory speeches, print disloyal books, and in other ways interfere with their comrades' fight for peace and plenty. Temporary controls were accordingly placed on treasonous talk, and exemplary executions were carried out. The burden of these duties proving onerous, the leaders found it necessary to retire to the more spacious estates surviving the holocaust, and to limit their diets to caviar, champagne, breast of chicken and other therapeutic items in order to keep up their strength for the battle against reaction. Malcontents naturally attributed the leaders' monopoly on limousines, palaces, custom tailoring and the company of trained nurses of appearance calculated to soothe the weary executive eye as evidence of decadence. Picture their fury and frustration when the State, refusing to tolerate sedition, hustled them off to remote areas where by performing useful labor under simple conditions, they received an opportunity to correct their thinking.

I called on the Prime Leader—affectionately known as the Dictator—and queried him as to his intentions, now that he had consolidated the economy, rooted out traitors, and established domestic tranquillity.

"I'm thinking about taking over the adjacent continent," he confided.

"Are they bothering us?" I inquired.

"You bet. Every time I see a good-looking broad on their side of the line and realize she's out of reach. . . ." He ground his teeth.

"Joking aside," I persisted. "Now that we have peace—"

"Next thing you know the mob will be getting restless," he said. "Wanting TV sets, cars, iceboxes—even refrigerators! Just because I and my boys have a few little amenities to help us over the intolerable burdens of leadership, they want to get into the act! What do those bums know about the problems we got? Did they ever have to mobilize along a frontier? Did they ever have to make up their minds: 'tanks or tractors'? Do they have to worry about the old international prestige? Not those bums! All they got to worry about is getting through enough groceries to stay alive long enough to have enough brats so there'll be somebody around to bury 'em—as if that was important.

I thought about it. I sighed. "I can't quite put my finger on it," I told the Dictator, "but somehow there's something lacking. It isn't exactly the Utopia I had in mind." I wiped him out and all his works and contemplated the desolation sadly. "Maybe the trouble was I let too many cooks into the broth," I reflected. "Next time I'll set the whole thing up, complete, just the way I like it—and then turn everybody loose in it."

It was a jolly thought. I did it. I turned the wilderness into a parkland, drained the bogs, planted flowers. I set up towns at wide intervals, each a jewel of design, with cozy dwellings and graceful trees and curving paths and fountains and reflecting pools and open-air theaters that fit into the landscape as if a part of it. I set up clean, well-lighted schools and swimming pools and dredged the rivers and stocked them with fish and provided abundant raw materials and a few discreet, well-concealed, nonpolluting factories to turn out the myriad simple, durable, miraculous devices that took all the drudgery out of my life, leaving humans free for the activities that only humans can perform, such as original research, art, massage, and prostitution, plus waiting on tables. Then I popped the population into the prepared setting and awaited the glad cries that would greet the realization that everything was perfect.

Somehow, there seemed to be a certain indifference right from the beginning. I asked a beautiful young couple strolling through a lovely park beside a placid lake if they weren't having a good time.

"I guess so," he said.

"There's nothing to do," she said.

"Think I'll take a nap," he said.

"You don't love me anymore," she said.

"Don't bug me," he said.

"I'll kill myself," she said.

"That'll be the day," he said, and yawned.

"You son of a bitch," she said.

I moved on. A child with golden curls a lot like mine was playing by the lake. It was drowning a kitten. It was just as well; it had already poked its eyes out. I resisted an impulse to tumble the tot in after the cat and approached an old gentleman with cherubic white locks who was standing on a stone bench, peering bemusedly at a large shrub. At close range I saw that he was peering *through* the shrub at two nubile maidens disporting themselves naked on the grass. He spun when he heard me coming.

"Scandalous," he quavered. "They've been doing that to each other for the better part of two hours, right out in public where a body can't help seeing them. Makes a body wonder if there aren't enough males to go around."

I had a moment of panic; had I overlooked that detail? But no, of course not. Male and female created i Them. It was something else that was wrong.

"I know," i cried. "i've been doing too much for Them; They're spoiled. What They need is a noble enterprise that They can tackle together, a brave crusade against the forces of evil, with the banners of Right floating overhead!"

We were arrayed in ranks, myself at the head, my loyal soldiery behind me. I rose in my stirrups and pointed to the walls of the embattled town ahead.

"There they are, lads," i cried. "The enemy —the killers, looters, rapists, vandals. Now's the time to get them! Forward once more into the breach, dear friends, for Harry, England and St. George!"

We charged, battered our way through the defenses; they surrendered; we rode triumphant into the city's streets. My lads leaped from their horses, began hacking at civilians, smashing windows and grabbing handfuls of costume jewelry, TV sets, and liquor. They raped all the females, sometimes killing them afterward and sometimes before. They set fire to what they couldn't eat, drink, or screw.

"God has won a glorious victory," my priests cried.

It annoyed me to have my name taken in vain; i caused a giant meteorite to crash down in the midst of the revelry. The survivors cited their survival as evidence of god's approval. I sent a plague of stinging flies, and half the people burned the other half at the stake to appease me. I sent a flood; they floated around, clinging to fragments of church pews, old TV chassis, and the swollen carcasses of dead cows, horses, and evangelists, yelling for help and making promises to me as to how they would behave if they only got out of this one.

I rescued a few and to my delight they set to work at once to save others, whom they immediately formed into platoons, congregations, labor unions, mobs, crowds, lobbies and political parties. Each group at once attacked another group, usually the one most similar to themselves. I gave a terrible yell and swept them all away under a tidal wave. The foaming of the waters around the ruins of temples, legislatures, court houses, clip joints, chemical factories, and the headquarters of large corporations amused me; I made bigger and better tidal waves, and washed away slums, eroded farmland, burned-off forest areas, silted-up rivers, and polluted seas. Adrenalin flooded my system; my lust to destroy was aroused. I pulverized the continents, shattered the crust, splashed around in the magma that boiled forth.

The moon caught my eye, riding aloof above my wrath. The bland smoothness of it annoyed me; I threw a handful of gravel at it, pocking the surface nicely. I grabbed the planet Oedipus and threw it at Saturn; it missed, but the close passage broke it up. Major chunks of rock went into orbit around Saturn and the dust formed rings; a few scraps were captured by Mars, and the rest trailed off around the sun.

I found that a satisfying spectacle, and turned to invite others to admire it, but of course there was no one there.

"This is the trouble with being god," i groaned. "I could set up a bunch of nincompoops to praise me, but what good is that? A fellow wants a response from an equal, dammit!"

Suddenly i was sick, and tired of the whole thing. It should have been easy, when you have all the power there is, to make things the

way you want them; but it wasn't. Part of the
trouble was that i didn't really know what i
wanted, and another part was that i didn't
know how to achieve what i wanted when i did
know what it was, and another part was that
when i got what i thought i wanted it turned
out not to be what i wanted. It was too hard,
too complicated, being god. It was a lot easier
just being a Man. There was a limit on a Man's
abilities, but there was also a limit on His
responsibilities.

"What i mean is," I told myself, "I'm only a
Human Being, no matter what kind of
thunderbolts I can throw. I need a few hundred thousand years more evolution, and then
maybe I can handle being god."

I stood—or floated, or drifted—in the midst
of the Ylem that was all that was left of all my
efforts, and remembered Van Wouk and Lard
Face and their big plans for me. They weren't
sinister anymore, only pathetic. I remembered Diss, the lizard man, and how frightened he had been just at the last. I thought of
the Senator, his cowardice and his excuses,
and suddenly he seemed merely human. And
then I thought about me, and what a shabby
figure I had cut, not just as god, but as a Man.

"You looked pretty good in there," i told
Me, "up to a point. You're all right as a loser,
but you're a lousy winner. Having it all your
way is the real problem. Success is the challenge nobody's ever met. Because no matter
how many you win, there's always a bigger
and harder and more complicated problem
ahead, and there always will be, and the
secret isn't Victory Forever but to keep on

doing the best you can one day at a time and remember you're a Man, not just god, and for you there aren't and never will be any easy answers, only questions, and no reasons, only causes, and no meaning, only intelligence, and no destination and no kindly magic smiling down from above, and no fires to goad you from below, only Yourself and the Universe and what You make out of the interface between the two equals."

And I rested from all my work which i had made.

* * *

I opened my eyes and she was sitting across the table from me.

"Are you all right?" she said. "You looked so strange, sitting here all alone, I thought perhaps you were sick."

"I feel like I've just made and destroyed the Universe," I said. "Or it's made and destroyed me. Or possibly both. Don't go away. There's one more detail I have to see to."

I got up and went across to the door and stepped through it into the Senator's study. He looked at me and gave me the smile that was as real as a billboard and as sincere.

"You've come," he said in a noble voice.

"I'm turning down the job," I said. "I just wanted you to know."

He looked dismayed. "You can't. I've counted on you."

"Not anymore," I said. "Come here; I want to show you something." I went over to the full-length mirror and he came reluctantly to stand beside me and I looked at the reflection:

the square jaw, the well-tailored shoulders, the level gaze.

"What do you see?" I asked.

"A four-flusher," I answered. "All they ever asked you to do was live one little old life. And did you do it? No. You copped out—or tried to. But it didn't work. You're in, like it or not. So you'd better like it."

I turned to object, but I was alone in the room.

* * *

I went to the door and opened it. Councillor Van Wouk looked up from the long table under the spiral chandelier.

"See here, Bardell," he started, but I unfolded the newspaper in my hand to the Sunday funnies, and dropped it in front of him with the *Florin—the Man of Steel* strip on top.

"He almost went for it," I said. "But he changed his mind."

"Then—that means . . . ?"

"It means forget the whole thing. It never happened."

"Well, in that case," Van Wouk said, and began to shrink. He dwindled down to the size of a monkey, a mouse, a *musca domestica*, and wasn't there anymore. Lard Face was gone too, and the Bird Man, and the rest.

In the corridor I ran into Trait and Eridani.

"You're fired," I told them. They tipped their hats and silently faded away.

"That leaves you," I said. "What are we going to do with you?"

The question seemed to echo along the gray-walled corridor, as if it hadn't been me that asked it. I tried to follow it to its source, but the walls turned to gray mist that swirled around me as palpable as gray draperies. Suddenly I was tired, too tired to stand. I sat down. My head was heavy. I held it tight in both hands and gave it a half-turn and lifted it off—

* * *

I was sitting behind my desk, holding the curious spiral artifact in my hands.

"Well," the Undersecretary for Science said. "Anything?"

"I thought for a moment you looked a bit odd," the Chief of Staff said stiffly, and almost let a smile mar the rigidity of his little round face.

"As I expected," my Science Adviser said, and curved the corners of his mouth down. It looked like a line drawn on a saucer of lard.

I got up and went over to the window and looked out at Pennsylvania Avenue and the cherry blossoms and the Washington Monument. I thought about turning it into a big cement doughnut, but nothing happened. It was a humid afternoon and the town looked hot and dirty and full of trouble, like I felt. I turned and looked at the men waiting expectantly, important men all, full of the affairs of the world and their roles therein.

"Let me get this straight," I said. "You people brought this gadget to me, claiming it was removed from the wreckage of an apparently alien space vessel which crash-landed and burned in Minnesota last night."

Half a dozen faces registered confirmation.

"You recovered the body of a small lizard-like animal, and this. No pilot was in evidence."

"I assure you, sir," the Director of the FBI said, "he won't get far—or *it* won't get far." He smiled grimly.

"Drop the search," I ordered. I put the spiral gadget on the desk. "Bury this thing at sea," I commanded.

"But—Mr. President—"

I silenced that with a look and glanced at the Chairman of the Joint Chiefs.

"Was there something you wanted to tell me, General Trait?"

He looked startled. "Why, as a matter of fact, sir. . . ." He cleared his throat. "It's no doubt a hoax—but I've had a report of a radio transmission from space—not from any of our installations, I'm assured. It seems to originate from just beyond the orbit of Mars." He smiled a sickly smile.

"Go on," I said.

"The, er, caller represents himself as a native of a planet he calls Grayfell. He states that we have, ah, passed preliminary inspection. He wants to open negotiations for a treaty of peace between the Lastrian Concord and Earth."

"Tell them we're willing," I said. "If they don't get too tricky."

There were other matters they wanted to present to me, each of vast importance, requiring my immediate attention. I waved it all away. They looked aghast when I stood and told them the Cabinet meeting was over.

She was waiting for me in our apartment.

* * *

It was twilight. We were walking together in the park. We sat on a bench in the cool of evening and watched the pigeons on the grass.

"How do we know this isn't a dream?" she asked.

"Perhaps it is," I said. "Perhaps nothing in life is real. But it doesn't matter. We have to live it as if it were."

THUNDERHEAD

Carnaby folded his cards without showing them, tossed them into the center of the table. "Time for me to make my TX." He pushed back his chair and rose, a tall, wide-shouldered, gray-haired man, still straight-backed, but thickening through the body now. "It's just as well. You boys pretty well cleaned me out for tonight."

"You still got the badge," a big-faced man with quick sly eyes said. "Play you a hand of showdown for it."

Carnaby rubbed a thumb across the tiny jeweled comet in his lapel and smiled slightly. "Fleet property, Sal," he said.

The big-faced man showed a glint of gold tooth, flicked his eyes at the others. "Yeah," he said. "I guess I forgot." He winked at a foxy man on his left.

"Say, uh, any promotions come through yet?" He was grinning openly at Carnaby now.

"Not yet." Carnaby pushed his chair in.

"Twenty-one years in grade," Sal said genially. "Must be some kind of record." He took out a toothpick and plied it on a back tooth.

"Shut up, Sal," one of the other men said. "Leave Jimmy make his TX."

"All these years, with no transfer, no replacement," Sal persisted. "Not even a letter from home. Looks like maybe they forgot you're out here, Carnaby."

"It's not Jim's fault if they don't get in touch," a white-haired man said. "Meantime, he's carrying out his orders."

"Some orders." Sal lolled back in his chair. "Kind of makes a man wonder if he ever really had any orders."

"I seen his orders myself, the day the cruiser dropped him in here," the white-haired man said. "He was to set up the beacon station and man it until he was relieved. It ain't his fault if they ain't been back for him."

"Yeah." Sal shot a hard glance at the speaker. "I know you 'claim.'"

The white-haired man frowned. "What do you mean, 'claim'?"

"Take it easy, Harry." Carnaby caught the big-faced man's eyes, held them. "He didn't mean anything—did you, Sal?"

Sal looked at Carnaby for a long moment. Then he grunted a laugh and reached to rake in the pot. "Nah, I didn't mean anything."

* * *

A cold wind whipped at Carnaby as he walked alone past the half-dozen ramshackle stores. They comprised the business district of the single surviving settlement on the frontier planet Longone.

At the foot of the unpaved street a figure detached itself from the shadow under a pole-mounted light.

"Hello, Lieutenant Carnaby," a youthful voice greeted him. "I been waiting for you."

"Hello, Terry." Carnaby swung his gate open. "You're out late."

"I been working on my Blue codes, Lieutenant." The boy followed him up the path, describing the difficulties he had encountered in mastering Fleet cryptographic theory. Inside the modest bungalow, Carnaby went into the small room he used as an office, took the gray dustcover from the compact Navy issue VFP transmitter set up on a small desk beside a rough fieldstone fireplace. He settled himself in the chair before it with a sigh, flicked on the SEND and SCR switches, studied the half-dozen instrument faces, carefully noted their readings in a dark-blue polyon-backed notebook.

The boy stood by as Carnaby depressed the tape key which would send the recorded call letters of the one-man station flashing out-ward as a shaped wavefront, propagated at the square of the speed of light.

"Lieutenant." The boy shook his head. "Every night you send out your call. How come you never get an answer?"

Carnaby shook his head. "I don't know, Terry. Maybe they're too busy fighting the Djann to check in with every little JN beacon station on the Outline."

"You said after five years they were sup-posed to come back and pick you up," the boy persisted. "Why—"

There was a sharp wavering tone from the round wire mesh-covered speaker. A dull red light winked on, blinked in a rapid flutter, settled down to a steady glow. The audio signal firmed to a raucous buzz.

"Lieutenant!" Terry blurted. "Something's coming in!"

* * *

For a moment Carnaby sat rigid. Then he thumbed the big S-R key to receive, flipped the selector lever to UNSC, snapped a switch tagged RCD.

"... *riority, to all stations,*" a voice faint with distance whispered through a rasp and crackle of star-static. "*Cincsec One-two-oh to ... Cincfleet Nine ... serial one-oh four ... stations copy ... Terem Aldo ... Terem ... pha ... this message ... two ... Part One ...*"

"What is it, Lieutenant?" The boy's voice broke with excitement.

"A Fleet Action signal," Carnaby said tensely. "An all-station, recorded. I'm taping it; if they repeat it a couple of times, I'll get it all."

They listened, heads close to the speaker grill; the voice faded and swelled. It reached the end of the message, began again: "Red priority ... tions ... incsec One-two. ..."

The message repeated five times; then the voice ceased. The wavering carrier hum went on another five seconds, cut off. The red light winked out. Carnaby flipped over the SEND key, twisted the selector to VOC-SQ.

"JN Thirty-seven Ace Trey to Cincsec One-two-oh," he transmitted in a tense voice.

"Acknowledging receipt Fleet TX One-oh-four. Request clarification."

Then he waited, his face taut, for a reply to his transmission, which had been automatically taped, condensed to a one-microsecond squawk, and repeated ten times at one second intervals.

Carnaby shook his head after a silent minute had passed. "No good. From the sound of the Fleet beam, Cincsec One-two-oh must be a long way from here."

"Try again, Lieutenant! Tell 'em you're here, tell 'em it's time they came back for you! Tell 'em—"

"They can't hear me, Terry." Carnaby's face was tight. "I haven't got the power to punch across that kind of distance." He keyed the playback. The filtered composite signal came through clearly now:

"Red priority to all stations. Cincsec One-two-oh to Rim HQ via Cincfleet Nine-two. All Fleet Stations copy. Pass to Terem Aldo Cerise, Terem Alpha Two and ancillaries. This message in two parts. Part one: CTF Forty-one reports breakthrough of Djann armed tender on standard vector three-three-seven, mark; three-oh-five, mark; oh-four-two. This is a Category One Alert. Code G applies. Class Four through Nine stations stand by on Status Green. Part Two. Inner Warning Line units divert all traffic lanes three-four through seven-one. Outer Beacon Line stations activate main beacon, pulsing code schedule gamma eight. Message ends. All stations acknowledge."

"What's all that mean, Lieutenant?" Terry's

eyes seemed to bulge with excitement.

"It means I'm going to get some exercise, Terry."

"Exercise, how?"

Carnaby took out a handkerchief and wiped it across his forehead. "That was a general order from Sector Command. Looks like they've got a rogue bogey on the loose. I've got to put the beacon on the air."

* * *

He turned to looked out through the curtained window beside the bookcase toward the towering ramparts of the nine-thousand-foot volcanic freak known as Thunderhead, gleaming white in the light of the small but brilliant moon. Terry followed Carnaby's glance.

"Gosh, Lieutenant! You mean you got to climb Old Thunderhead?"

"That's where I set the beacon up, Terry," Carnaby said mildly. "On the highest ground around."

"Sure—but your flitter was working then!"

"It's not such a tough climb, Terry. I've made it a few times, just to check on things." He was studying the rugged contour of the moonlit steep, which resembled nothing so much as a mass of snowy cumulus. There was snow on the high ledges, but the wind would have scoured the east face clear. . . .

"Not in the last five years, you haven't, Lieutenant!" Terry sounded agitated.

"I haven't had a Category-One Alert, either." Carnaby smiled.

"Maybe they didn't mean you," Terry said.

"They called for Outer Beacon Line stations. That's me."

"They don't expect you to do it on foot," Terry protested. "This time o' year!"

Carnaby looked at the boy, smiling slightly. "I guess maybe they do, Terry."

"Then they're wrong!" Terry's thin face looked pale. "Don't go, Lieutenant!"

"It's my job, Terry. It's what I'm here for. You know that."

"What if you never got the message?" Terry countered.

"What if the radio went on the blink, like all the rest of the stuff you brought in here with you—the flitter, and the food unit, and the scooter? Then nobody'd expect you to get yourself killed!" The boy whirled suddenly. He grabbed up a poker from the fireplace, swung it against the front of the communicator, brought it down a second time before Carnaby caught his arm.

"You shouldn't have done that, Terry," he said softly. His eyes were on the smashed instrument faces.

"That . . . hurts . . ." the lad gasped.

"Sorry." Carnaby released the boy's thin arm. He stooped, picked up a fragment of a broken nameplate with the words FLEET SIGNAL ARM.

Terry stared at him; his mouth worked as though he wanted to speak, but couldn't find the words. "I'm going with you," he said at last.

Carnaby shook his head. "Thanks, Terry. But you're just a boy. I need a man along on this trip."

Terry's narrow face tightened. "Boy, hell," he said defiantly. "I'm seventeen."

"I didn't mean anything, Terry. Just that I need a man who's had some trail experience."

"How'm I going to get any trail experience, Lieutenant, if I don't start sometime?"

"Better to start with an easier climb than Thunderhead," Carnaby said gently. "You better go along home now, Terry. Your uncle will be getting worried."

"When . . . when you leaving, Lieutenant?"

"Early. I'll need all the daylight I can get to make Halliday's Roost by sundown."

* * *

After the boy had gone, Carnaby went to the storage room at the rear of the house and checked over the meager store of issue supplies. He examined the cold suit, shook his head over the brittleness of the wiring. At least it had been a loose fit; he'd still be able to get into it.

He left the house then, walked down to Maverik's store. The game had broken up, but half a dozen men still sat around the old hydrogen space heater. They looked up casually.

"I need a man," Carnaby said without preamble. "I've got a climb to make in the morning."

"What's got into you?" Yank Pepper rocked his chair back, glanced toward Sal Maverik. "Never knew you to go in for exercises before breakfast."

"I got an Alert Signal just now," Carnaby said. "From a Fleet unit in Deep Space. They've scared up a Djann blockade-runner. My orders are to activate the beacon."

Maverik clattered a garbage can behind the bar. "Kind of early in the evening for falling out of bed with a bad dream, ain't it?" he inquired loudly.

"You got a call in from the Navy?" The white-haired man named Harry frowned at Carnaby. "Hell, Jimmy, I thought. . . ."

"I just need a man along to help me pack gear as far as Halliday's Roost. I'll make the last leg alone."

"Ha!" Pepper looked around. "That's all: just as far as Halliday's Roost!"

"You gone nuts, Carnaby?" Sal Maverik growled. "Nobody in his right mind would tackle that damned rock after first snow, even if he had a reason."

"Halliday's hut ought to still be standing," Carnaby said. "We can overnight there, and—"

"Jimmy, wait a minute," Harry said. "All this about orders, and climbing old Thunderhead; it don't make sense! You mean after all these years they pick you to pull a damn fool stunt like that?"

"It's a general order to all Outer Line stations. They don't know my flitter's out of action."

Harry shook his head. "Forget it, Jimmy. Nobody can make a climb like that at this time of year."

"Fleet wants that beacon on the air," Carnaby said. "I guess they've got a reason;

maybe a good reason."

Maverik spat loudly in the direction of a sand-filled can. "You're the one's been the big-shot Navy man for the last twenty years around here," he said. "The big man with the fancy badge. Okay, your brass want you to go run up a hill, go ahead. Don't come in here begging for somebody to do your job for you."

"Listen, Jim," Harry said urgently. "I remember when you first came here, a young kid in your twenties, fresh out of the Academy. Five years you was to be here; they've left you here to rot for twenty. Now they come in with this piece of tomfoolery. Well, to hell with 'em! After five years, all bets were off. You got no call to risk your neck—"

"It's still my job, Harry."

Harry rose and came over to Carnaby. He put a hand on the big man's shoulder. "Let's quit pretending, Jim," he said softly. "They're never coming back for you, you know that. The high tide of the Concordiat dropped you here. For twenty years the traffic's been getting sparser, the transmitters dropping off the air. Adobe's deserted now, and Petreac. Another few years and Longone'll be dead, too."

"We're not dead yet."

"That message might have come from the other end of the galaxy, Jim! For all you know, it's been on the way for a hundred years!"

Carnaby faced him, a big solidly-built man with a lined face. "You could be right on all counts," he said. "It wouldn't change any-thing."

Harry sighed, turned away. "If I was twenty years younger, I might go along, just to keep you company, Jimmy. But I'm not. I'm old."

He turned to face Carnaby. "Like you, Jim. Just too old."

"Thanks anyway, Harry." Carnaby looked at the other men in the room, nodded slowly. "Sal's right," he said. "It's my lookout, and nobody else's." He turned and pushed back out into the windy street.

* * *

Aboard the Armed Picket *Malthusa*, five million tons, nine months out of Fleet HQ on Van Dieman's World on a routine Deep Space sweep, Signal Lieutenant Pryor, Junior Communications Officer on message deck duty, listened to the playback of the brief transmission the Duty NCOIC had called to his attention:

"JN Thirty-seven Ace Trey to Cincsec One . . . Fleet TX . . . clarification," the voice came through with much crackling.

"That's all I could get out of it Lieutenant," the signalman said. "I wouldn't have picked it up if I hadn't been filtering the Y band looking for AKs on One-oh-four."

The officer punched keys, scanning a listing that flashed onto the small screen on his panel.

"There's no JN Thirty-seven Ace Trey listed, Charlie," he said. He keyed the playback, listened to the garbled message again.

"Maybe it's some outworld sheepherder amusing himself."

"With WFP equipment? On Y channel?"

The NCO furrowed his forehead.

"Yeah." The lieutenant frowned. "See if you can get back to him with a station query, Charlie. See who this guy is."

"I'll try, sir, but he came in with six millisec lag. That puts him halfway from here to Rim."

The lieutenant crossed the room with the NCO, stood by as the latter sent the standard Confirm ID code. There was no reply.

"I guess we lost him, sir. You want me to log him?"

"No, don't bother."

The big repeater panel chattered then, and the officer hurried back to his console, settled down to the tedious business of transmitting follow-up orders to the fifty-seven hundred Fleet Stations of the Inner Line.

* * *

The orange sun of Longone was still below the eastern horizon when Carnaby came out the gate to the road. Terry Sickle was there, waiting for him.

"You got to get up early to beat me out, Lieutenant," he said in a tone of forced jocularity.

"What are you doing here, Terry?"

"I heard you still need a man," the lad said, less cocky now.

Carnaby started to shake his head, and Terry cut in with, "I can help pack some of the gear you'll need to try the high slope."

"Terry, go on back home, son. That high slope's no place for you."

"How'm I going to qualify for the Fleet when your ship comes, Lieutenant, if I don't start getting some experience?"

"I appreciate it, Terry. It's good to know I have a friend. But—"

"Lieutenant—what's a friend, if he can't help you when you need it?"

"I need you here when I get back, to have a hot meal waiting for me, Terry."

"Lieutenant. . . ." All the spring had gone from the boy's stance. "I've known you all my life. All I ever wanted was to be with you on Navy business. If you go up there, alone. . . ."

Carnaby looked at the boy, the dejected slump of his thin shoulders.

"Your uncle know you're here, Terry?"

"Sure. Uh, he thought it was a fine idea, me going with you."

"All right, then, Terry, if you want to. As far as Halliday's Roost. Thanks."

"Oh, boy, Lieutenant! We'll have a swell time. I'm a good climber, you'll see!" He grinned from ear to ear, squinting through the early gloom at Carnaby.

"Hey, Lieutenant, you're rigged out like a real . . ." he broke off. "I thought you'd, uh, wore out all your issue gear," he finished lamely.

"Seemed like for this trek I ought to be in uniform," Carnaby said. "And the coldsuit will feel good, up on the high slopes."

* * *

The two moved off down the dark street. There were lights on in Sal Maverik's general store. The door opened as they came up: Sal emerged, carrying a flour sack, his mackinaw collar turned up around his ears. He grunted a greeting, then swung to stare at Carnaby.

"Hey, by God! Look at him, dressed fit to kill."

"The Lieutenant got a hot-line message in from Fleet Headquarters last night," Terry said. "We got no time to jaw with you, Maverik." He brushed past the heavy-set man.

"You watch your mouth, boy," Sal snapped. "Carnaby," he raised his voice, "this poor kid the best you could get to hold your hand?"

"What do you mean, 'poor kid'?" Terry started back. Carnaby caught his arm.

"We're on official business, Terry," he said. "Eyes front and keep them there."

"Playing Navy, hah? That's a hot one," the storekeeper called after the two. "What kind of orders you get? To take a goonybird census up in the foothills?"

"Don't pay him no attention, Lieutenant," Terry said, his voice unsteady. "He's as full of meanness as a rotten mealspud is of weevils."

"He's had some big disappointments in his life, Terry. That makes a man bitter."

"I guess you did too, Lieutenant. It ain't made *you* mean." Terry looked sideways at Carnaby. "I don't reckon you beat out the competition to get an Academy appointment and then went through eight years of training just for this." He made a gesture that took in the sweep of the semiarid landscape stretching away to the big world's far horizon, broken only by the massive outcroppings of the pale, convoluted lava cores spaced at intervals of a few miles along a straight fault line that extended as far as men had explored the desolate world.

Carnaby laughed softly. "No, I had big ideas about seeing the galaxy, making fleet admiral, and coming home covered with gold braid and glory."

"You leave any folks behind, Lieutenant?" Terry inquired, waxing familiar in the comradeship of the trail.

"No wife. There was a girl. And my half-brother, Tom. A nice kid. He'd be over forty, now."

"Lieutenant—I'm sorry I busted up your transmitter. You might have got through, gotten yourself taken off this Godforsaken place—"

"Never mind, Terry."

The dusky sun was up now, staining the rounded, lumpy flank of Thunderhead a deep scarlet.

Carnaby and Sickle crossed the first rock-slope, entered the broken ground where the prolific rock-lizards eyed them as they approached, then heaved themselves from their perches, scuttled away into the black shadows of the deep crevices opened in the porous rock by the action of ten million years of wind and sand erosion on thermal cracks.

Five hundred feet above the plain Carnaby looked back at the settlement. Only a mile away, it was almost lost against the titanic spread of empty wilderness.

"Terry, why don't you go back now?" he said. "Your uncle will have a nice breakfast waiting for you."

"I'm looking forward to sleeping out," the boy said confidently. "We better keep pushing, or we won't make the Roost by dark."

* * *

In the officers' off-duty bay Signal Lieutenant Pryor straightened from over the billiard table as the nasal voice of the command deck yeoman broke into the recorded dance music: "Now hear this. Commodore Broadly will address ship's company."

"Ten to one he says we've lost the bandit." Supply Lieutenant Aaron eyed the annunciator panel.

"Gentlemen." The sonorous tones of the ship's commander sounded relaxed, unhurried. "We now have a clear track on the Djann blockade runner, which indicates he will attempt to evade our Inner Line defenses and lose himself in Rim territory. In this I propose to disappoint him. I have directed Colonel Lancer to launch interceptors to take up stations along a conic, subsuming thirty degrees on axis from the presently constructed vector. We may expect contact in approximately three hours' time."

A record bos'un's whistle shrilled the end-of-message signal.

"So?" Aaron raised his eyebrows. "A three-million-tonner swats a ten-thousand-ton sideboat. Big deal."

"That boat can punch just as big a hole in the blockade as a Super-D," Pryor said. "Not that the Djann have any of those left to play with."

"We kicked the damned spiders back into their home system ten years ago," Aaron said tiredly. "In my opinion, the whole Containment operation's a boondoggle to justify a ten-million-man fleet."

"As long as there are any of them alive, they're a threat," Pryor repeated the slogan.

"Well, Bradley sounds as though he's got the bogey in the bag." Aaron yawned.

"Maybe he has." Pryor addressed the ball carefully, sent the ivory sphere cannoning against the target.

"He wouldn't go on record with it if he didn't think he was on to a sure thing."

"He's a disappointed 'ceptor-jockey. What makes him think that pirate won't duck back of some kind of a blind spot and go dead?"

"It's worth a try—and if he nails it, it will be a feather in his cap."

"Another star on his collar, you mean."

"Uh-huh, that too."

"We're wasting our time," Aaron said.

"But that's his lookout. Six ball in the corner pocket."

* * *

As Commodore Broadly turned away from the screen on which he had delivered his position report to the crew of the great war vessel, his eye met that of his executive officer. The latter shifted his gaze uneasily.

"Well, Roy, you expect me to announce to all hands that Cincfleet has committed a major blunder letting this bandit slip through the picket line?" he demanded with some asperity.

"Certainly not, sir." The officer looked

worried. "But in view of the seriousness of the breakout. . . ."

"There are some things better kept in the highest command channels," the commodore said shortly. "You and I are aware of the grave consequences of a new release of their damned seed in an uncontaminated sector of the Eastern Arm. But I see no need to arouse the parents, aunts, uncles, and cousins of every apprentice technician aboard in an overly candid disclosure of the facts!"

"I thought Containment had done its jobs by now," the captain said. "It's been three years since the last Djann sighting outside the Reservation. It seems we're not the only ones who're keeping things under our hats."

Broadly frowned. "Mmmm. I agree. I'm placed at something of a disadvantage in my tactical planning by the oversecretiveness of the General Staff. However, there can be no two opinions as to the correctness of my present course."

The exec glanced ceilingward. "I hope so, sir."

"Having the admiral aboard makes you nervous, does it, Roy?" Broadly said in a tone of heartiness. "Well, I regard it merely as an opportunity better to display *Malthusa*'s capabilities!"

"Commodore, you don't think it would be wise to coordinate with the admiral on this—"

"I'm in command of this vessel," Broadly said sharply. "I'm carrying the vice admiral as supercargo, nothing more!"

"He's still Task Group CINC. . . ."

"I'm conning this ship, Roy, not old

Carbuncle!" Broadly rocked on his heels, watching the screen where a quadrangle of bright points representing his interceptor squadron fanned out, on an intersecting course with the fleeing Djann vessel. "I'll pinch off this breakthrough single-handed; and all of us will share in the favorable attention the operation will bring us!"

* * *

In his quarters on the VIP deck, the vice admiral studied the Utter Top Secret dispatch which had been handed to him five minutes earlier by his staff signal major.

"It looks as though this is no ordinary boatload of privateers." He looked soberly at the elderly communicator. "They're reported to be carrying a new weapon of unassessed power and a cargo of spore racks that will knock Containment into the next continuum."

"It doesn't look good, sir." The major wagged his head.

"I note that the commodore has taken action according to the manual." The admiral's voice was noncommittal.

The major frowned. "Let's hope that's sufficient, Admiral."

"It should be. The bogey's only a converted tender. She couldn't be packing much in the way of firepower in that space, secret weapon or no secret weapon."

"Have you mentioned this aspect to the commodore, sir?"

"Would it change anything, Ben?"

"Nooo. I suppose not."

"Then we'll let him carry on without any

more cause for jumpiness than the presence of a vice admiral on board is already providing."

                         * * *

Crouched in his fitted acceleration cradle aboard the Djann vessel, the One-Who-Commands studied the motion of the charged molecules in the sensory tank.

"Now the Death-Watcher dispatches his messengers," he communed with the three link-brothers who formed the Chosen Crew. "Now is the hour of the testing of Djann."

"Profound is the rhythm of our epic," the One-Who-Records sang out. "We are the Chosen-To-Be-Heroic, and in our tiny cargo, Djann lives still, his future glory inherent in the convoluted spores!"

"It was a grave risk to put the destiny of Djann at hazard in this wild gamble," the One-Who-Refutes reminded his link-brothers. "If we fail, the generations yet unborn will slumber on in darkness or perish in ice or fire."

"Yet if we succeed! If the New Thing we have learned serves well its function—then will Djann live anew!"

"Now the death-messengers of the Water-Being approach," the One-Who-Commands pointed out. "Link well, brothers! The energy-aggregate waits for our directing impulse. Now we burn away the dross of illusions from the hypothesis of the theorists in the harsh crucible of reality!"

"In such a fire the flame of Djann coruscates in unparalleled glory!" the One-Who-

Records exulted. "Time has ordained this conjunction to try the timbre of our souls!"

"Then channel your trained faculties, brothers." The One-Who-Commands gathered his forces, feeling out delicately to the ravening nexus of latent energy contained in the thought-shell poised at the center of the stressed-space field enclosing the fleeting vessel. "Hold the sacred fire sucked from the living bodies of a million of our fellows," he exhorted. "Shape it and hurl it in well-directed bolts at the death-bringers, for the future and glory of Djann!"

* * *

At noon, Carnaby and Sickle rested on a nearly horizontal slope of rock that curved to meet the vertical wall that swelled up and away overhead. Their faces and clothes were gray with the impalpable dust whipped up by the brisk wind. Terry spat grit from his mouth, passed a can of hot stew and a plastic water flask to Carnaby.

"Getting cool already," he said. "Must not be more'n ten above freezing."

"We might get a little more snow before morning." Carnaby eyed the milky sky. "You'd better head back now, Terry. No point in you getting caught in a storm."

"I'm in for the play," the boy said shortly. "Say Lieutenant, you got another transmitter up there at the beacon station you might get through on?"

Carnaby shook his head. "Just the beacon tube, the lens generators, and a power pack. It's a stripped-down installation. There's a code receiver, but it's only designed to receive classified instruction input.''

"Too bad." They ate in silence for a few minutes, looking out over the plain below. "Lieutenant, when this is over," Sickle said suddenly, "we got to do something. There's got to be some way to remind the Navy about you being here!"

Carnaby tossed the empty can aside and stood. "I put a couple of messages on the air, sublight, years ago," he said. "That's all I can do."

"Heck, Lieutenant, it takes six years just to make the relay station on Goy! Then if somebody happens to pick up the call and boost it, in another ten years some Navy brass might even see it. And then if he's in a good mood, he might tell somebody to look into it, next time they're out this way!"

"Best I could do, Terry, now that the liners don't call any more."

Carnaby finished his stew and dropped the can. He watched it roll off downslope, clatter over the edge, a tiny sound lost in the whine and shrill of the wind. He looked up at the rampart ahead.

"We better get moving," he said. "We've got a long climb to make before dark."

* * *

Signal Lieutenant Pryor awoke to the strident buzz of his bunkside telephone.

"Sir, the commodore's called a Condition Yellow," the message deck NCO informed him. "It looks like that bandit blasted through our intercept and took out two Epsilon-classes while he was at it. I got a standby from command deck, and—"

"I'll be right up," Pryor said quickly.

Five minutes later he stood with the on-duty signals crew, reading out an incoming from fleet. He whistled.

"Brother, they've got something new!" he looked at Captain Aaron. "Did you check out the vector they had to make to reach their new position in the time they've had?"

"Probably a foul-up in tracking." Aaron looked ruffled, routed out of a sound sleep.

"The commodore's counting off the scale," the NCO said. "He figured he had 'em boxed."

The annunciator beeped. The yeoman announced *Malthusa*'s commander.

"All right, you men!" The voice had a rough edge to it now. "The enemy has an idea he can maul Fleet units and go his way unmolested. I intend to disabuse him of that notion! I'm ordering a course change. I'll maintain contact with this bandit until such time as units designated for the purpose have reported his neutralization! This vessel is under a Condition Yellow at this time and I need not remind you that relevant sections of the manual will be adhered to with full rigor!"

Pryor and Aaron looked at each other, eyebrows raised. "He must mean business if he's willing to risk straining seams with a full-vector course change," the former said.

"So we pull six on and six off until he gets it out of his system," Aaron growled. "I knew this cruise wasn't going to work out as soon as I heard Old Carbuncle would be aboard."

"What's *he* got to do with it? Broadly's running this action."

"Don't worry, he'll be in it before we're through."

* * *

On the slope, three thousand feet above the plain, Carnaby and Terry hugged the rock-face, working their way upward. Aside from the steepness of the incline, the going was of no more than ordinary difficulty here: the porous rock, resistant though it was to the erosive forces that had long ago stripped away the volcanic cone of which the remaining mass had formed the core, had deteriorated in its surface sufficiently to afford easy hand- and footholds. Now Terry paused, leaning against the rock. Carnaby saw that under the layer of dust, the boy's face was pale and drawn.

"Not much farther, Terry," he said. He settled himself in a secure position, his feet wedged in a cleft. His own arms were feeling the strain now; there was the beginning of a slight tremble in his knees after the hours of climbing.

"I didn't figure to slow you down, Lieutenant." Terry's voice showed the strain of his fatigue.

"You've been leading me a tough chase, Terry." Carnaby grinned across at him. "I'm glad of a rest." He noted the dark hollows under the lad's eyes, the pallor of his cheeks.

Sickle's tongue came out and touched his lips. "Lieutenant—you made a try—a good try. Turn back now. It's going to snow. You can't make it to the top in a blizzard."

Carnaby shook his head. "It's too late in the day to start down; you'd be caught on the slope. We'll take it easy up to the Roost. In the morning you'll have an easy climb down."

"Sure, Lieutenant. Don't worry about me." Terry drew a breath, shivered with the bitter wind that plucked at his snow jacket, started upward.

* * *

"What do you mean, lost him!" the bull roar of the commodore rattled the screen. "Are you telling me that this ragtag refugee has the capability to drop off the screens of the best-equipped tracking deck in the fleet?"

"Sir," the stubborn-faced tracking officer repeated, "I can only report that my screens register nothing within the conic of search. If he's there—"

"He's there, mister!" The commodore's eyes glared from under a bushy overhang of brows. "Find that bandit or face a court, Captain! I haven't diverted a ship of the fleet line from her course for the purpose of becoming the object of an effectiveness inquiry!"

The tracking officer turned away from the screen as it went white, met the quizzical gaze of the visiting signal-lieutenant.

"The old devil's bit off too big a bite this time," he growled. "Let him call a court; he wouldn't have the gall."

"If we lose the bogey now, he won't look good back on Vandy," Pryor said. "This is serious business, diverting from cruise plan to chase rumors. I wonder if he really had a positive ID on this track."

"Hell, no! There's no way to make a positive at this range, under these conditions! After three years without any action for the news-tapes, the brass are grabbing at straws."

"Well, if I were you, Gordie, I'd find that track, even if it turns out to be a tramp with a load of bootleg *dran*."

"Don't worry, if he's inside the conic, I'll find him."

* * *

"I guess . . . it's dropped twenty degrees . . . in the last hour." Terry Sickle's voice was almost lost in the shriek of the wind that buffeted the two men as they inched their way up the last yards toward the hut on the narrow rock shelf called Halliday's Roost.

"Never saw snow falling at this temperature before." Carnaby brushed at the ice caked around his eyes. Through the swirl of crystals as fine as sand, he discerned the sagging outline of the shelter above.

Ten minutes later, inside the crude lean-to built of rock slabs, he set to work chinking the gaping holes in the five-foot walls with packed snow. Behind him, Terry lay huddled against the back wall, breathing hoarsely.

"Guess . . . I'm not in as good shape . . . as I thought I was," he said.

"You'll be okay, Terry." Carnaby closed the gap through which the worst of the icy draft was keening, paused long enough to open a can of stew for the boy. The fragrance of the hot meat and vegetables made his jaws ache.

"Lieutenant, how are you going to climb in

this snow?" Sickle's voice shook to the chattering of his teeth. "In good weather, you might have made it. Like this, you haven't got a chance!"

"Maybe it'll be blown clear by morning," Carnaby said mildly. He opened a can for himself. Terry ate slowly, shivering uncontrollably. Carnaby watched him worriedly.

"Lieutenant," the boy said, "even if that call you picked up was meant for you—even if this ship they're after is headed out this way— what difference will it make one way or another if one beacon's on the air or not?"

"Probably none," Carnaby said. "But if there's one chance in a thousand he breaks this way—well, that's what I'm here for, isn't it?"

"But what's a beacon going to do, except give him something to steer by?"

Carnaby smiled. "It's not that kind of beacon, Terry. My station's part of a system— a big system that covers the surface of a sphere of space a hundred lights in diameter. When there's an alert, each station locks in with the others that flank it and sets up what's called a stressed field. There's a lot of things you can do with this field. You can detect a drive, monitor communications—"

"What if these other stations you're talking about aren't working?" Terry cut in.

"Then my station's not going to do much good," Carnaby said.

"If the other stations are still on the air, why haven't any of them picked up your TXs and answered?"

Carnaby shook his head. "We don't use the

beacon field to chatter back and forth, Terry. This is a top-security system. Nobody knows about it except the top command levels—and of course, the men manning the beacons."

"Maybe that's how they came to forget about you. Somebody lost a piece of paper, and nobody else knew!"

"I shouldn't be telling you about it," Carnaby said with a smile. "But I guess you'll keep it under your hat."

"You can count on me, Lieutenant," Terry said solemnly.

"I know I can, Terry," Carnaby said.

* * *

The clangor of the general quarters alarm shattered the tense silence of the chart deck like a bomb through a plate-glass window. The navigation officer whirled abruptly from the grametric over which he had been bending, collided with the deck chief. Both men leaped for the master position monitor, caught just a glimpse of a vivid scarlet tracer lancing toward the emerald point targeted at the center of the plate before the apparatus exploded from its mounting, mowed the two men down in a hail of shattered plastic fragments.

Smoke boiled, black and pungent, from the gutted cavity. The duty NCO, bleeding from a dozen gashes, stumbled toward the two men, turned away in horror, reached an emergency voice phone. Before he could key it, the deck under him canted sharply. He screamed, clutched at a table for support, saw it tilt, come crashing down on top of him. . . .

On the message deck Lieutenant Pryor clung to an operator's stool, listening, through the stridency of the alarm bell, to the frantic voice from command deck:

"All sections, all sections, combat stations! We're under attack! My God, we've taken a hit—"

The voice cut off, to be replaced by the crisp tones of Colonel Lancer, first battle officer:

"As you were. Section G-Nine-eight-seven and Nine-eight-nine damage control crews report! Forward armaments, safety interlocks off, stand by for firing orders! Message center, flash a Code Six to Fleet and TF Command. Power section, all selectors to gate, rig for full emergency power. . . ."

Pryor hauled himself hand over hand to the main message console. The body of the code yeoman hung slackly in the seat harness, blood dripping from the fingertips of his dangling hand, Pryor freed him, took his place. He keyed the Code Six alarm into the pulse-relay tanks, triggered an emergency override signal, beamed the message outward toward the distant Fleet Headquarters.

On the command deck, Commodore Broadly clutched a sprained wrist to his chest, stood, teeth bared, feet braced apart, staring into the forward image-screen at the dwindling point of light that was the Djann blockade runner.

"The effrontery of the damned scoundrel!" he roared. "Lancer, launch another convey of U-Ninety-fives! You've got over five hundred megaton/seconds of firepower, man! Use it!"

"He's out of range, Commodore," Lancer

said coolly. "He boobytrapped us very neatly."

"It's your job to see that we don't blunder into traps, by God, Colonel!" the commodore rounded on the battle officer. "You'll stop that pirate, or I'll rip those eagles off your shoulders myself!"

Lancer's mouth was a hard line; his eyes were ice chips.

"You can relieve me, Commodore," his voice grated. "Until you do, I'm battle commander aboard this vessel."

"By God, you're relieved, sir!" Broadly yelled. He whirled on the startled exec standing by. "Confine this officer to his quarters! Order full emergency acceleration! This vessel's on Condition Red at full combat alert until we overtake and destroy that sneaking snake in the grass!"

"Commodore—at full emergency without warning, there'll be men injured, even killed—"

"Carry out my commands, Captain, or I'll find someone who will!" The admiral's bellow cut off the exec. "I'll show that filthy sneaking pack of spiders what it means to challenge a Terran fighting ship!"

On the power deck, Chief Powerman Joe Arena wiped the cut on his forehead, stared at the bloody rag, hurled it aside with a curse.

"All right, you one-legged deck-apes!" he roared. "You heard it! We're going after the bandit, full gate, and if we melt our linings down to slag, I'll have every man of you sign a statement of charges that'll take your grandchildren two hundred years to pay off!"

* * *

In the near darkness of the Place of Observation aboard the Djann vessel, the ocular complex of the One-Who-Commands glowed with a dim red sheen as he studied the apparently black surface of the sensitive plate. "The Death-Watcher has eaten our energy weapon," he communicated to his three link-brothers. "Now our dooms are in the palms of the fate-spinner."

"The Death-Watcher of the Water-Beings might have passed us by," the One-Who-Anticipates signaled. "It was an act of rashness to hurl the weapon at it."

"It will make a mighty song." The One-Who-Records thrummed his resonator plates, tried a melancholy bass chord.

"But what egg-carrier will exude the brood-nourishing honeys of strength and sagacity in response to these powerful rhymes, if the stimulus to their creation leads us to quick extinction?" the One-Who-Refutes attested.

"The Death-Watcher shakes himself," the One-Who-Commands stated. "Now he turns in pursuit."

The One-Who-Records emitted a booming tone. "Gone are the great suns of Djann," he sang. "Lost are the fair worlds that knew their youth. But the spark of their existence glows still!"

"Now we fall outward, toward the Great Awesomeness," the One-Who-Anticipates commented. "Only the blackness will know your song."

"Draw in your energies from that - which -

is - extraneous," the One - Who - Commands ordered. "Focus the full poignancy of your intellects on the urgency of our need for haste! All else is vain, now. Neither singer nor song will survive the vengeance of the Death-Watcher if he outstrips our swift fight!"

"Though Djann and Water-Being perish, my poem is eternal." The One-Who-Records emitted a stirring assonance. "Fly, Djanni! Pursue, Death-Watcher! Let the suns observe how we comport ourselves in this hour!"

"Exhort the remote nebulosities to attend our plight, if you must," the One-Who-Refutes commented. "But link your energies to ours or all is lost!"

Silent now, the Djann privateer fled outward toward the Rim.

* * *

Carnaby awoke, lay in darkness listening to the wheezing of Terry Sickle's breath. The boy didn't sound good. Carnaby sat up, suppressing a grunt at the stiffness of his limbs. The icy air seemed stale. He moved to the entry, lifted the polyon flap. A cascade of powdery snow poured in. Beyond the opening a faint glow filtered down through banked snow.

He turned back to Terry as the latter coughed deeply.

"Looks like the snow's quit," Carnaby said. "It's drifted pretty bad, but there's no wind now. How are you feeling, Terry?"

"Not so good, Lieutenant," Sickle said weakly. He breathed heavily, in and out. "I don't know what's got into me. Feel hot and cold at the same time."

Carnaby stripped off his glove, put his hand on Sickle's forehead. It was scalding hot.

"You just rest easy here for a while, Terry. There's a couple more cans of stew and plenty of water. I'll make it up to the top as quickly as I can. Soon as I get back, we'll go down. With luck, I'll have you to Doc Lin's house by dark."

"I guess . . . I guess I should have done like Doc said." Terry's voice was a thin whisper.

"What do you mean?"

"I been taking these hyposprays. Two a day. He said I better not miss one, but heck, I been feeling real good lately—"

"What kind of shots, Terry?" Carnaby's voice was tight.

"I don't know. Heck, Lieutenant, I'm no invalid!" His voice trailed off.

"You should have told me, Terry!"

"Gosh, Lieutenant—don't worry about me! I didn't mean nothing! Hell, I feel. . . ." He broke off to cough deeply, rackingly.

"Terry, Terry!" Carnaby put a hand on the boy's thin shoulder.

"I'm okay," Sickle gasped. "It's just asthma. It's nothing."

"It's nothing—if you get your medicine on schedule," Carnaby said. "But—"

"I butted in on this party, Lieutenant," Terry said. "It's my own fault . . . if I come down sick." He paused to draw a difficult breath. "You go ahead, sir . . . do what you got to do . . . I'll be okay."

"I've got to get you back, Terry. But I've got to go up first," Carnaby said. "You understand that, don't you?"

Terry nodded. "A man's got to do his job . . . Lieutenant. I'll be waiting . . . for you . . . when you get back."

"Listen to me carefully, Terry." Carnaby's voice was low. "If I'm not back by this time tomorrow, you'll have to make it back down by yourself. You understand? Don't wait for me."

"Sure, Lieutenant, I'll just rest a while. Then I'll be okay."

"Sooner I get started, the sooner I'll be back." Carnaby took a can from the pack, opened it, handed it to Terry. The boy shook his head.

"You eat it, Lieutenant. You need your strength. I don't feel like I . . . could eat anything anyway."

"Terry, I don't want to have to pry your mouth open and pour it in."

"All right. But open one for yourself too."

"All right, Terry."

Sickle's hand trembled as he spooned the stew to his mouth. He ate half of the contents of the can, then leaned back against the wall, closed his eyes. "That's all . . . I want. . . ."

"All right, Terry. You get some rest now. I'll be back before you know it." Carnaby crawled out through the open flap, pushed his way up through loosely drifted snow. The cold struck his face like a spiked club. He turned the suit control up another notch, noticing as he did that the left side seemed to be cooler than the right.

The near-vertical rise of the final crown of the peak thrust up from the drift, dazzling white in the morning sun. Carnaby examined the rockface for twenty feet on either side of the hut, picked a spot where a deep crack angled upward, started the last leg of the climb.

On the message deck, Lieutenant Pryor frowned into the screen from which the saturnine features of Lieutenant Aaron gazed back sourly.

"The commodore's going to be unhappy about this," Pryor said. "If you're sure your extrapolation is accurate—"

"It's as good as the data I got from plotting," Aaron snapped. "The bogey's over the make-or-break line; we'll never catch him now. You know your trans-Einsteinian physics as well as I do."

"I never heard of the Djann having anything capable of that kind of acceleration," Pryor protested.

"You have now." Aaron switched off and keyed command deck, passed his report to the exec, then sat back with a resigned expression to await the reaction.

Less than a minute later, Commodore Broadly's irate face snapped into focus on the screen.

"You're the originator of this report?" he growled.

"I did the extrapolation." Aaron stared back at his commanding officer.

"You're relieved for incompetence," Broadly said in a tone as harsh as a handsaw.

"Yes, sir," Aaron said. His face was pale, but he returned the commodore's stare. "But my input data and comps are a matter of record. I'll stand by them."

Broadly's face darkened. "Are you telling me these spiders can spit in our faces and skip off, scot-free?"

"All I'm saying, sir, is that the present acceleration ratios will put the target ahead of us by a steadily increasing increment."

Broadly's face twitched. "This vessel is at full emergency gain!" he growled. "No Djann has ever outrun a fleet unit in a straightaway run."

"This one is . . . sir."

The commodore's eyes bored into Aaron's. "Remain on duty until further notice," he said, and switched off. Aaron smiled crookedly and buzzed the message deck.

"He backed down," he said to Pryor. "We've got a worried commodore on board."

"I don't understand it myself," Pryor said. "How the hell is that can outgaining us?"

"He's not," Aaron said complacently. "From a standing start, we'd overhaul him in short order. But he got the jump on us by a couple of minutes, after he lobbed the fish into us. If we'd been able to close the gap in the first half-hour or so, we'd have had him; but at trans-L velocities, you get some strange effects. One of them is that our vectors become asymptotic. We're closing on him—but we'll never overtake him."

Pryor whistled. "Broadly could be busted for this fiasco."

"Uh-huh," Aaron grinned. "Could be—unless the bandit stops for a quick one. . . ."

After Aaron rang off, Pryor turned to study the position repeater screen. On it *Malthusa* was represented by a bright point at the center, the fleeing Djann craft by a red dot above.

"Charlie," Pryor called the NCOIC. "That garbled TX we picked up last watch; where did you R and D it?"

"Right about here, Lieutenant." The NCO flicked a switch and turned knobs; a green dot appeared near the upper edge of the screen.

"Hey," he said. "It looks like maybe our bandit's headed out this way."

"You picked him up on Y band. Have you tried to raise him again?"

"Yeah, but nothing doing, Lieutenant. It was just a fluke—"

"Get a Y beam on him, Charlie. Focus it down to a cat's whisker and work a pattern over a one-degree radius centered around his MPP until you get an echo."

"If you say so, sir—but—"

"I do say so, Charlie! Find that transmitter, and the drinks are on me!"

* * *

Flat against the windswept rockface, Carnaby clung with his fingertips to a tenuous hold, feeling with one booted toe for a purchase higher up. A flake of stone broke away, and for a moment he hung by the fingers of his right hand, his feet dangling over emptiness; then, swinging his right leg far out, he hooked a knob with his knee, caught at a rocky rib with his free hand, pulled himself up to a more secure rest. He clung, his cheek against the iron-cold stone; out across the vast expanse of featureless grayish-tan plain the gleaming whipped-cream shape of the next core rose, ten miles to the south.

A wonderful view up here—of nothing. Funny to think it could be his last. He was out of condition. It had been too long since his last climb. . . .

But that wasn't the way to think. He had a job to do—the first in twenty-one years. For a moment, ghostly recollections rose up before him: the trim Academy lawns, the spit-and-polish of inspection, the crisp feel of the new uniform, the glitter of the silver comet as Anne pinned it on. . . .

That was no good either. What counted was here: the station up above. One more push, and he'd be there.

He rested for another half-minute, then pulled himself up and forward, onto the relatively mild slope of the final approach to the crest. Fifty yards above, the dull-gleaming plastron-coated dome of the beacon station squatted against the exposed rock, looking no different than it had five years earlier.

Five minutes later he was at the door, flicking the combination latch dial with cold-numbed fingers.

Tumblers clicked, and the panel slid aside. The heating system, automatically reacting to his entrance, started up with a busy hum to bring the interior temperature up to comfort level. He pulled off his gauntlets, ran his hands over his face, rasping the stubble there. There was coffee in the side table, he remembered. Fumblingly, with stiff fingers, he got out the dispenser, twisted the control cap, poured out a steaming mug, gulped it down. It was hot and bitter. The grateful warmth of it made him think of Terry, waiting down below in the chill of the half-ruined hut.

"No time to waste," he muttered to himself. He stamped up and down the room, swinging his arms to warm himself, then seated himself at the console, flicked keys with a trained ease rendered only slightly rusty by the years of disuse. He referred to an index, found the input instructions for Code Gamma Eight, set up the boards, flipped in the Pulse lever. Under his feet, he felt the faint vibration as the power pack buried in the rock stored its output for ten microseconds, fired it in a single millisecond burst, stored and pulsed again. Dim instrument lights winked on, indicating normal readings all across the board.

Carnaby glanced at the wall clock. He had been here ten minutes now. It would take another quarter hour to comply with the manual's instructions—but to hell with that gobbledegook. He'd put the beacon on the air; this time the Navy would have to settle for that. It would be pushing it to get back to the boy and pack him down to the village by nightfall as it was. Poor kid; he'd wanted to help so badly. . . .

* * *

"That's correct, sir," Pryor said crisply. "I haven't picked up any comeback on my pulse, but I'll definitely identify the echo as coming from a JN-type installation."

Commodore Broadly nodded curtly. "However, inasmuch as your instruments indicate that this station is operating solo—not linked in with a net to set up a defensive field—it's of no use to us." The commodore looked at Pryor coldly.

"I think perhaps there's a way, sir," Pryor said. "The Djann are known to have strong tribal feelings. They'd never pass up what they thought was an SOS from one of their own. Now, suppose we signal this JN station to switch over to the Djann frequencies and beam one of their own signal-patterns at them. They just might stop to take a look. . . ."

"By God!" Broadly looked at the Signal-Lieutenant. "If he doesn't, he's not human!"

"You like the idea, sir?" Pryor grinned.

"A little rough on the beacon station if they reach it before we do, eh, Lieutenant? I imagine our friends the Djann will be a trifle upset when they learn they've been duped."

"Oh . . . " Pryor looked blank. "I guess I hadn't thought of that, sir."

"Never mind," Broadly said briskly. "The loss of a minor installation such as this is a reasonable exchange for an armed vessel of the enemy."

"Well. . . ."

"Lieutenant, if I had a few more officers aboard who employed their energies in something other than assembling statistics proving we're beaten, this cruise might have made a record for itself—" Broadly cut himself off, remembering the degree of aloofness due every junior officer—even juniors who may have raked some very hot chestnuts out of the fire.

"Carry on, Lieutenant," he said. "If this works out, I think I can promise you a very favorable endorsement on your next ER."

As Pryor's pleased grin winked off the screen, the commodore flipped up the red-line key, snapped a brusque request at the bored log room yeoman.

"This will make Old Carbuncle sing another tune," he remarked almost gaily to the Exec, standing by with a harassed expression.

"Maybe you'd better go slow, Ned," the latter cautioned, gauging his senior's mood. "It might be as well to get a definite confirmation on this installation's capabilities before we go on record—"

Broadly turned abruptly to the screen as it chimed. "Admiral, as I reported, I've picked up one of our forward beacon towers," Broadly's hearty voice addressed the screen from which the grim visage of the task force commander eyed him. "I'm taking steps to complete the intercept that are, if I may say so, rather ingenious."

"It's my understanding the target is receding on an I-curve, Broadly," the admiral said flatly. "I've been anticipating a Code Thirty-three from you."

"Break off action?" Broadly's jaw dropped. "Now, Tom—"

"It's a little irregular to use a capital ship of the line to chase a ten-thousand-ton yacht." The task force commander ignored the interruption. "I can understand your desire to break the monotony with a little activity; good exercise for the crew, too. But at the rate the signal is attenuating, it's apparent you've lost her." His voice hardened. "I'm beginning to wonder if you've forgotten that your assignment is the containment of enemy forces supposedly pinned down under tight quarantine!"

"This yacht, as you put it, Admiral, blew two of my detached units out of space!" Broadly came back hotly. "In addition, he planted a missile squarely in my fore lazaret—"

"I'm not concerned with the details of your operation at this moment, Commodore." The other bit off the words like bullets. "I'm more interested in maintaining the degree of surveillance over my assigned quadrant that Concordiat security requires. Accordingly—"

"Just a minute, Tom, before you commit yourself!" Broadly's florid face was pale around the ears. "Perhaps you failed to catch my first remark: I have a forward station directly in the enemy's line of retreat. The intercept is in the bag—unless you countermand me."

"You're talking nonsense! The target's well beyond the Inner Line."

"He's not beyond the Outer Line!"

The admiral frowned. His tight well-chiseled face was still youthful under the mask of authority. "The system was never extended into the region under discussion," he said harshly. "I suggest you recheck your instruments. In the interim, I want to see an advice of a course-correction for station in the length of time it takes you to give the necessary orders to your navigation section."

Broadly drew a breath, hesitated. If Old Carbuncle was right—if that infernal signal-lieutenant had made a mistake—but the boy seemed definite enough about it. He clamped his jaw. He'd risked his career on a wild throw; maybe he'd acted a little too fast; maybe he'd been a little too eager to grab a chance at some favorable notice; but the die was cast now. If he turned back empty-handed the entire affair would go into the record as a major fiasco. But if this scheme worked out. . . .

"Unless the admiral wishes to make that a direct order," he heard himself saying firmly, "I intend to hold my course and close with the enemy. It's my feeling that neither the admiralty nor the general public will enjoy hearing of casualties inflicted by a supposedly neutralized enemy who was then permitted to go his way unhindered." He returned the other's stare, feeling a glow of pride at his own decisiveness and a simultaneous sinking sensation at the enormity of the insubordination.

The vice admiral looked back at him through narrowed eyes. "I'll leave that decision to you, Commodore," he said tightly. "I think you're as aware as I of what's at stake here."

Broadly stiffened at what was almost an open threat. "Instruct your signals officer to pass full information on this supposed station to me immediately," the senior concluded curtly and then disappeared from view on the screen.

Broadly turned away, feeling all eyes on him. "Tell Pryor to copy his report to G at once," he said in a harsh voice. His eyes strayed to the exec's. "And if this idea of his doesn't work, God help him." *And all of us*, he added under his breath.

* * *

As Carnaby reached for the door, to start the long climb down, a sharp *beep!* sounded from the panel behind him.

He looked back, puzzled. The bleat repeated, urgent, commanding. He swung the pack down, went to the console, flipped down the REC key.

". . . Thirty-seven Ace Trey," an excited voice came through loud and clear. "I repeat, cut your beacon immediately! JN Thirty-seven Ace Trey, Cincsec One-oh- four to JN Thirty-seven Ace Trey. Shut down beacon soonest! This is an Operational Urgent! JN Thirty-seven Ace Trey, cut beacon and stand by for further operational urgent instructions. . . ."

* * *

On the fleet command deck aboard the flagship, Vice Admiral Thomas Carnaby, otherwise known as Old Carbuncle, studied the sector triagram as his communications chief pointed out the positions of the flagship *Malthusa*, the Djann refugee, and the reported JN beacon station.

"I've researched the call letters, sir," the gray-haired signals major said. "They're not shown on any listing as an active station. In fact, the entire series of which this station would be a part is coded null: never reported in commission."

"So someone appears to be playing pranks, is that your conclusion, Henry?"

The signals officer pulled at his lower lip. "No, sir, not that, precisely. I've done a full-

analytical on the recorded signal that young
Pryor first intercepted. It's plainly directed to
Cincsec in response to the alert; and the ID is
confirmed. Now, as I say, this series was
dropped from the register. But at one time,
such a designation *was* assigned *en bloc* to a
proposed link in the Out Line. However, the
planned installations never came to fruition
due to changes in the strategic position."

The vice admiral frowned. "What changes
were those?"

"The task force charged with the establishment of the link encountered heavy enemy
pressure. In fact, the cruiser detailed to carry
out the actual placement of the units was lost
in action with all hands. Before the program
could be reinitiated, a withdrawal from the
sector was ordered. The new link was never
completed, and the series was retired, unused."

"So?"

"So . . . just possibly, sir, one of those old
stations *was* erected before *Redoubt* was
lost—"

"What's that?" The admiral rounded on the
startled officer. "Did you say . . . *Redoubt*?"
His voice was a hiss between set teeth.

"Y—yessir!"

"*Redoubt* was lost with all hands before she
planted her first station!"

"I know that's what we've always thought,
Admiral—"

The admiral snatched the paper from the
major's hand. "JN Thirty-seven Ace-Trey," he
read aloud. "Why the hell didn't you say so
sooner?" He whirled to his chief of staff.

"What's Broadly got in mind?" he snapped the question.

The startled officer began a description of the plan to decoy the Djann vessel into range of *Malthusa's* batteries.

"*Decoy?*" the vice admiral snarled. The exec took a step backwark, shocked at the expression on his superior's face. The latter spun to face his battle officer, standing by on the bridge.

"General, rig out an interceptor and get my pressure gear into it! I want it on the line, ready for launch in ten minutes! Assign your best torchman as copilot!"

"Yessir!" The general spoke quickly into a lapel mike. The admiral flicked a key beside the hot-line screen.

"Get Broadly," he said in a voice like doom impending.

* * *

In the Djann ship, the One-Who-Commands stirred and extended a contact to his crewmembers. "Tune keenly in the scarlet regions of the spectrum," he communicated. "And tell me whether the spinners weave a new thread in the tapestry of our fates."

"I sensed it but now and felt recognition stir within me!" the One-Who-Records thrummed a mighty euphony. "A voice of the Djann, sore beset, telling of mortal need!"

"I detect a strangeness," the One-Who-Refutes indicated. "This is not the familiar voice of They-Who-Summon."

"After the passage of ninety cycles, it is not surprising that new chords have been added to the voice and others withdrawn," the One-Who-Anticipates pointed out. "If the link-cousins are in distress, our path is clear!"

"Shall I then bend our fate-line to meet the new voice?" the One-Who-Commands called for a weighing. "The pursuers press us closely."

"The voice calls. Will we pervert our saga by shunning it?"

"This is a snare of the Water-Beings, calculated to abort our destinies!" the One-Who-Refutes warned. "Our vital energies are drained to the point of incipient coma by the weapon-which-feeds-on-life! If we turn aside now, we place ourselves in the jaws of the destroyer!"

"Though the voice lies, the symmetry of our existence demands that we answer its appeal," the One-Who-Anticipates declared.

"I accede," The One-Who-Records sounded a booming arpeggio, combining triumph and defeat. "Let the Djann flame burn brightest in its hour of extinction!"

* * *

"By God, they've fallen for it!" Commodore Broadly smacked his fist into his hand and beamed at the young signal-lieutenant. He rocked back on his heels, studying the position chart the plot officer had set up for him on the message deck. "We'll make the intercept about here." His finger stabbed at a point of fractional light from the calculated position of the newfound OL station.

He broke off as an excited voice burst from the intercom screen.

"Commodore Broadly, sir! Urgent from task—" The yeoman's face disappeared from the screen to be replaced by the fierce visage of the vice admiral.

"Broadly, sheer off and take up course for station and then report yourself under arrest! Commodore Baskov will take command: I've countermanded your damnfool orders to the OL station! I'm on my way out there now to see what I can salvage—and when I get back, I'm preferring charges against you that will put you on the beach for the rest of your miserable life!"

* * *

In the beacon station atop the height of ground known as Thunderhead, Carnaby waited before the silent screen. The modification to the circuitry had taken half an hour; setting up the new code sequences, another fifteen minutes. Then another half-hour had passed while the converted beacon beamed out the alien signal.

He'd waited long enough. It had been twenty minutes now since the last curt order to stand by; and in the hut a thousand feet below, Terry had been waiting now for nearly five hours, every breath he drew a torture of strangulation. The order had been to put the signal on the air, attempt to delay the enemy ship. Either it had worked, or it hadn't. If Fleet had any more instructions for him, they'd have to damn well deliver them in person. He'd done what was required. Now he had to see to the boy.

Carnaby rose, again donned the backpack,

opened the door. As he did so, a faint deep-toned rumble of distant thunder rolled. He stepped outside, squinted up at the sky, a dazzle of mist-gray. Maybe the snow squall was headed back this way. That would be bad luck: it would be close enough as it was.

A bright point of light caught his eye, winking from high above, almost at zenith.

Carnaby felt his heart take a leap in his chest that almost choked off his breath. For a moment he stood, staring up at it; then he whirled back through the door.

" . . . termand previous instructions!" A new voice was rasping from the speaker. "Terminate all transmissions immediately! JN Thirty-seven, shut down power and vacate station! Repeat, an armed enemy vessel is believed to be vectored in on your signal! This is, repeat, a hostile vessel! You are to cease transmission and abandon station immediately—"

Carnaby's hand slapped the big master lever. Lights died on the panel. Underfoot, the minute vibration jelled into immobility. Sudden silence pressed in like a tangible force —a silence broken by a rising mutter from above.

"Like that, eh?" Carnaby said to himself through clenched teeth. "Abandon station, eh?" He took three steps to a wall locker, yanked the door wide, took out a short, massive power rifle, still encased in its plastic protective cover. He stripped the oily sheath away, checked the charge indicator; it rested on FULL.

There were foot-square windows set on

each side of the twenty-foot room. Carnaby
went to one. By putting his face flat against
the armorplast panel he was able to see the
ship, now a flaring fireball dropping in along
a wide approach curve. As it descended
swiftly the dark body of the vessel took shape
above the glare of the drive. It was a small
blunt-ended ovoid of unfamiliar design, a
metallic black in color, decorated fore and aft
with the scarlet blazons of a Djann war vessel.

The ship was close now, maneuvering to a
position a thousand feet directly overhead.
Now a small landing craft detached itself
from the parked ship and plummeted down-
ward like a stone with a shrill whistling of
high-speed rotors, to settle in across the expanse of broken rock in a cloud of pale dust.
The black plastic bubble atop the landing sled
split like a clamshell.

A shape came into view, clambered over the
cockpit rim and stood, a cylindrical bronze-
black body slung by leather mesenteries from
the paired U frames that were its ambulatory
members, two pairs of grasping limbs folded
above.

A second Djann emerged, a third, a fourth.
They stood together, immobile, silent, while a
minute ticked past. Sweat trickled down the
side of Carnaby's face. He breathed shallowly,
rapidly, feeling the almost painful thudding of
his heart.

One of the Djann moved suddenly, its
strange, jointless limbs moving with twink-
ling grace and speed. It flowed across to
a point from which it could look down across
the plain, then angled to the left and recon-

noitered the entire circumference of the
mountaintop. Carnaby moved from window
to window to watch it. It rejoined the other
three; briefly, they seemed to confer. Then
one of the creatures, whether the same one or
another Carnaby wasn't sure, started across
toward the hut.

Carnaby moved back into a position in the
lee of a switch-gear cabinet. A moment later
the Djann appeared at the door. At a distance
of fifteen feet Carnaby saw the lean limbs,
like leather-covered metal; the heavy body;
the immense faceted eyes that caught the light
and sent back fiery glints. For thirty seconds
the creature scanned the interior of the structure. Then it withdrew.

Carnaby let out a long shaky breath,
watched the alien lope back to rejoin its com-
panions. Again, the Djann conferred; then one
turned to the landing craft.

For a long moment Carnaby hesitated. He
could stay where he was, do nothing, and the
Djann would reboard their vessel and go their
way; and in a few hours a fleet unit would
heave into view off Longone, and he'd be
home safe.

But the orders had been to delay the
enemy. . . .

He centered the sights of the power gun on
the alien's body, just behind the fore-legs, and
pushed the firing stud.

A shaft of purple fire blew the window from
its frame, lanced out to smash the uprearing
alien against the side of the sled, sent it skid-
ding in a splatter of molten rock and metal.
Carnaby swung the rifle, fired at a second

Djann as the group scattered; the stricken
creature went down, rolled, came up,
stumbling on three limbs. He fired again,
knocked the creature spinning, dark fluid
spattering from a gaping wound in the barrel-
like body. Carnaby swung to cover a third
Djann, streaking for the plateau's edge; his
shot sent a shower of molten slag arcing high
from the spot where it disappeared.

He lowered the gun, stepped outside, ran to
the corner of the building. The fourth Djann
was crouched in the open, thirty feet away;
Carnaby saw the glitter of a weapon gripped
in the handlike members springing from its
back. He brought the gun up, fired in the same
instant that light etched the rocks, and a
hammer-blow struck him crushingly in the
side, knocked him back against the wall. He
tasted dust in his mouth, was aware of a high,
humming sound that seemed to blank out his
hearing, his vision, his thoughts. . . .

He came to, lying on his side against the
wall. Forty feet away the Djann sprawled, its
stiff limbs outthrust at awkward angles.
Carnaby looked down at his side.

The Djann particle-gun had torn a gaping
rent in his suit, through which he could see
bright crimson beads of frozen blood. He
groped, found the rifle, dragged it to him. He
shook his head to clear away the mist that
seemed to obscure his vision. At every move, a
terrible sharp pain stabbed outward from his
chest. *Ribs broken*, he thought. *Something
smashed inside, too.* It was hard for him to
breathe. The cold stone on which he lay
seemed to suck the heat from his body.

Across the hundred-foot stretch of frost-shattered rock, a soot-black scar marked the spot where the escaping Djann had gone over the edge. Painfully, Carnaby propped the weapon to cover the direction from which attack might come. Then he slumped, his face against the icy rock, watching down the length of the rifle barrel for the next move from the enemy.

* * *

"Another four hours to shift, Admiral," said General Drew, the battle commander acting as copilot aboard the racing interceptor. "That's if we don't blow our linings before then."

"Bandit still holding position?" The admiral's voice was a grate as of metal against metal.

Drew spoke into his lip mike, frowned at the reply. "Yes, sir, *Malthusa* says he's still stationary. Whether his focus is identical with the LN beacon's fix or not, he isn't sure at that range."

"He could be standing by off-planet, looking over the ground," the admiral muttered half to himself.

"Not likely, Admiral. He knows we're on his tail."

"I know it's not likely, damn it!" the admiral snarled. "But if he isn't, we haven't got a chance."

"I suppose the Djann conception of honor requires these beggars to demolish the beacon and hunt down the station personnel, even if it means letting us overhaul them,"

Drew said. "A piece of damn foolishness on their part, but fortunate for us."

"For us, General? I take it you mean yourself and me, not the poor devil that's down there alone with them!"

"Just the one man? Well, we'll get off more cheaply than I imagined." The general glanced sideways at the admiral, intent over the controls. "After all, he's Navy. This is his job, what he signed on for."

"Kick the converter again, General," Admiral Carnaby said between his teeth. "Right now you can earn your pay by squeezing another quarter light out of this bucket."

* * *

Crouched in a shallow crevice below the rim of the mesa where the house of the Water-Beings stood, the One-Who-Records quivered under the appalling impact of the death-emanations of his link-brothers.

"Now it lies with you alone," the fading thought came from the One-Who-Commands. "But the Water-Being, too, is alone, and in this . . . there is . . . a certain euphony. . . ." The last fragile tendril of communication faded.

The One-Who-Records expelled a gust of the planet's noxious atmosphere from his ventral orifice-array, with an effort freed his intellect of the shattering extinction-resonances it had absorbed. Cautiously, he probed outward, sensing the strange fiery mind-glow of the alien. . . .

Ah, he too was injured! The One-Who-

Records shifted his weight from his scalded forelimb, constricted further the flow of vital fluids through the damaged section of his epidermal system. He was weakened by the searing blast that had scored his flank, but still capable of action; and up above the wounded Water-Being waited.

Deftly, the Djann extracted the hand-weapon from the sheath strapped to his side, holding it in a two-handed grip, its broad base resting on his dorsal ridge, its ring-lenses aligned along his body. He wished briefly that he had spent more *li* periods in the gestalt-tanks, impressing the weapon's use-syndromes on his reflex system; but reckless regrets made poor scansion. Now indeed the display-podium of existence narrowed down to a single confrontation: a brief and final act in a century-old drama, with the fate of the mighty epic of Djann resting thereon. The One-Who-Records sounded a single trumpet-like resonance of exultation and moved forward to fulfill his destiny.

* * *

At the faint bleat of sound, Carnaby raised his head. How long had he lain here, waiting for the alien to make its move? Maybe an hour, maybe longer. He had passed out at least twice, possibly for no more than a second or two; but it could have been longer. The Djann might even have gotten past him—or crawled along below the ridge, ready now to jump him from a new angle. . . .

He thought of Terry Sickle, waiting for him, counting on him. Poor kid; time was running out for him. The sun was dropping low, and the shadows would be closing in. It would be icy cold inside the hut; and down there in the dark the boy was slowly strangling, maybe calling for him. . . .

He couldn't wait any longer. To hell with the alien. He'd held him long enough. Painfully, using the wall as a support, Carnaby got to his hands and knees. His side felt as though it had been opened and packed with red-hot stones—or were they ice-cold? His hands and feet were numb. His face ached. Frostbite. He'd look fine with a frozen ear. Funny how vanity survived as long as life itself. . . .

He got to his feet, leaned against the building, worked on breathing. The sky swam past him, fading and brightening. His feet felt like blocks of wood; that wasn't good. He had a long way to go. But the activity would warm him, get the blood flowing, except where the hot stones were. He would be lighter if he could leave them here. His hands moved at his side, groping over torn polyon, the sharp ends of broken wires. . . .

He brought his mind back to clarity with an effort. Wouldn't do to start wandering now. The gun caught his eye, lying at his feet. Better pick it up; but to hell with it, too much trouble. Navy property. Can't leave it here for the enemy to find. Enemy. Funny dream about a walking oxy tank, and—

He was looking at the dead Djann, lying, awkward, impossible, thirty feet away. No dream. The damn things were real. He was here, alone, on top of Thunderhead—

But he couldn't be. Flitter was broken

down. Have to get another message off via the next tramp steamer that made planetfall. Hadn't been one for . . . how long?

Something moved, a hundred feet away, among the tumble of broken rock.

Carnaby ducked, came up with the blast rifle, fired in a half-crouch from the hip, saw a big dark shape scramble up and over the edge, saw the wink of yellow light, fired again, cursing the weakness that made the gun buck and yaw in his hands, the darkness that closed over his vision. With hands that were stiff, clumsy, he fired a third time at the swift-darting shape that charged toward him; and then he was falling, falling. . . .

* * *

Stunned by the direct hit from the energy weapon of the Water-Being, the One-Who-Records fought his way upward through a universe shot through with whirling shapes of fire, to emerge on a plateau of mortal agony.

He tried to move, was shocked into paralysis by the cacophony of conflicting motor and sense impressions from shattered limbs and organs.

Then I, too, die, the thought came to him with utter finality. *And with me dies the once-mighty song of Djann.*

Failing, his mind groped outward, calling in vain for the familiar touch of his link-brothers —and abruptly, a sharp sensation impinged on his sensitivity-complex. Concepts of strange and alien shape drifted into his mind, beating at him with compelling urgency from a foreign brain:

Youth, aspirations, the ringing bugle of the call-to-arms. A white palace rearing up into yellow sunlight; a bright banner, rippling against blue sky, and the shadows of great trees ranked on green lawns. The taste of grapes, and an odor of flowers; night, and the moon reflected from still water; the touch of a soft hand and the face of a woman, invested with a supernal beauty; chords of a remote music that spoke of the inexpressibly desirable, the irretrievably lost. . . .

"Have we warred then, Water-Beings?" the One-Who-Records sent his thought outward. "We who might have been brothers?" With a mighty effort, he summoned his waning strength, sounded a final chord in tribute to that which had been, and was no more.

* * *

Carnaby opened his eyes and looked at the dead Djann lying in the crumpled posture of its final agony, not six feet from him. For a moment, a curious sensation of loss plucked at his mind.

"Sorry, fellow," he muttered aloud. "I guess you were doing what you had to do, too."

He stood, felt the ground sway under his feet. His head was light, hot; a sharp, clear humming sounded in his ears. He took a step, caught himself as his knees tried to buckle.

"Damn it, no time to fall out now," he grunted. He moved past the alien body, paused by the door to the shed. A waft of warm air caressed his cold-numbed face.

"Could go inside," he muttered. "Wait

there. Ship along in a few hours, maybe. Pick me up. . . ." He shook his head angrily. "Job's not done yet," he said clearly, addressing the white gleam of the ten-mile distant peak known as Creamtop. "Just a little longer, Terry," he added. "I'm coming."

Painfully, Carnaby made his way to the edge of the plateau, pulled himself up and over and started down.

* * *

"We'd better shift to sub-L now, Admiral," Drew said, strain showing in his voice. "We're cutting it fine as it is."

"Every extra minute at full gain saves a couple of hours," the vice admiral came back.

"That won't help us if we kick out inside the Delta limit and blow ourselves into free ions," the general said coolly.

"You've made your point, General!" The admiral kept his eyes fixed on his instruments. Half a minute ticked past. Then he nodded curtly.

"All right, kick us out," he snapped, "and we'll see where we stand."

The hundred-ton interceptor shuddered as the distorters whined down the scale, allowing the stressed space field that had enclosed the vessel to collapse. A star swam suddenly into the visible spectrum, blazing at planetary distance off the starboard bow at three-o'clock high.

"Our target's the second body, there." The copilot punched the course into the panel.

"What would you say—another hour?" The admiral bit off the words.

"Make it two," the other replied shortly. He glanced up, caught the admiral's eye on him.

"Kidding ourselves won't change anything," he said steadily.

Admiral Carnaby narrowed his eyes, opened his mouth to speak, then clamped his jaw shut.

"I guess I've been a little snappy with you, George," he said. "I'll ask your pardon. That's my brother down there."

"Your . . . ?" the general's features tightened. "I guess I said some stupid things myself, Tom." He frowned at the instruments, busied himself adjusting course for an MIT approach to the planet.

* * *

Carnaby half jumped, half fell the last few yards to the narrow ledge called Halliday's Roost, landed awkwardly in a churn of powdered wind-driven snow. For a moment he lay sprawled, then gathered himself, made it to his feet, tottered to the hollow concealing the drifted entrance to the hut. He lowered himself, crawled down into the dark clammy interior.

"Terry," he called hoarsely. A wheezing breath answered him. He felt his way to the boy's side, groped over him. He lay on his side, his legs curled against his chest.

"Terry!" Carnaby pulled the lad to a sitting position, he felt him stir feebly. "Terry, I'm back! We have to go now, Terry. . . ."

"I knew"—the boy stopped to draw an agonizing breath—"you'd come. . . ." He groped, found Carnaby's hand.

Carnaby fought the dizziness that threatened to close in on him.

He was cold—colder than he had ever been. The climbing hadn't warmed him. The side wasn't bothering him much now; he could hardly feel it. But he couldn't feel his hands and feet, either. They were like stumps, good for nothing.... Clumsily, he backed through the entry, bodily hauling Terry along with him.

Outside, the wind lashed at him like frozen whips. Carnaby raised Terry to his feet. The boy leaned against him, slid down, crumpled to the ground.

"Terry, you've got to try," Carnaby gasped out. His breath seemed to freeze in his throat. "No time to waste...got to get you to... Doc Lin...."

"Lieutenant...I...can't...."

"Terry...you've got to try!" He lifted the boy to his feet.

"I'm...scared...Lieutenant...." Terry stood swaying, his slight body quivering, his knees loose.

"Don't worry, Terry." Carnaby guided the boy to the point from which they would start the climb down. "Not far now."

"Lieutenant...." Sickle caught at Carnaby's arm, clung. "You...better...leave... me."

His breath sighed in his throat.

"I'll go first." Carnaby heard his own voice as from a great distance. "Take...it easy. I'll be right there...to help...."

He forced a breath of sub-zero air into his lungs. The bitter wind moaned around the shattered rock. The dusky afternoon sun shed a reddish light but no heat on the long slope below.

"It's late." He mouthed the words with stiff lips. "It's late. . . ."

* * *

Two hundred thousand feet above the surface of the outpost world Longone, the fleet interceptor split the stratosphere, its receptors fine-tuned to the Djann energy-cell emission spectrum.

"Three hundred million square miles of desert," Admiral Carnaby said. "Except for a couple of deserted townsites, not a sign that life ever existed here."

"We'll find it, Tom," Drew said. "If they'd lifted, *Malthusa* would have known—hold it!" He looked up quickly. "I'm getting something —yes! It's the typical Djann idler output!"

"How far from us?"

"Quite a distance. . . . Now it's fading. . . ."

The admiral put the ship into a screaming deceleration curve that crushed both men brutally against the restraint of their shock-frames.

"Find that signal, George," the vice admiral grated. "Find it and steer me to it, if you have to pick it out of the air with psi!"

"I've got it!" Drew barked. "Steer right, on Oh-three-oh. I'd range it at about two thousand kilometers. . . ."

* * *

On the bald face on an outcropping of wind-scored stone Carnaby clung one-handed to a scanty hold, supporting Terry with the other arm. The wind shrieked, buffeting at him; sand-fine snow whirled into his face, slashing at his eyes, already half-blinded by the glare. The boy slumped against him, barely conscious.

His mind seemed as sluggish now as his half-frozen limbs. Somewhere below there was a ledge, with shelter from the wind. How far? Ten feet? Fifty?

It didn't matter. He had to reach it. He couldn't hold on here in this wind; in another minute he'd be done for.

Carnaby pulled Terry closer, got a better grip with a hand that seemed no more a part of him than the rock against which they clung. He shifted his purchase with his right foot—and felt it slip. He was falling, grabbing frantically with one hand at the rock, then dropping through open air—

The impact against drifted snow drove the air from his lungs. Darkness shot through with red fire threatened to close in on him; he fought to draw a breath, struggling in the claustrophobia of suffocation. With a desperate lunge, he caught a ridge of hard ice, pulled himself back from the brink, then groped, found Terry, lying on his back under the vertically rising wall of rock. The boy stirred.

"So . . . tired . . ." he whispered. His body arced as he struggled to draw breath.

Carnaby pulled himself to a position beside the boy, propped himself with his back against the rock. Dimly, through ice-rimmed eyes, he could see the evening lights of the settlement, far below; so far. . . .

He put his arm around the thin body, settled the lad's head gently in his lap, leaned over him to shelter him from the whirling snow. "It's all right, Terry," he said. "You can rest now."

*　*　*

Supported on three narrow pencils of beamed force, the fleet interceptor slowly circuited the Djann yacht, hovering on its idling null-G generators a thousand feet above the towering white mountain.

"Nothing alive there," the co-pilot said. "Not a whisper on the life-detection scale."

"Take her down." Vice Admiral Carnaby squinted through S-R lenses which had darkened almost to opacity in response to the frost-white glare from below. "The shack looks all right, but that doesn't look like a Mark Seven flitter parked beside it."

The heavy fleet boat descended swiftly under the expert guidance of the battle officer. At fifty feet, he leveled off, orbited the station.

"I count four dead Djann," the admiral said in a brittle voice.

"Tracks," the general pointed. "Leading off there. . . ."

"Put her down, George!" The hundred-foot boat settled in with a crunching of rock and ice, its shark's prow overhanging the edge of the tiny plateau. The hatch cycled open; the two men emerged.

At the spot where Carnaby had lain in wait for the last of the aliens, they paused, staring silently at the glossy patch of dark blood, and at the dead Djann beside it. Then they followed the irregularly spaced footprints across to the edge.

"He was still on his feet—but that's about all," the battle officer said.

"George, can you operate that Spider boat?" The admiral indicated the Djann landing sled.

"Certainly."

"Let's go."

* * *

It was twilight half an hour later when the admiral, peering through the obscuring haze, saw the show-drifted shapes huddled in the shadow of an overhang. Fifty feet lower, the general settled the sled into a precarious landing on a narrow shelf. It was a ten-minute climb back to their objective.

Vice Admiral Carnaby pulled himself up the last yard, looked across the icy ledge at the figure in the faded-blue polyon cold suit. He saw the weathered and lined face, glazed with ice; the closed eyes, the gnarled and bloody hands, the great wound in the side.

The general came up beside him, stared silently, then went forward.

"I'm sorry, Admiral," he said a moment later. "He's dead. Frozen. Both of them."

The admiral came up, went to Carnaby's side.

"I'm sorry, Jimmy," he said. "Sorry."

"I don't understand," the general said. "He could have stayed up above, in the station. He'd have been all right there. What in the world was he doing down here?"

"What he always did," Admiral Carnaby said. "His duty."

THE LAST COMMAND

I came to awareness, sensing a residual oscillation traversing me from an arbitrarily designated heading of 035. From the damping rate I compute that the shock was of intensity 8.7, emanating from a source within the limits 72 meters/46 meters. I activate my primary screens, trigger a return salvo. There is no response. I engage reserve energy cells, bring my secondary battery to bear—futilely. It is apparent that I have been ranged by the Enemy and severely damaged.

My positional sensors indicated that I am resting at an angle of 13 degrees 14 seconds, deflected from a base line at 21 points from median. I attempt to right myself, but encounter massive resistance. I activate my forward scanners, shunt power to my IR microstrobes. Not a flicker illuminates my surroundings. I am encased in utter blackness.

Now a secondary shock wave approaches, rocks me with an intensity of 8.2. It is apparent that I must withdraw from my position—but my drive trains remain inert under full thrust. I shift to base emergency power, try again.

Pressure mounts; I sense my awareness fading under the intolerable strain; then, abruptly, resistance falls off and I am in motion.

It is not the swift maneuvering of full drive, however; I inch forward, as if restrained by massive barriers. Again I attempt to penetrate the surrounding darkness and this time perceive great irregular outlines shot through with fracture planes. I probe cautiously, then more vigorously, encountering incredible densities.

I channel all available power to a single ranging pulse, direct it upward. The indication is so at variance with all experience that I repeat the test at a new angle. Now I must accept the fact: I am buried under 207.6 meters of solid rock!

I direct my attention to an effort to orient myself to my uniquely desperate situation. I run through an action-status check list of thirty thousand items, feel dismay at the extent of power loss. My main cells are almost completely drained, my reserve units at no more than .4 charge. Thus my sluggishness is explained. I review the tactical situation, recall the triumphant announcement from my commander that the Enemy forces were annihilated, that all resistance had ceased. In memory, I review the formal procession; in company with my comrades of the Dinochrome Brigade, many of us deeply scarred by Enemy action, we parade before the Grand Commandant, then assemble on the depot ramp. At command, we bring our music storage cells into phase and display our Battle Anthem. The near-by star radiates over a full spectrum unfiltered by atmospheric haze. It is a moment of glorious triumph. Then the final command is given—

The rest is darkness. But it is apparent that the victory celebration was premature. The Enemy has counterattacked with a force that has come near to immobilizing me. The realization is shocking, but the .1 second of leisurely introspection has clarified my position. At once, I broadcast a call on Brigade Action wave length:

"Unit LNE to Command, requesting permission to file VSR."

I wait, sense no response, call again, using full power. I sweep the enclosing volume of rock with an emergency alert warning. I tune to the all-units band, await the replies of my comrades of the Brigade. None answers. Now I must face the reality: I alone have survived the assault.

I channel my remaining power to my drive and detect a channel of reduced density. I press for it and the broken rock around me yields reluctantly. Slowly, I move forward and upward. My pain circuitry shocks my awareness center with emergency signals; I am doing irreparable damage to my overloaded neural systems, but my duty is clear: I must seek out and engage the Enemy.

* * *

Emerging from behind the blast barrier, Chief Engineer Pete Reynolds of the New Devonshire Port Authority pulled off his rock mask and spat grit from his mouth.

"That's the last one; we've bottomed out at

just over two hundred yards. Must have hit a hard stratum down there."

"It's almost sundown," the paunchy man beside him said shortly. "You're a day and a half behind schedule."

"We'll start backfilling now, Mr. Mayor. I'll have pilings poured by oh-nine hundred tomorrow, and with any luck the first section of pad will be in place in time for the rally."

"I'm—" The mayor broke off, looked startled. "I thought you told me that was the last charge to be fired. . . ."

Reynolds frowned. A small but distinct tremor had shaken the ground underfoot. A few feet away, a small pebble balanced atop another toppled and fell with a faint clatter.

"Probably a big rock fragment falling," he said. At that moment, a second vibration shook the earth, stronger this time. Reynolds heard a rumble and a distant impact as rock fell from the side of the newly blasted excavation. He whirled to the control shed as the door swung back and Second Engineer Mayfield appeared.

"Take a look at this, Pete!"

Reynolds went across to the hut, stepped inside. Mayfield was ending over the profiling table.

"What do you make of it?" he pointed. Superimposed on the heavy red contour representing the detonation of the shaped charge that had completed the drilling of the final pile core were two other traces, weak but distinct.

"About .1 intensity." Mayfield looked puzzled. "What—"

The tracking needle dipped suddenly, swept up the screen to peak at .21, dropped back. The hut trembled. A stylus fell from the edge of the table. The red face of Mayor Dougherty burst through the door.

"Reynolds, have you lost your mind? What's the idea of blasting while I'm standing out in the open? I might have been killed!"

"I'm not blasting," Reynolds snapped. "Jim, get Eaton on the line, see if they know anything." He stepped to the door, shouted. A heavy-set man in sweat-darkened cover-alls swung down from the seat of a cable-lift rig.

"Boss, what goes on?" he called as he came up. "Damn near shook me out of my seat!"

"I don't know. You haven't set any trim charges?"

"Jesus, no, boss. I wouldn't set no charges without your say-so."

"Come on." Reynolds started out across the rubble-littered stretch of barren ground selected by the Authority as the site of the new spaceport. Halfway to the open mouth of the newly blasted pit, the ground under his feet rocked violently enough to make him stumble. A gout of dust rose from the excavation ahead. Loose rock danced on the ground. Beside him, the drilling chief grabbed his arm.

"Boss, we better get back!"

Reynolds shook him off, kept going. The drill chief swore and followed. The shaking of the ground went on, a sharp series of thumps interrupting a steady trembling.

"It's a quake!" Reynolds yelled over the low rumbling sound.

He and the chief were at the rim of the core now.

"It can't be a quake, boss," the latter shouted. "Not in these formations!"

"Tell it to the geologists—" The rock slab they were standing on rose a foot, dropped back. Both men fell. The slab bucked like a small boat in choppy water.

"Let's get out of here!" Reynolds was up and running. Ahead, a fissure opened, gaped a foot wide. He jumped it, caught a glimpse of black depths, a glint of wet clay twenty feet below—

A hoarse scream stopped him in his tracks. He spun, saw the drill chief down, a heavy splinter of rock across his legs. He jumped to him, heaved at the rock. There was blood on the man's shirt. The chief's hands beat the dusty rock before him. Then other men were there, grunting, sweaty hands gripping beside Reynolds. The ground rocked. The roar from under the earth had risen to a deep, steady rumble. They lifted the rock aside, picked up the injured man, and stumbled with him to the aid shack.

The mayor was there, white-faced.

"What is it, Reynolds? By God, if you're responsible—"

"Shut up!" Reynolds brushed him aside, grabbed the phone, punched keys.

"Eaton! What have you got on this temblor?"

"Temblor, hell." The small face on the four-inch screen looked like a ruffled hen. "What in the name of Order are you doing out there? I'm reading a whole series of displacements originating from that last core of yours! What did you do, leave a pile of trim charges lying around?"

"It's a quake. Trim charges, hell! This thing's broken up two hundred yards of surface rock. It seems to be traveling north-northeast—"

"I see that; a traveling earthquake!" Eaton flapped his arms, a tiny and ridiculous figure against a background of wall charts and framed diplomas. "Well—do something, Reynolds! Where's Mayor Dougherty?"

"Underfoot!" Reynolds snapped, and cut off.

Outside, a layer of sunset-stained dust obscured the sweep of level plain. A rock-dozer rumbled up, ground to a halt by Reynolds. A man jumped down.

"I got the boys moving equipment out," he panted. "The thing's cutting a trail straight as a rule for the highway!" He pointed to a raised roadbed a quarter mile away.

"How fast is it moving?"

"She's done a hundred yards; it hasn't been ten minutes yet!"

"If it keeps up another twenty minutes, it'll be into the Intermix!"

"Scratch a few million cees and six months' work then, Pete!"

"And Southside Mall's a couple miles farther."

"Hell, it'll damp out before then!"

"Maybe. Grab a field car, Dan."

"Pete!" Mayfield came up at a trot. "This thing's building! The centroid's moving on a heading of 022—"

"How far sub-surface?"

"It's rising; started at two-twenty yards, and it's up to one-eighty!"

"What the hell have we stirred up?" Reynolds stared at Mayfield as the field car skidded to a stop beside them.

"Stay with it, Jim. Give me anything new. We're taking a closer look." He climbed into the rugged vehicle.

"Take a blast truck—"

"No time!" He waved and the car gunned away into the pall of dust.

* * *

The rock car pulled to a stop at the crest of the three-level Intermix on a lay-by designed to permit tourists to enjoy the view of the site of the proposed port, a hundred feet below. Reynolds studied the progress of the quake through field glasses. From this vantage point, the path of the phenomenon was a clearly defined trail of tilted and broken rock, some of the slabs twenty feet across. As he watched, the fissure lengthened.

"It looks like a mole's trail." Reynolds handed the glasses to his companion, thumbed the send key on the car radio.

"Jim, get Eaton and tell him to divert all traffic from the Circular south of Zone Nine. Cars are already clogging the right-of-way. The dust is visible from a mile away, and when the word gets out there's something going on, we'll be swamped."

"I'll tell him, but he won't like it!"

"This isn't politics! This thing will be into the outer pad area in another twenty minutes!"

"It won't last—"

"How deep does it read now?"

"One-five!" There was a moment's silence. "Pete, if it stays on course, it'll surface at about where you're parked!"

"Uh-huh. It looks like you can scratch one Intermix. Better tell Eaton to get a story ready for the press."

"Pete—talking about news hounds—" Dan said beside him. Reynolds switched off, turned to see a man in a gay-colored driving outfit coming across from a battered Monojag sportster which had pulled up behind the rock car. A big camera case was slung across his shoulder.

"Say, what's going on down there?" he called.

"Rock slide," Reynolds said shortly. "I'll have to ask you to drive on. The road's closed to all traffic—"

"Who're you?" The man looked belligerent.

"I'm the engineer in charge. Now pull out, brother." He turned back to the radio. "Jim, get every piece of heavy equipment we own over here, on the double." He paused, feeling a minute trembling in the car. "The Intermix is beginning to feel it," he went on. "I'm afraid we're in for it. Whatever that thing is, it acts like a solid body boring its way through the ground. Maybe we can barricade it."

"Barricade an earthquake?"

"Yeah—I know how it sounds—but it's the only idea I've got."

"Hey—what's that about an earthquake?" The man in the colored suit was still there.

"By gosh, I can feel it—the whole damned bridge is shaking!"

"Off, mister—now!" Reynolds jerked a thumb at the traffic lanes where a steady stream of cars were hurtling past. "Dan, take us over to the main track. We'll have to warn this traffic off—"

"Hold on, fellow." The man unlimbered his camera. "I represent the New Devon *Scope*. I have a few questions—"

"I don't have the answers." Pete cut him off as the car pulled away.

"Hah!" The man who had questioned Reynolds yelled after him. "Big shot! Think you can . . ." His voice was lost behind them.

* * *

In a modest retirees' apartment block in the coast town of Idlebreeze, forty miles from the scene of the freak quake, an old man sat in a reclining chair, half dozing before a yammering Tri-D tank.

" . . . Grandpa," a sharp-voiced young woman was saying. "It's time for you to go in to bed."

"Bed? Why do I want to go to bed? Can't sleep anyway. . . ." He stirred, made a pretense of sitting up, showing an interest in the Tri-D. "I'm watching this show. Don't bother me."

"It's not a show, it's the news," a fattish boy said disgustedly. "Ma, can I switch channels—"

"Leave it alone, Bennie," the old man said. On the screen, a panoramic scene spread out, a stretch of barren ground across which a furrow showed. As he watched, it lengthened.

". . . up here at the Intermix we have a fine view of the whole curious business, lazangemmun," the announcer chattered. "And in our opinion it's some sort of publicity stunt staged by the Port Authority to publicize their controversial port project—"

"Ma, can I change channels?"

"Go ahead, Bennie—"

"Don't touch it," the old man said. The fattish boy reached for the control, but something in the old man's eye stopped him. . . .

* * *

"The traffic's still piling in here," Reynolds said into the phone. "Damn it, Jim, we'll have a major jam on our hands—"

"He won't do it, Pete! You know the Circular was his baby—the super all-weather pike that nothing could shut down. He says you'll have to handle this in the field—"

"Handle, hell! I'm talking about preventing a major disaster! And in a matter of minutes, at that!"

"I'll try again—"

"If he says no, divert a couple of the big ten-yard graders and block it off yourself. Set up field arcs, and keep any cars from getting in from either direction."

"Pete, that's outside your authority!"

"You heard me!"

Ten minutes later, back at ground level, Reynolds watched the boom-mounted poly-arcs swinging into position at the two roadblocks a quarter of a mile apart, cutting off the threatened section of the raised expressway. A hundred yards from where he stood on the rear cargo deck of a light grader rig, a section of rock fifty feet wide rose slowly, split, fell back with a ponderous impact. One corner of it struck the massive pier supporting the extended shelf of the lay-by above. A twenty-foot splinter fell away, exposing the reinforcing-rod core.

"How deep, Jim?" Reynolds spoke over the roaring sound coming from the disturbed area.

"Just sub-surface now, Pete! It ought to break through—" His voice was drowned in a rumble as the damaged pier shivered, rose up, buckled at its mid-point, and collapsed, bringing down with it a large chunk of pavement and guard rail, and a single still-glowing light pole. A small car that had been parked on the doomed section was visible for an instant just before the immense slab struck. Reynolds saw it bounce aside, then disappear under an avalanche of broken concrete.

"My God, Pete—" Dan started. "That damned fool news hound . . . !"

"Look!" As the two men watched, a second pier swayed, fell backward into the shadow of the span above. The roadway sagged, and two more piers snapped. With a bellow like a burst dam, a hundred-foot stretch of the road fell into the roiling dust cloud.

"Pete!" Mayfield's voice burst from the car radio. "Get out of there! I threw a reader on that thing and it's chattering off the scale . . . !"

Among the piled fragments, something

stirred, heaved, rising up, lifting multi-ton pieces of the broken road, thrusting them aside like so many potato chips. A dull blue radiance broke through from the broached earth, threw an eerie light on the shattered structure above. A massive, ponderously irresistible shape thrust forward through the ruins. Reynolds saw a great blue-glowing profile emerge from the rubble like a surfacing submarine, shedding a burden of broken stone, saw immense treads ten feet wide claw for purchase, saw the mighty flank brush a still-standing pier, send it crashing aside.

"Pete—what—what is it . . . ?"

"I don't know." Reynolds broke the paralysis that had gripped him. "Get us out of here, Dan, fast! Whatever it is, it's headed straight for the city!"

* * *

I emerge at last from the trap into which I had fallen, and at once encounter defensive works of considerable strength. My scanners are dulled from lack of power, but I am able to perceive open ground beyond the barrier, and farther still, at a distance of 5.7 kilometers, massive walls. Once more I transmit the Brigade Rally signal; but as before, there is no reply. I am truly alone.

I scan the surrounding area for the emanations of Enemy drive units, monitor the EM spectrum for their communications. I detect nothing; either my circuitry is badly damaged, or their shielding is superb.

I must now make a decision as to possible courses of action. Since all my comrades of the

Brigade have fallen, I compute that the fortress before me must be held by Enemy forces. I direct probing signals at them, discover them to be of unfamiliar construction, and less formidable than they appear. I am aware of the possibility that this may be a trick of the Enemy; but my course is clear.

I reengage my driving engines and advance on the Enemy fortress.

* * *

"You're out of your mind, Father," the stout man said. "At your age—"

"At your age, I got my nose smashed in a brawl in a bar on Aldo," the old man cut him off. "But I won the fight."

"James, you can't go out at this time of night . . ." an elderly woman wailed.

"Tell them to go home." The old man walked painfully toward his bedroom door. "I've seen enough of them for today." He passed out of sight.

"Mother, you won't let him do anything foolish?"

"He'll forget about it in a few minutes; but maybe you'd better go now and let him settle down."

"Mother—I really think a home is the best solution."

"Yes," the young woman nodded agreement. "After all, he's past ninety—and he has his veteran's retirement. . . ."

Inside his room, the old man listened as they departed. He went to the closet, took out clothes, began dressing. . . .

* * *

City Engineer Eaton's face was chalk-white on the screen.

"No one can blame me," he said. "How could I have known—"

"Your office ran the surveys and gave the PA the green light," Mayor Dougherty yelled.

"All the old survey charts showed was 'Disposal Area,'" Eaton threw out his hands. "I assumed—"

"As City Engineer, you're not paid to make assumptions! Ten minutes' research would have told you that was a 'Y' category area!"

"What's 'Y' category mean?" Mayfield asked Reynolds. They were standing by the field comm center, listening to the dispute. Near by, boom-mounted Tri-D cameras hummed, recording the progress of the immense machine, its upper turret rearing forty-five feet into the air, as it ground slowly forward across smooth ground toward the city, dragging behind it a trailing festoon of twisted reinforcing iron crusted with broken concrete.

"Half-life over one hundred years," Reynolds answered shortly. "The last skirmish of the war was fought near here. Apparently this is where they buried the radioactive equipment left over from the battle."

"But, what the hell—that was seventy years ago—"

"There's still enough residual radiation to contaminate anything inside a quarter-mile radius."

"They must have used some hellish stuff." Mayfield stared at the dull shine half a mile distant.

"Reynolds, how are you going to stop this thing?" the mayor had turned on the PA engineer.

"Me stop it? You saw what it did to my heaviest rigs: flattened them like pancakes. You'll have to call out the military on this one, Mr. Mayor."

"Call in Federation forces? Have them meddling in civic affairs?"

"The station's only sixty-five miles from here. I think you'd better call them fast. It's only moving at about three miles per hour but it will reach the south edge of the Mall in another forty-five minutes."

"Can't you mine it? Blast a trap in its path?"

"You saw it claw its way up from six hundred feet down. I checked the specs; it followed the old excavation tunnel out. It was rubble-filled and capped with twenty-inch compressed concrete."

"It's incredible," Eaton said from the screen. "The entire machine was encased in a ten-foot shell of reinforced armocrete. It had to break out of that before it could move a foot!"

"That was just a radiation shield; it wasn't intended to restrain a Bolo Combat Unit."

"What was, may I inquire?" The mayor glared from one face to another.

"The units were deactivated before being buried," Eaton spoke up, as if he were eager to talk. "Their circuits were fused. It's all in the report—"

"The report you should have read somewhat sooner," the mayor snapped.

"What—what started it up?" Mayfield looked bewildered. "For seventy years it was down there, and nothing happened!"

"Our blasting must have jarred something," Reynolds said shortly. "Maybe closed a relay that started up the old battle reflex circuit."

"You know something about these machines?" The mayor beetled his brows at him.

"I've read a little."

"Then speak up, man. I'll call the station, if you feel I must. What measures should I request?"

"I don't know, Mr. Mayor. As far as I know, nothing on New Devon can stop that machine now."

The mayor's mouth opened and closed. He whirled to the screen, blanked Eaton's agonized face, punched in the code for the Federation station.

"Colonel Blane!" he blurted as a stern face came onto the screen. "We have a major emergency on our hands! I'll need everything you've got! This is the situation . . ."

* * *

I encounter no resistance other than the flimsy barrier, but my progress is slow. Grievous damage has been done to my main drive sector due to overload during my escape from the trap; and the failure of my sensing circuitry has deprived me of a major portion of my external receptivity. Now my pain circuits project a continuous signal to my awareness center; but it is my duty to my commander and to my fallen comrades of the Brigade to press forward at my best speed; but my performance is a poor shadow of my former ability.

And now at last the Enemy comes into action! I sense aerial units closing at supersonic velocities; I lock my lateral batteries to them and direct salvo fire; but I sense that the arming mechanisms clatter harmlessly. The craft sweep over me, and my impotent guns elevate, track them as they release detonants that spread out in an envelopmental pattern which I, with my reduced capabilities, am powerless to avoid. The missiles strike; I sense their detonations all about me; but I suffer only trivial damage. The Enemy has blundered if he thought to neutralize a Mark XXVIII Combat Unit with mere chemical explosives! But I weaken with each meter gained.

Now there is no doubt as to my course. I must press the charge and carry the walls before my reserve cells are exhausted.

* * *

From a vantage point atop a bucket rig four hundred yards from the position the great fighting machine had now reached, Pete Reynolds studied it through night glasses. A battery of beamed polyarcs pinned the giant hulk, scarred and rust-scaled, in a pool of blue-white light. A mile and a half beyond it, the walls of the Mall rose sheer from the garden setting.

"The bombers slowed it some," he reported to Eaton via scope. "But it's still making better than two miles per hour. I'd say another twenty-five minutes before it hits the main ring-wall. How's the evacuation going?"

"Badly! I get no cooperation! You'll be my witness, Reynolds, I did all I could—"

"How about the mobile batteries; how long before they'll be in position?" Reynolds cut him off.

"I've heard nothing from Federation Central—typical militaristic arrogance, not keeping me informed—but I have them on my screens. They're two miles out—say three minutes."

"I hope you made your point about N-heads."

"That's outside my province!" Eaton said sharply. "It's up to Brand to carry out this portion of the operation!"

"The HE Missiles didn't do much more than clear away the junk it was dragging." Reynold's voice was sharp.

"I wash my hands of responsibility for civilian lives," Eaton was saying when Reynolds shut him off, changed channels.

"Jim, I'm going to try to divert it," he said crisply. "Eaton's sitting on his political fence; the Feds are bringing artillery up, but I don't expect much from it. Technically, Brand needs Sector OK to use nuclear stuff, and he's not the boy to stick his neck out—"

"Divert it how? Pete, don't take any chances—"

Reynolds laughed shortly. "I'm going to get around it and drop a shaped drilling charge in its path. Maybe I can knock a tread off. With luck, I might get its attention on me and draw it away from the Mall. There are still a few thousand people over there, glued to their Tri-

D's. They think it's all a swell show."

"Pete, you can't walk up on that thing! It's hot—" He broke off. "Pete—there's some kind of nut here—he claims he has to talk to you; says he knows something about that damned juggernaut. Shall I . . . ?"

Reynolds paused with his hand on the cut-off switch. "Put him on," he snapped. Mayfield's face moved aside and an ancient, bleary-eyed visage stared out at him. The tip of the old man's tongue touched his dry lips.

"Son, I tried to tell this boy here, but he wouldn't listen—"

"What have you got, old-timer?" Pete cut in. "Make it fast."

"My name's Sanders. James Sanders. I'm . . . I was with the Planetary Volunteer Scouts, back in '71—"

"Sure, Dad," Pete said gently. "I'm sorry, I've got a little errand to run—"

"Wait . . ." The old man's face worked. "I'm old, son—too damned old. I know. But bear with me. I'll try to say it straight. I was with Hayle's squadron at Toledo. Then afterwards, they shipped us—but hell, you don't care about that! I keep wandering, son; can't help it. What I mean to say is—I was in on that last scrap, right here at New Devon—only we didn't call it New Devon then. Called it Hellport. Nothing but bare rock and Enemy emplacement—"

"You were talking about the battle, Mr. Sanders," Pete said tensely, "Go on with that part."

"Lieutenant Sanders," the oldster said. "Sure, I was Acting Brigade Commander. See, our major was hit at Toledo—and after Tommy Chee stopped a sidewinder at Belgrave—"

"Stick to the point, Lieutenant!"

"Yessir!" The old man pulled himself together with an obvious effort. "I took the Brigade in; put out flankers, and ran the Enemy into the ground. We mopped 'em up in a thirty-three-hour running fight that took us from over by Crater Bay all the way down here to Hellport. When it was over, I'd lost sixteen units, but the Enemy was done. They gave us Brigade Honors for that action. And then . . ."

"Then what?"

"Then the triple-dyed yellow-bottoms at Headquarters put out the order the Brigade was to be scrapped; said they were too hot to make decon practical. Cost too much, they said! So after the final review—" he gulped, blinked—"they planted 'em deep, two hundred meters, and poured in special High-R concrete."

"And packed rubble in behind them," Reynolds finished for him. "All right, Lieutenant, I believe you! Now for the big one: What started that machine on a rampage?"

"Should have known they couldn't hold down a Bolo Mark XXVIII!" The old man's eyes lit up. "Take more than a few million tons of rock to stop Lenny when his battle board was lit!"

"Lenny?"

"That's my old command unit out there, son. I saw the markings on the Tri-D. Unit LNE of the Dinochrome Brigade!"

"Listen!" Reynolds snapped out. "Here's what I intend to try . . ." He outlined his plan.

"Ha!" Sanders snorted. "It's a gutsy notion, mister, but Lenny won't give it a sneeze."

"You didn't come here to tell me we were licked," Reynolds cut in. "How about Brand's batteries?"

"Hell, son, Lenny stood up to point-blank Hellbore fire on Toledo, and—"

"Are you telling me there's nothing we can do?"

"What's that? No, son, that's not what I'm saying . . ."

"Then what!"

"Just tell those johnnies to get out of my way, mister. I think I can handle him."

* * *

At the field comm hut, Pete Reynolds watched as the man who had been Lieutenant Sanders of the Volunteer Scouts pulled shiny black boots over his thin ankles and stood. The blouse and trousers of royal blue polyon hung on his spare frame like wash on a line. He grinned, a skull's grin.

"It doesn't fit like it used to; but Lenny will recognize it. It'll help. Now, if you've got that power pack ready . . ."

Mayfield handed over the old-fashioned field instrument Sanders had brought in with him.

"It's operating, sir—but I've already tried everything I've got on that infernal machine; I didn't get a peep out of it."

Sanders winked at him. "Maybe I know a couple of tricks you boys haven't heard about." He slung the strap over his bony shoulder and turned to Reynolds.

"Guess we better get going, mister. He's getting close."

In the rock car, Sanders leaned close to Reynolds' ear. "Told you those Federal guns wouldn't scratch Lenny. They're wasting their time."

Reynolds pulled the car to a stop at the crest of the road, from which point he had a view of the sweep of ground leading across to the city's edge. Lights sparkled all across the towers of New Devon. Close to the walls, the converging fire of the ranked batteries of infinite repeaters drove into the glowing bulk of the machine, which plowed on, undeterred. As he watched, the firing ceased.

"Now, let's get in there, before they get some other damn-fool scheme going," Sanders said.

The rock car crossed the rough ground, swung wide to come up on the Bolo from the left side. Behind the hastily rigged radiation cover, Reynolds watched the immense silhouette grow before him.

"I knew they were big," he said. "But to see one up close like this—" He pulled to a stop a hundred feet from the Bolo.

"Look at the side ports," Sanders said, his voice crisper now. "He's firing anti-personnel charges—only his plates are flat. If they weren't, we wouldn't have gotten within half a mile." He unclipped the microphone and spoke into it:

"Unit LNE, break off action and retire to ten-mile line!"

Reynolds' head jerked around to stare at the old man. His voice had rung with vigor and authority as he spoke the command.

The Bolo ground slowly ahead. Sanders shook his head, tried again.

"No answer, like that fella said. He must be running on nothing but memories now. . . ." He reattached the microphone, and before Reynolds could put out a hand, had lifted the anti-R cover and stepped off on the ground.

"Sanders—get back in here!" Reynolds yelled.

"Never mind, son. I've got to get in close. Contact induction." He started toward the giant machine. Frantically, Reynolds started the car, slammed it into gear, pulled forward.

"Better stay back." Sanders' voice came from his field radio. "This close, that screening won't do you much good."

"Get in the car!" Reynolds roared. "That's hard radiation!"

"Sure; feels funny, like a sunburn, about an hour after you come in from the beach and start to think maybe you got a little too much." He laughed. "But I'll get to him. . . ."

Reynolds braked to a stop, watched the shrunken figure in the baggy uniform as it slogged forward, leaning as if against a sleet storm.

* * *

"I'm up beside him." Sanders' voice came through faintly on the field radio. "I'm going to try to swing up on his side. Don't feel like trying to chase him any farther."

Through the glasses, Reynolds watched the small figure, dwarfed by the immense bulk of the fighting machine, as he tried, stumbled, tried again, swung up on the flange running across the rear quarter inside the churning bogie wheel.

"He's up," he reported. "Damned wonder the track didn't get him. . . ."

Clinging to the side of the machine, Sanders lay for a moment, bent forward across the flange. Then he pulled himself up, wormed his way forward to the base of the rear quarter turret, wedged himself against it. He unslung the communicator, removed a small black unit, clipped it to the armor; it clung, held by a magnet. He brought the microphone up to his face.

In the Comm shack, Mayfield leaned toward the screen, his eyes squinted in tension. Across the field, Reynolds held the glasses fixed on the man lying across the flank of the Bolo. They waited. . . .

* * *

The walls are before me, and I ready myself for a final effort, but suddenly I am aware of trickle currents flowing over my outer surface. Is this some new trick of the Enemy? I tune to the wave energies, trace the source. They originate at a point in contact with my aft port armor. I sense modulation, match receptivity to a computed pattern. And I hear a voice:

"Unit LNE, break it off, Lenny. We're pulling back now, boy. This is Command to LNE; pull back to ten miles. If you read me, Lenny, swing to port and halt."

I am not fooled by the deception. The order appears correct, but the voice is not that of my commander. Briefly I regret that I cannot spare energy to direct a neutralizing power flow at the device the Enemy has attached to me. I continue my charge.

"Unit LNE! Listen to me, boy; maybe you don't recognize my voice, but it's me. You see, boy—some time has passed. I've gotten old. My voice has changed some, maybe. But it's me! Make a port turn, Lenny. Make it now!"

I am tempted to respond to the trick, for something in the false command seems to awaken secondary circuits which I sense have been long stilled. But I must not be swayed by the cleverness of the Enemy. My sensing circuitry has faded further as my energy cells drain; but I know where the Enemy lies. I move forward, but I am filled with agony, and only the memory of my comrades drives me on.

"Lenny, answer me. Transmit on the old private band—the one we agreed on. Nobody but me knows it, remember?"

Thus the Enemy seeks to beguile me into diverting precious power. But I will not listen.

"Lenny—not much time left. Another minute and you'll be into the walls. People are going to die. Got to stop you, Lenny. Hot here. My God, I'm hot. Not breathing too well, now. I can feel it; cutting through me like knives. You took a load of Enemy power, Lenny; and now I'm getting my share. Answer me, Lenny. Over to you. . . ."

It will require only a tiny allocation of power to activate a communication circuit. I realize that it is only an Enemy trick, but I compute that by pretending to be deceived, I may achieve some trivial advantage. I adjust circuitry accordingly and transmit:

"Unit LNE to Command. Contact with Enemy defensive line imminent. Request supporting fire!"

"Lenny . . . you can hear me! Good boy, Lenny! Now make a turn, to port. Walls . . . close. . . ."

"Unit LNE to Command. Request positive identification; transmit code 685749."

"Lenny—I can't . . . don't have code blanks. But it's me. . . ."

"In absence of recognition code, your transmission disregarded," I send. And now the walls loom high above me. There are many lights, but I see them only vaguely. I am nearly blind now.

"Lenny—less'n two hundred feet to go. Listen, Lenny. I'm climbing down. I'm going to jump down, Lenny, and get around under your fore scanner pickup. You'll see me, Lenny. You'll know me then."

The false transmission ceases. I sense a body moving across my side. The gap closes. I detect movement before me, and in automatic reflex fire anti-P charges before I recall that I am unarmed.

A small object has moved out before me, and taken up a position between me and the wall behind which the Enemy conceal themselves. It is dim, but appears to have the shape of a man. . . .

I am uncertain. My alert center attempts to engage inhibitory circuitry which will force

*me to halt, but it lacks power. I can override it.
But still I am unsure. Now I must take a last
risk; I must shunt power to my forward scanner to examine this obstacle more closely. I do
so, and it leaps into greater clarity. It is indeed
a man—and it is enclothed in regulation blues
of the Volunteers. Now, closer, I see the face
and through the pain of my great effort, I
study it. . . .*

                    * * *

"He's backed against the wall," Reynolds said
hoarsely. "It's still coming. A hundred feet to
go—"

"You were a fool, Reynolds!" the mayor
barked. "A fool to stake everything on that old
dotard's crazy ideas!"

"Hold it!" As Reynolds watched, the mighty
machine slowed, halted, ten feet from the
sheer wall before it. For a moment, it sat, as
though puzzled. Then it backed, halted again,
pivoted ponderously to the left, and came
about.

On its side, a small figure crept up, fell
across the lower gun deck. The Bolo surged
into motion, retracing its route across the
artillery-scarred gardens.

"He's turned it." Reynolds let his breath out
with a shuddering sigh. "It's headed out for
open desert. It might get twenty miles before
it finally runs out of steam."

The strange voice that was the Bolo's came
from the big panel before Mayfield:

*"Command. . . . Unit LNE reports main
power cells drained, secondary cells drained;*

now operating at .037 per cent efficiency, using Final Emergency Power. Request advice as to range to be covered before relief maintenance available."

"It's a long way, Lenny. . . ." Sanders' voice was a bare whisper. *"But I'm coming with you. . . ."*

Then there was only the crackle of static. Ponderously, like a great mortally stricken animal, the Bolo moved through the ruins of the fallen roadway, heading for the open desert.

"That damned machine," the mayor said in a hoarse voice. "You'd almost think it was alive."

"You would at that," Pete Reynolds said.